Re:ZeRo
-Starting Life in Another World-

Characters

Re:ZERO -Starting Life in Another World-

The only ability Subaru Natsuki gets when he's summoned to another world is time travel via his own death. But to save her, he'll die as many times as it takes.

Flop

A Volakian merchant. Travels around the empire with his sister.

Medium

Flop's younger sister. Wields two swords.

Todd

Imperial soldier. Coolheaded and willing to do whatever is necessary to achieve his goal.

Louann

A binge-drinking alcoholic. Skilled with a sword and possessed of excellent judgment.

A figure was visible through the black smoke, slowly emerging from the flames. It was a man with a wet cloth wrapped around his face and an ax in one hand.

"Wh-who are you? Why are you doing this?"

Dance

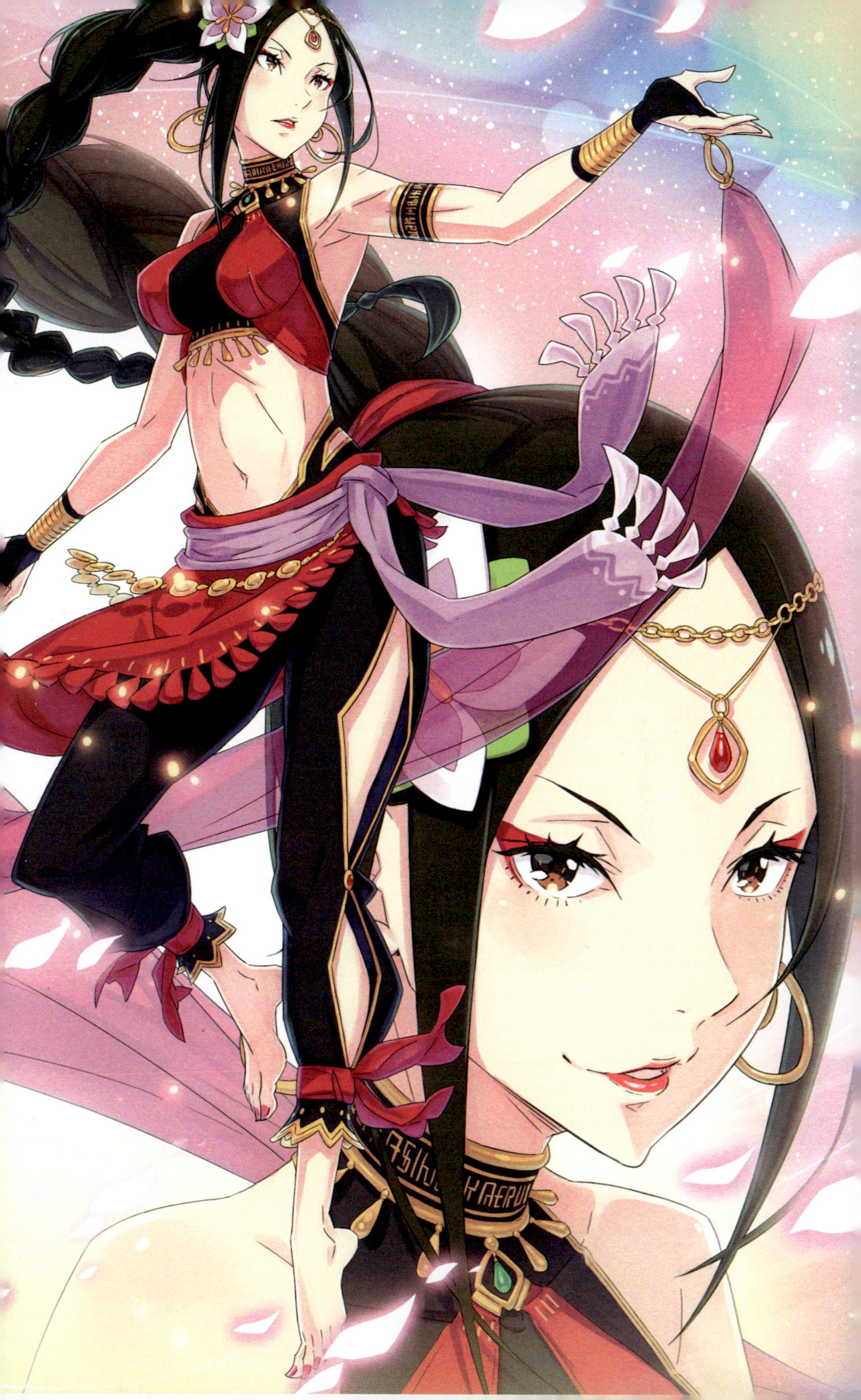

Re:ZERO -Starting Life in Another World-

The only ability Subaru Natsuki gets when he's summoned to another world is time travel via his own death. But to save her, he'll die as many times as it takes.

CONTENTS

Chapter 1
Something I Want to Protect
001

Chapter 2
Creeping Malignancy
037

Chapter 3
The Battle of Fortress City Guaral
077

Chapter 4
Emperor, Merchant, Subaru Natsuki
105

Chapter 5
The Musician Natsumi Schwartz
155

Chapter 6
A Haughty Crimson
197

Re:ZeRo

-Starting Life in Another World-

VOLUME 27

TAPPEI NAGATSUKI
ILLUSTRATION: SHINICHIROU OTSUKA

Yen ON

New York

Re:ZERO Vol. 27
TAPPEI NAGATSUKI

Translation by Dale DeLucia
Cover art by Shinichirou Otsuka

This book is a work of fiction. Names, characters, places, and incidents are the product of the author's imagination or are used fictitiously. Any resemblance to actual events, locales, or persons, living or dead, is coincidental.

Re:ZERO KARA HAJIMERU ISEKAI SEIKATSU Vol. 27
©Tappei Nagatsuki 2021
First published in Japan in 2021 by KADOKAWA CORPORATION, Tokyo.
English translation rights reserved by YEN PRESS, LLC under the license from KADOKAWA CORPORATION, Tokyo through Tuttle-Mori Agency, Inc., Tokyo.

English translation © 2025 by Yen Press, LLC

Yen Press, LLC supports the right to free expression and the value of copyright. The purpose of copyright is to encourage writers and artists to produce the creative works that enrich our culture.

The scanning, uploading, and distribution of this book without permission is a theft of the author's intellectual property. If you would like permission to use material from the book (other than for review purposes), please contact the publisher. Thank you for your support of the author's rights.

Yen On
150 West 30th Street, 6th Floor
New York, NY 10001

Visit us at yenpress.com
facebook.com/yenpress
twitter.com/yenpress
yenpress.tumblr.com
instagram.com/yenpress

First Yen On Edition: May 2025
Edited by Yen On Editorial: Ivan Liang
Designed by Yen Press Design: Jane Sohn, Andy Swist

Yen On is an imprint of Yen Press, LLC.
The Yen On name and logo are trademarks of Yen Press, LLC.

The publisher is not responsible for websites (or their content) that are not owned by the publisher.

Library of Congress Cataloging-in-Publication Data
Names: Nagatsuki, Tappei, 1987– author. | Otsuka, Shinichirou, illustrator. | ZephyrRz, translator. | DeLucia, Dale, translator.
Title: Re:ZERO starting life in another world / Tappei Nagatsuki ; illustration by Shinichirou Otsuka ; translation by ZephyrRz ; translation by DeLucia, Dale
Other titles: Re:ZERO kara hajimeru isekai seikatsu. English
Description: First Yen On edition. | New York, NY : Yen On, 2016– |
Audience: Ages 13 & up.
Identifiers: LCCN 2016031562 | ISBN 9780316315302 (v. 1 : pbk.)
Subjects: CYAC: Science fiction. | Time travel—Fiction.
Classification: LCC PZ7.1.N34 Re 2016 | DDC [Fic]—dc23
LC record available at https://lccn.loc.gov/2016031562

ISBNs: 978-1-9753-7846-2 (paperback)
978-1-9753-7847-9 (ebook)

10 9 8 7 6 5 4 3 2 1

LSC-C

Printed in the United States of America

Chapter 1

SOMETHING I WANT TO PROTECT

1

—Swaying, wobbling, spinning.

His consciousness rocked gently, like a ship adrift at sea. It was unsteady, heavy—enough to make his head spin even behind closed eyelids.

Something was missing. No, everything was missing. It felt like all the pieces had leaked out somewhere.

He had to gather them, put them back in place, and stand up again. There was somewhere he had to go. A thought pushed him forward— a reason to live, a wish so intense it compelled him to shout, *I want to live!*

Even if he lacked everything, even if he was incomplete, he had to keep going.

And for that, Subaru Natsuki…

Right after waking up, as if on cue…

"…This is a new ceiling," Subaru murmured.

His body was drenched in night sweat. It felt like waking up after a nightmare—which wasn't far from the truth. The bed beneath him wasn't particularly comfortable, either.

The ceiling above was crude, and the hard bed was no better—both clearly made without regard for modern construction standards. A hut, put together by brute force and crude building techniques.

Subaru slowly pieced together his foggy memories to recall why he was sleeping there.

"I got summoned to another world on the way back from a convenience store, met Emilia-tan, et cetera, et cetera…"

Of course, that was going too far back, but the joke helped clear his head.

Subaru Natsuki had been summoned into a different world, met a silver-haired beauty, embarked on a series of incredible adventures, cleared a tower in the desert, and then got sent flying to a neighboring country.

Even in his own head, it sounded absurd. But thinking it over helped jog his memory.

"Rem…!"

The precious girl who had been sent to this strange land alongside Subaru. She was the one he needed to protect. Yet somehow, they'd been separated…

"What am I, stupid? No, I'm an idiot…! I have to save Rem—"

"Why are you thrashing around?"

Subaru, ready to jump out of bed, froze at the unexpected voice. He turned, and an "Ah" slipped out as his eyes went wide. A blue-eyed girl sat beside the uncomfortable bed, watching him.

"Rem…?"

"…Yes, though I am not particularly inclined to answer to that name. I still haven't accepted that I'm the Rem you're speaking of," she replied flatly, her tone wooden.

Subaru swallowed hard. This wasn't a dream. It wasn't a hallucination. Rem was here, speaking to him. Her warmth was real—he could feel it in her hand beneath the ragged cloth covering him.

"Did you…hold my hand until I woke up?"

"Huh? Do your eyes work? You grabbed my hand and wouldn't let go."

"Ah, right…that makes sense. Okay, yeah! I'm the one who reached out, huh…?"

His hopes and reality blurred together, earning Rem's clear annoyance. Of course she wouldn't willingly hold his hand—not the way she was doing now. But the fact that she hadn't pulled it away brought him some small relief.

"Why are you looking at me like that?"

"I-it's nothing. Nothing at all."

"Is that so? Then please let go. Your hand is sweaty and gross."

"Oof, saying that's, like, an automatic critical hit for boys…!"

That sort of remark could leave a lasting scar on someone. But emotional well-being ranked below physical safety, especially when it came to Rem's safety.

At a glance, at least, she seemed okay.

"You're not injured anywhere, are you? Tell me if anything feels off… Huh? Why are you looking at me like that?"

"…Are you really asking? You came this close to dying."

Despite his concern, her reaction was even colder than before. And, seeing his bewilderment, Rem sighed disappointedly.

"It's clear you don't even understand that much. I really can't trust you."

"…"

Her blunt rejection broke Subaru's heart.

Because she had lost her memories and because of the stench of the miasma clinging to him, Rem remained distant and cold. He hadn't been able to bridge the gap this time, as he'd been too focused on saving her from the imperial camp.

"…Oh."

Another memory clicked into place.

Rem had been imprisoned in the imperial camp. To rescue her, Subaru had gambled everything. In the process, he'd encountered the Shudrak people in the jungle and been captured. He'd participated in their rituals alongside another prisoner.

And...

"...My right arm isn't black..."

He raised his arm, staring at the exposed limb where his sleeve had been torn. The hideous black pattern—the mark left by an Archbishop of the Witch Cult in Pristella—was gone. Not a trace remained.

The black mark had fused with his battered arm, healing its wounds, and now it was as if it had never existed. It hadn't been just a nightmare, though it had certainly felt like one.

Subaru flexed his arm, which was no longer useless. Rem was here, safe. It meant he'd survived the Shudrak ritual and saved her, though at great cost.

"...You look awful. Go back to sleep," Rem muttered, watching him sit there in silence.

Kindness? Or just a reflection of how lifeless Subaru appeared?

But I can't. There's too much I have to figure out.

"Thanks for the concern, but I can't stay laid up in here...This is the Shudrak village, right? Where are Mizelda and the others?"

After hesitating, Rem finally answered, her gaze softening reluctantly.

"...Outside. They said to bring you if you woke up."

That settled one question, but Subaru had one more.

"What about...Louis?"

"...What an unpleasant expression. Why do you push her away so?"

"It's hard to explain. You probably wouldn't believe me even if I did."

Every conversation about Louis was guaranteed to incur Rem's displeasure. Even though it pained him, Subaru did not think it was something he could get through in words.

"...Please turn around," Rem replied, clearly exasperated.

Confused, Subaru looked back at the bed—

"Zzzz, zzzz..."

On the other side, Louis lay asleep, her head nestled near Subaru's stomach. She was drooling profusely onto the blanket, adding to the already damp mess of night sweats.

"AAAHHH!!!"
Subaru's scream shook the entire Shudrak village.

2

"Still, it's great that you woke up without any problems," Mizelda said with a bold, heroic smile.

The young chief of the Shudrak, her black hair dyed red, embodied an Amazonian lifestyle. Her straightforward, carefree demeanor was infectious, and it made Subaru naturally want to cut loose, too.

"It's thanks to you that I'm still kicking. Sorry for making you worry," Subaru replied.

"Don't worry about it. If you had died, your valiant Shudrak soul would have returned to the heavens, and your body to the earth. Nothing more. The fact that your soul remains here is something to celebrate."

Subaru scratched his cheek awkwardly, unsure how to respond to her unflinching sincerity. He'd been prepared to die when first captured by the Shudrak, but the bond they'd developed after all the twists and turns was deeply gratifying.

"It's a shame you already have partners. Have you thought about taking another after Rem and Louis?" Mizelda teased with a mischievous glint in her eye.

"Mizelda!"

Rem's sharp voice cut through the air. She approached with a new staff for support, Louis clinging tightly to her arm now that she was awake. After surprising Louis with her sudden shout, she gently patted the girl's head before glaring at Mizelda.

"That's too much. I neither trust nor understand this man."

"Then can I have him?" Mizelda asked playfully.

"Yes, of course. I'll gladly give him to you," Rem said coldly, without hesitation.

"What about what I want?!" Subaru exclaimed.

"Aauu!" Louis shouted, adding to the commotion. The bizarre exchange left Subaru flustered, but it was clear that Mizelda looked on Subaru favorably now. The rest of the tribe, including Mizelda's younger sister, seemed to share her opinion—likely due to his having survived their ritual of blood.

However...

"That doesn't mean my opinion of *you* has necessarily improved," Subaru said to a masked man standing nearby.

"Hmph. Such arrogance. Are you claiming you could have achieved the same results alone? If so, your conceit is laughable," the man shot back.

"I wouldn't say that. I don't even think it. It's just..." Subaru's lips curled into a frown.

"What?" the man asked, irritation clear in his voice.

Subaru shrugged, meeting his provocative gaze. "It's hard to take anything seriously from a guy wearing a mask."

The man wore a red-and-white oni-style mask that Subaru found unnerving. Since there were already people called oni in this world, it probably had a different name here, but that didn't matter—it was intimidating, plain and simple.

The two of them stood in the largest structure of the Shudrak village, a simple wooden gathering hall. Mizelda and her sister Talitta represented the Shudrak, while Subaru was accompanied by Rem, leaning on her staff, and Louis, who clung to her arm. And right in the middle of them all stood the masked man.

"I received this mask and had always intended to keep my face hidden," the masked man said. "Rewrapping the bandages whenever I washed my face was a hassle."

"I bet it got itchy when it was dirty, too..." Subaru grimaced before narrowing his eyes. "But that's not what I wanted to talk about. I want to talk with you one-on-one, *Vincent Abelks*."

"_____"

Though the mask obscured his expression, the air grew heavy, and the temperature seemed to drop. Subaru's declaration filled the room with tension, but he held his ground despite the pressure.

The masked man slowly shook his head. "I let it slide the first time because you weren't fully lucid, but I will not repeat myself. There won't be a third time. Do not speak my name so freely."

"And if I said I didn't want to stop?"

"Then you would receive a fitting punishment. I know any number of ways to make you admit defeat."

Subaru instinctively understood that the man wasn't bluffing. Even with limited options, he would do whatever he deemed necessary.

"You're a real irritating guy..."

"Do you wish to test me a third time?"

"—No. I'll leave it at that. I didn't come here to pick a fight...Abel," Subaru said, conceding for now.

The masked man—Abel, as Subaru had decided to go along with for now—nodded at Subaru's decision.

"Wise. If you had persisted, blood would surely have been spilled," Abel replied coolly.

"You've got a lot of nerve," Subaru muttered. "But if we went at it, I'd say it's a coin flip."

"Let us see if you still believe that after you take a look behind you," Abel countered.

Turning, Subaru saw Rem coldly observing their argument.

"Uhhh, Rem? Your face..."

"Oh, it's nothing. I'm just watching someone who spent three days on the brink of death trying his hardest to get himself injured again over pointless stubbornness. Why don't you just die in a gutter somewhere and save us all the trouble?"

Faltering under Rem's withering gaze, Subaru desperately apologized. "Sorry! I was wrong! I won't do it again!"

While he clearly failed to regain what little trust Rem had had in him, Subaru did have a realization. He'd likely survived his near-mortal wounds due to healing magic, and there was only one person who could have cast it.

"The handling of that matter is precisely why we need to talk," Abel interjected, reading Subaru's thoughts. "Mizelda, have everyone else leave. I and this man alone will be sufficient."

"Awfully bossy. If you weren't so handsome, I'd be angry."

"Sister, please be angry even if he is handsome...," Talitta muttered, her shoulders slumping as Mizelda breezily accepted Abel's instructions. But she didn't argue. As the chief, Mizelda made the final decision, and she and Talitta left the meeting place. Only Rem and Louis remained, the latter staring blankly, not comprehending the situation.

"Rem, could you please give us a moment? He's got...something really important to talk about," Subaru said.

"...And what if I said no?"

"Eh?!"

Rem's sharp response left Subaru reeling. He had prepared himself for the difficulty of dealing with Abel, but her resistance caught him completely off guard. Truthfully, he was powerless against her criticism, always wanting to fulfill her every wish, no matter how small. But...

"...I'd rather you...not hear this...I guess?"

It was the best answer he could muster under her piercing gaze.

Just then, Louis tugged on Rem's sleeve and let out a small groan. The tiny girl seemed to be trying to drag Rem out of the meeting place with her meager strength. Subaru watched in surprise as a faint smile crept onto Rem's face.

"Sorry. I just wanted to vent a little at this smelly person before we leave," Rem said to Louis, her words calm but cutting.

"Smelly...," Subaru muttered, feeling the sting of her remark but choosing not to respond.

True to her word, Rem left the room hand in hand with Louis. As they disappeared, Subaru exhaled deeply.

I can't tell if she's starting to trust me or if she actually hates me more than ever.

"Obviously, I'd love to be trusted, but I'm not getting my hopes up. That's just my style..."

"What trifling perseverance and hubris. Come, I shall listen to your story," Abel interjected.

Now alone, Subaru and Abel sat facing each other, the firelight flickering between them. Subaru sat cross-legged, while Abel reclined with one knee propped up, his mask still in place.

"The first thing I want to know is how much of all that was real and how much was a dream," Subaru began cautiously.

"Ha. That is a question only you can answer. Were I to tell you it was an ephemeral, fleeting dream, and the situation unfolded peacefully, would you be satisfied?"

"There's a girl among the Shudrak named Utakata, so I'd say your hypothetical is kind of distracting…"

The girl's name sounded just like the Japanese word for *ephemeral*, but that clearly wasn't what Abel meant. Subaru knew he wouldn't let him avoid the subject with pointless jokes.

"I have no intention of indulging your timidity, Subaru Natsuki."

"…Yeah, I know. So the attack on that camp was real, then?"

"Of course. The military camp outside of the Badheim Jungle was completely destroyed by the Shudrak. What you saw was no illusion or dream."

Abel's confirmation hit Subaru hard. His chest felt tight, and he was having trouble breathing. He had desperately wanted it to be a nightmare, something he could wake up from. But reality didn't offer him that escape.

"…I see. So you led the Shudrak and attacked the imperial camp and drove them off."

"Yes. However, that alone was not the reason for our success. That achievement belongs to you."

"Huh?"

"Do you not understand? Our ability to crush the enemy was due to knowing the details of their deployment. Those details came from none other than you," Abel said, resting his chin in his palm and his elbow on his knee.

Subaru froze, his mind struggling to process what he had just heard. His mouth opened and closed as he tried to form a response, but no words came out.

"What…what are you saying? I…I didn't…"

"The formation, the positions of the enemy forces—knowing these details drastically improved our chances of success. Thanks to that, we achieved victory without losses. That was your contribution. You even secured a reward for your efforts."

"..."

"That is what saved your woman. I reward performance, but there is no reward for the dead. I acted quickly while you still drew breath. Hmph. You are a lucky man."

Abel's words landed like daggers. Subaru couldn't believe what he was hearing. Perhaps to Abel that was a compliment, but Subaru was from a culture that disagreed fundamentally.

What kind of reward was being a tool of war?

"I said something...about the camp? Why would I...?"

"The side effects of treatment. You were on the verge of death after the ritual of blood. Medicine was administered to keep you alive long enough to meet your woman. In your semilucid state, you answered the questions put to you."

"So I just...told you everything while I was out of it?"

Subaru buried his face in his hands, his voice trembling.

It was true. He knew the camp's layout fairly well. During his time as an errand boy, he had memorized details about troop numbers and weapon locations—information any commander would kill for. But so what?

"What medicine?! You forced some crap down my throat to make me talk?!" Subaru snapped.

"Without it, you would have died before reuniting with your woman. Her healing magic would not have helped you. A dead man has no right to complain about being saved."

"Of course I do! I didn't want to be part of a war! So many people died...and you—!"

"You misunderstand," Abel interrupted, his voice icy.

"Misunderstand? What exactly am I getting wrong?"

"Even without the medicine, you needed the Shudrak's help to save your woman. That would have required sharing your knowledge."

"I...agh..."

"Whether you were lucid or not, the outcome remains the same.

The camp's secrets would still have been revealed, and the soldiers would still have died."

Subaru tried to argue but found himself unable to refute Abel's logic. Even assuming he had come out of the trial in better shape, he still would've had to share what he knew about the camp.

"At the very least, if I had been involved in the planning, I wouldn't have agreed to any plan that led to deaths."

"You think you could have convinced them? That you could persuade those who know no method beyond killing to devise a plan without bloodshed? One that could have saved your woman still?"

"That's… I…"

"It is a flight of fancy."

Abel's words pierced Subaru's heart. The gap between their values was insurmountable, and there had been no magic solution.

Even if there were, I probably wouldn't have been able to find it in what little time I had before Rem was gone.

"Still, I didn't want to give up," Subaru muttered through clenched teeth.

"And in exchange for your refusal to give up, someone else would die. Perhaps a stranger, or perhaps your other half. Standing still and indulging in foolish ideals allows such deaths to occur."

"And who are you to decide who lives and who dies? Do you think you're a god?"

"Fool. I am neither god nor hero. Nor am I some detached observer. I am a king. A king among kings," Abel declared, his tone as unshakable as his gaze.

"…"

"The people call he who stands at the summit *emperor*," Abel declared, placing a hand to his chest. "That is I."

Though his mask concealed his expression, Subaru could imagine the face beneath—a fearless smile and blazing eyes. His voice and words were so regal, they left little room for doubt.

While Subaru froze up, Abel—Vincent Abelks—spoke with unwavering authority.

"The seventy-seventh emperor of the Holy Volakian Empire. That is who I am."

"..."

"Though at present I have been removed from the summit and my throne."

3

The seventy-seventh emperor of the Holy Volakian Empire.

Subaru's thoughts blanked as the weight of Abel's title settled in. From the moment he had encountered Abel in the jungle clearing, Subaru had known he wasn't just some ordinary guy. But discovering that Abel was the emperor? That was far beyond anything Subaru had imagined.

"Assuming what you're saying is actually true..." Subaru said, narrowing his eyes.

"You doubt my words?"

"Of course I do. Why would the most important dude in the entire country be wandering around in the jungle? Sure, you've got emperor-class guts, but..." Subaru scowled, pointing at Abel's oni mask. "Like I said before, how can I trust someone who hides his face?"

The accusation brought back a hazy memory for Subaru—a memory of when they had looked down at the burning camp together. At that time, Abel had wrapped his face in rags instead of wearing a mask. Subaru had made a similar remark then, and Abel had responded by revealing his face.

"You fixate on the most inconsequential things," Abel said with a sigh, removing his mask and setting it aside, just as he had done before.

"..."

"What is that insolent gaze? My face is no different from yours."

"...The building blocks maybe, but the difference in how they were put together convinces me that the gods are fickle," Subaru muttered, averting his eyes.

Abel's face was striking—his glossy black hair and sharp, dignified eyes exuded an aura of authority. It was a face that commanded respect, so imposing it felt almost magical. This was the face of an emperor.

Yet it didn't look familiar to Subaru. As a knight of one of Lugunica's royal candidates, he'd expected to at least recognize a neighboring nation's ruler.

"Is that just how it is? You're a head of state, but I wouldn't…"

"You have no reason to know my face. It is not something that should be seen beyond the capital. There are far too many in this country who would have my head."

"Self-defense? You pissed off that many people?"

"No. In Volakia, power is everything. The weak, the frail, and the cowardly deserve death. The strong take all. The throne of the emperor is no exception."

Resting his chin in his hand and his elbow on his knee, Abel explained the ruthless creed of Volakia. After living among the soldiers in the imperial camp, Subaru knew it wasn't a lie. Todd and the others fully embodied this ideology.

It was the imperial way. They would make whatever sacrifices were needed for…

"Wait, that's weird," Subaru said, a thought striking him.

"What is?"

"If, for the sake of argument, you really are the emperor, then why would you attack an imperial camp? Couldn't you just meet with their commander and—?"

"Fool. Unlike you, I have no desire to die."

"I don't want to die either, but…why is that suicidal?" Subaru paused, confusion mounting. Why would an emperor meeting with his own soldiers be a death sentence? Unless…

"…You said earlier you'd been removed from the throne. Is that right?"

"So you did not miss that. As I said before, do not make me repeat myself."

"Quit joking around! This is important! If the emperor has been deposed, then..." Subaru hesitated as it dawned on him. If his guess was right, Abel's situation was dire beyond belief.

"Your line of thought is correct," Abel said calmly with a nod, confirming Subaru's suspicion.

Subaru's breath hitched. Abel's gaze dropped slightly, and he stared into the fire between them. A log cracked and burst, the noise echoing the tension in the air.

"The force stationed outside of the Badheim was sent by my political enemies. Their mission was to eliminate me. You and your woman were simply in the wrong place at the wrong time."

"But…the people in the camp didn't mention anything about that. They said their goal was to negotiate with the Shudrak."

Subaru had no ability to detect lies, but it seemed implausible that dozens of soldiers came up with an elaborate ruse and went to the effort of getting all their stories straight just to deceive a few outsiders. Most likely, they genuinely believed that they had come for the Shudrak.

"If their real goal was capturing you…"

"Do not embellish. You said yourself they planned to attack. To protect yourself and your woman, you placed the Shudrak and the soldiers on the scales."

"You're wr—"

"I am not mistaken. Battles happen, and those who die do not return. The dead do not speak, nor can they influence the living."

"…"

"The dead do not come back to life."

Subaru shut his eyes tightly against Abel's harsh words.

That's a lot of shit coming from a guy who doesn't know anything. There is *a way to bring back the dead.*

Subaru's unique power allowed him to reverse death itself. If he had died, there was a chance he would have returned to a point before the camp was destroyed and warned the soldiers. He might have saved them. But that would have put the Shudrak in danger.

He couldn't stand on both sides at once. Saving everyone was impossible.

And more than that, Subaru lacked the resolve to use his power in this case. What were the odds of a better outcome, even if he tried again? It had not gone the way he had wanted, but he and Rem were safe. There was no telling what it would take to get a better result.

How far would I have to grind myself down to make that happen?

"You are a foolish man gripped by strange anguish," Abel said, interrupting Subaru's spiraling thoughts.

Subaru's eyes snapped open with astonishment. Abel was watching him from across the fire, his expression almost sympathetic.

"Why do you wish only to curry favor with others?"

"Curry favor… Me?"

"You focus solely on others. You have intentionally honed yourself, cloaking it in the guise of charity. It is no different from a warrior honing his skills—you've blotted out your own heart."

"Shut up! Don't act like you know me!" Subaru snapped, anger flaring.

There's no way someone like him—someone who doesn't know about Return by Death—could understand even a fraction of what I've endured.

"Answer my question! The soldiers were looking for the Shudrak, and there wasn't one word about you…"

"It is not the sort of thing that would be shared with common soldiers. Word of the emperor's exile must not leave the capital. My enemies cannot afford to let the empire waver."

"…"

"And the Shudrak were a natural target. They are the only group an exiled emperor could ally with. Killing the Shudrak would be the same as cutting off my arms and legs as I struggled to keep my head afloat."

Abel's explanation resolved Subaru's lingering doubts—about the soldiers' motives, their encirclement of the jungle, and their attempts to either negotiate with or annihilate the Shudrak.

"Why the Shudrak, though?"

"Long ago, an emperor of Volakia saved the Shudrak during their time of need. They do not forget such debts. That, along with the ritual of blood, makes them my chance at reclaiming the throne."

Abel's gamble had been audacious, relying on the Shudrak's loyalty to ancient obligations and their respect for rituals after he escaped from the capital. His enemies in the government had deployed the army to the jungle to eliminate him before he could capitalize on them, but Abel had won this round.

"However, this battle isn't going to end just because the first wave of the enemy was driven back, right?" Subaru asked.

"Of course not. If I die, that is the end. Yet I still live. I will do everything in my power to reclaim those things that were stolen from me and are rightfully mine," Abel replied calmly.

That was Abel's—Vincent Abelks's—choice as the emperor of Volakia.

When he spoke, Subaru could tell that "things" meant his country. That was a scale far beyond what Subaru was used to considering.

"So what, then…? You're going to lead the Shudrak into war?!"

"That's right. They have promised their support in accordance with the result of the ritual of blood and in honor of the oath sworn with the emperor of old. Those who celebrate pride and honor are simple to use. They will fight alongside me."

"With all they've already done…that still isn't enough?!" Subaru's voice rose sharply.

Retaking the throne meant countless more battles, an endless cycle of conflict. That was war—a fierce, unrelenting struggle that left a trail of untold suffering and countless deaths.

"…"

As far as Subaru knew, there had been over a hundred soldiers in the burned-out imperial camp. In the few hours he had been unconscious, more than a hundred lives had been snuffed out.

"Why do you kill…?" Subaru muttered.

"Because there is no other means. Nothing more."

"…Is that really true? Have you seriously tried looking for another way?" Subaru's voice trembled as he asked, "Any other way before you killed someone and robbed them of all possibilities?"

Abel's eyes narrowed.

His gaze didn't suggest serious consideration of Subaru's question. Instead, it seemed to ask why Subaru would even question the necessity of such actions.

It was a fundamental clash of values.

Until now, Subaru Natsuki had been fortunate. He hadn't been forced to navigate relationships with people whose values were fundamentally at odds with his own.

Most of the people he'd met in this world, despite their differences from him, had been rational. The witches and Archbishops were exceptions—extremes whose values were so alien that Subaru didn't even attempt to engage with them meaningfully. He defined them as clearly wrong and acted against them accordingly.

But Abel was different. So were the Shudrak. And the soldiers in the camp. They weren't evil. They didn't treat life and death as sport, nor did they wield power out of gross self-interest. Aside from their differing views, they were people much like Subaru himself.

And yet…

"…I just want to take Rem and go home."

Abel's battle to reclaim the throne was beginning. If this were a page out of a legend or a history book, it might be thrilling. But this was reality, and Subaru had no desire to participate in a historic battle in a land where he had nothing to rely on.

His goal was to return Rem to Lugunica. To meet up with Emilia, Beatrice, and everyone else at Roswaal Manor. To celebrate Rem's recovery and plan their next steps together.

He couldn't afford to deal with anything else.

Slapping his cheeks with both hands, Subaru forced himself to focus. He narrowed his objectives down to a single, unshakable goal.

"Can you please tell me the closest town or village? I'll figure out a way back myself from there."

"Ho," Abel breathed out softly. "A sensible decision. However, the path you choose will not be an easy one."

"I'll walk whatever path I have to, easy or hard. Preferably on a paved road, though," Subaru said, biting the inside of his cheek. The pain helped sharpen his thoughts.

He turned to Abel—the solitary emperor determined to continue his fight.

"I didn't thank you yet... The method aside, thank you for rescuing Rem. I am grateful for that."

"I did not just save her; I saved the other one, too," Abel said dryly.

"That was uncalled for... Thanks to that, my worries have to stick around awhile."

Of course, if Louis had been lost in the camp, Subaru's already tenuous relationship with Rem might have become even more precarious. He couldn't say which outcome would have been better.

So...

"I'll choose the path I can live with... Anyway, it sounds like it'll be complicated, but good luck with whatever road you go down. Just...don't..."

"Do not get the Shudrak involved?" Abel finished for him. "If neither of us had intervened, their fate would have been to burn along with this jungle. This is already their fight."

Subaru couldn't deny that. The Shudrak had no choice but to fight for their survival.

But...

"It's impossible for me. I can't ever become like you," Subaru said, shaking his head.

Abel looked at him and blinked—but only with one eye. Subaru had noticed this quirk. Abel never closed both eyes at once, even for a moment.

Subaru realized it was a survival instinct, a habit born from a life spent in the highest halls of the swordwolf empire. He was awed by the emperor who lived in a world where such vigilance was required to survive. And he was terrified.

"Of course. Neither you nor anyone can take my place," Abel said, his voice quiet but firm.

That was the only response he gave Subaru.

4

Leave the Shudrak and head to the town closest to the Badheim Jungle.

To Subaru's surprise, the Shudrak did not react strongly to his decision.

"I see. Unfortunate, but if that is our brother's decision, then so be it," Mizelda said with calm acceptance.

Subaru had braced himself for scorn, expecting to be criticized for refusing to fight alongside them. Instead, Mizelda respected his choice, and the lack of judgment left him both relieved and uneasy.

Utakata took the news much harder than Mizelda. Her reaction weighed on him more than he'd expected.

"Suu is leaving. That's so sad…"

"Yeah, sorry… Um, Utakata, do you know what's going to happen now?" Subaru asked softly, gently patting her head as she clung to his sleeve.

The Shudrak's values and solidarity were unshakeable, and Mizelda's decisions represented the will of the tribe. But Utakata was still young. Subaru couldn't help but worry that she might be swept up in the heat of the moment without fully understanding the gravity of what lay ahead.

"The fight is going to start. I'm going to fight with Mii and Taa and everyone," Utakata said confidently, pointing to the bow slung across her back.

"…I see," Subaru said with a sigh.

A part of him wished a child like her could stay blissfully ignorant at times like these. But such sentiments had no place in this jungle. Utakata was a Shudrak through and through. She had the resolve to fight—and to kill. Subaru himself had been killed by one of her poison arrows before.

Even so…

"Don't die, Utakata."

"Uu won't die! You try hard not to die, too, Suu," Utakata replied brightly.

Subaru could only manage a weak smile in response.

In truth, he couldn't fathom what chances Abel and the Shudrak had in this fight. Abel, the deposed emperor, faced enemies who could wield the might of the entire imperial army. No matter how ingenious Abel's strategies might be, could they really overcome such overwhelming odds?

"I'm ready."

"Whoa!" Subaru yelped, startled by the sudden voice.

"...What is it? Why are you so surprised?" Rem asked, holding a wooden staff in one hand and wearing a small bag slung over her back. She looked at him quizzically, clearly prepared for travel.

Subaru stared, stunned by how readily she seemed to have accepted that they were leaving.

After his tense exchange with Abel, Subaru had expected convincing Rem to leave to be the hardest part. He'd even prepared himself to drag her away in the middle of the night if it came to that. Yet when he had broached the subject directly, expecting resistance, she had surprised him.

"*...Understood. I'll prepare for tomorrow,*" she had said simply.

Even now, seeing her dressed and ready, Subaru still struggled to believe it was happening.

"So..."

"Ah! No, sorry, it's fine. Yeah, you've even got your travel clothes on. Cute."

"Huh?"

"Sorry! Not what I meant! I mean, you're prepared and reliable, and that really helps. I'm happy about that," Subaru stammered awkwardly.

Rem's dubious glare deepened, making it clear his clumsy attempt to recover had failed.

I'm not trying to suck up, Subaru thought. Still, if she wasn't resisting, that was a huge relief. Ideally, he'd like to open things up between them more.

"So are you ready? You seemed reluctant to leave earlier..."

"Yeah, don't worry about that. We didn't have much to pack, and you're carrying most of it anyway."

"...But you're going to be carrying me," Rem pointed out, glancing at the handmade wooden frame.

It was a crude but sturdy device made from thick branches lashed together with vines, designed to allow Subaru to carry Rem on his back. While Rem could walk short distances with her staff, traveling to the nearest town—several days away—was another matter entirely.

"It's got that handmade vibe, but it's strong. We tested it with Talitta, and she's heavier than you," Subaru said.

"I'm not particularly concerned about heavy or light, but I believe you're being rude to Talitta."

Scratching his cheek awkwardly, Subaru shifted his gaze behind Rem to Louis. She would be joining them on this journey as well, of course. If Subaru was taking Rem, Louis had to come, too.

"And it's too much to leave a ticking time bomb like her with the Shudrak..."

Even if the Shudrak were willing, letting an Archbishop off the leash was unthinkable. There had been several times already that he had let her out of his sight, giving her plenty of chances to reveal her true nature, but he wouldn't let that happen again.

Even if he was starting to believe that Louis's behavior was not just an act.

"Ah, uuu."

Louis stood quietly, her long hair tied neatly behind her head. Her once-tattered white dress had been mended, giving her a cleaner and softer appearance. The Shudrak doted on her, and they had fixed her clothes as a gift.

Mizelda approached to see them off.

"Sorry for needing your help with everything," Subaru said.

"Don't apologize, Subaru. You overcame the ritual of blood and proved the radiance of your soul. It is only natural to honor a brother and offer what help we can," Mizelda said.

"'Brother'...," Subaru echoed, lowering his gaze.

He couldn't bring himself to meet Mizelda's eyes. The tribe was preparing for a brutal battle, yet here he was, leaving them behind.

Would a proud and honorable Shudrak do something like this?

"Do not fret over it, Subaru," Mizelda said, sensing his hesitation.

"Mizelda..."

"We will fight and prove our worth. But protecting what's important is how we secure the future of the tribe. Never forget that."

"..."

"You must protect Rem and Louis. That is what I expect of our honored brother."

Her straightforward encouragement stirred something in Subaru. He felt a heat rise in the backs of his eyes but held it at bay.

He didn't bother correcting Mizelda about Louis. At the very least, he owed it to them to fulfill that expectation.

And I might never see them again...

"We're ready. It's time to go," Holly called out, waving a large hand. The lively Shudrak woman with the tips of her hair dyed yellow stood alongside Kuna, a quieter figure with green-dyed hair.

The two had been chosen to escort Subaru and his group to Guaral, the nearest town.

"I didn't want to ask for protection, but..."

In this unfamiliar land, Subaru had already died several times in just a few days. Better to be safe than sorry. Relying on Rem or Louis for support wasn't an option, and Subaru's own strength wasn't enough to ensure their safety.

I dunno about Kuna but I've seen Holly lift a boulder up like it didn't weigh anything. She's plenty strong.

And...

"It doesn't hurt anywhere, does it, Rem?" Subaru asked as he adjusted the frame on his back. Because they were back-to-back, it wasn't possible for Subaru to see Rem's face. In order to keep her fixed in place, they had tried to pack it with the softest leaves and cloth they could manage, but there would surely be plenty of discomfort on a long hike.

"I'm fine...but are you going to manage?"

"I'm technically trained up, so don't worry. My stamina's not fully back, but I'll manage. I'd rather not have Holly or Kuna too distracted in case something does happen."

It was already a huge help that they were coming along. No matter how hard it was, he couldn't ask them to carry Rem as well.

With Rem securely on his back and Louis ready at his side, Subaru stood. Holly and Kuna finished their preparations and joined them, dressed lightly for travel.

The rest of the village had already gathered.

"To the safety of our worthy brother Subaru Natsuki and to his success!" Mizelda cried out.

"—To his success!" the Shudrak women shouted in unison.

Feeling the chill breeze, Subaru managed a grateful smile.

"Yeah! Thank you, everyone. Take care!"

The words felt hollow and inadequate, considering the battles awaiting the Shudrak. But they were sincere. He wanted these bright, charming women to survive.

"..."

As the group began their journey, Subaru searched the crowd for the distinctive oni mask. But, perhaps unsurprisingly, Abel was nowhere to be seen.

Bearing the weight of his shame and gratitude…

"I'm going now!" Subaru called out.

"Ooo!" Louis echoed him with a loud shout.

With that, Subaru, Rem, Louis, Holly, and Kuna left the Shudrak village, taking their first steps toward the town of Guaral—away from the flames of the war that was sure to come.

5

THUD.

The loud sound echoed across the plain, startling a herd of animals in a small thicket of trees. The creatures, which resembled deer with imposing antlers and sleek black fur, were called black deer—large herbivores that grazed on the leaves.

The impact scattered the group, leaving one black deer lying motionless on the ground. A thick arrow protruded from its torso. It had pierced the animal's heart in a single, precise shot.

"I took down the meat!" Holly exclaimed triumphantly.

"...Meat? At least call it a black deer," muttered Kuna.

"Huh? Did you just say something? Your voice is so soft, I can't hear you, Kuna," Holly said, her tone as cheerful as ever. It was her heavy bow that had brought down the prey.

Kuna pursed her lips and snapped, "Never mind! Drain the blood! Let's get this over with."

"Ah, wait for me!" Holly called as Kuna stomped over to the deer. Holly paused mid-step, saying "Whoops," before turning around.

"We're going to take a break. Is that all right with you, Subaru?"

"...Y-yeah, no problem. I'm absolutely A-OK, but a break would be fine," Subaru replied, drenched in sweat and breathing heavily.

"Great," Holly said, dashing after Kuna.

Watching them leave, Subaru slowly knelt, his exhaustion plain to see. Behind him, perched in the wooden frame on his back, Rem let out a small sigh.

"...Stubborn...," she murmured softly, too faintly for Subaru to hear.

"Whew, I seriously underestimated this a bit. If I weren't the eldest son, I'd probably start complaining already. I can manage because I'm the eldest, but if I was second or even youngest, there's no way I could take this," Subaru rambled as he began gathering twigs for a campfire.

"I don't understand. Does having siblings have anything to do with perseverance?" Rem asked coldly.

Beneath her withering gaze, Subaru let out a groan.

"It's just a joke, but I do think having siblings changes how much you can persevere. Everyone says parents are stricter with the oldest and spoil the youngest, right?"

"Don't say 'right' as if I know what everyone says. Wouldn't that not apply to an only child?"

"In that case, you get pampered and raised strictly all at once. As an only child, I'm both the oldest and the youngest," Subaru quipped.

Considering how close his parents were, it was surprising he didn't have siblings. They showered their only child with love, and he sometimes wondered how different things might have been if he did have a brother or sister, but it didn't change reality.

"And there's no guarantee I haven't gotten any younger siblings while I've been away...," Subaru muttered, his imagination running wild.

"Aauaa," Louis cooed, playing on Rem's lap.

The wooden frame supporting Rem doubled as a seat when Subaru wasn't carrying it, sparing her the trouble of constantly getting on and off. Despite any embarrassment she might feel about relying on him, she would have to tolerate the arrangement for now.

While playing with Louis, Rem murmured absentmindedly, "Siblings... Did I have any?"

Subaru froze, his breath catching. Her question was unexpected. He looked up to meet Rem's gaze, her blue eyes tinged with a flicker of emotion she likely didn't fully understand herself.

"That's a first—you asking me about your memories," Subaru said.

"I've already asked you plenty of questions. *Where is this? Who are you? Who am I? What are you doing? How shameless can you be?*" Rem countered.

"I meant other than the negative ones. Also, I don't think you've asked about my shamelessness before just now," Subaru replied with a wan smile.

Despite her sharp words, her question felt like progress. This was the first time she had asked anything positive, and Subaru took it as a step forward.

Ever since they left the Shudrak village, Subaru had been bracing for a disaster. Rem, who had once been so blunt in her distrust and animosity toward him, was now surprisingly cooperative. It made him uneasy, as if calmness was merely the prelude to a storm.

Yet here she was, behaving herself. She had even scolded Louis when she got restless and got in the way during the day's travel. They were small gestures, but she was obviously trying to lighten Subaru's burden.

"..."

"What is it? Does that mean you have no intention of talking?" Rem asked.

"No, no, you've got it wrong. It's just...we've been kind of awkward this whole time, haven't we?"

"We still are. And the correct word is not *awkward*, but *cold*," Rem corrected him.

"I was thinking that coldness might be thawing, just a little!" Subaru replied.

Rem's disgusted look was another blow to Subaru's already battered heart, but he found a strange comfort in it—it was, after all, something he had received from her.

"I don't know everything about you," Subaru said. "But I do know more than you do at the moment. So if there's something you want to ask, I'll answer whatever I can. But..."

"It is up to me how much I believe you..."

"Yeah, pretty much." Subaru nodded, glancing at her.

Rem combed Louis's hair with her fingers, her brow furrowed in thought. After a moment of deliberation, she met Subaru's gaze again.

"I don't know."

"Of course not. You can't remember, after all."

"Not about me. About you... I cannot comprehend what sort of person you are at all. What I feel and what I see do not match," Rem said, her lips pursed and her blue eyes serious.

There was no malice in her words. Instead, her gaze was sharp as she tried to unravel the mystery that was Subaru.

At the very least, it was a sign of Rem's willingness to entertain the possibility of evaluating Subaru's humanity.

"...Considering you were treating me like the embodiment of all evil without letting me explain, that feels like a pretty big step forward," Subaru said.

"My doubt has not been cleared up... I simply thought there might be a sliver of leeway to reconsider it," Rem replied bluntly.

"All right, so with a single sheet of paper added to support the thin ice of our relationship, is there anything you want to ask me?" Subaru offered.

"...Allow me more time to think," Rem said after a pause.

Subaru, ready for a heart-to-heart, had to accept that Rem was not. She wasn't ready to trust him yet—not fully, anyway.

I'd be lying if I said I wasn't impatient, but...

"Got it. Then I'll wait for you to be ready," he said.

"Please don't say that as if it's not up to you as well. It wouldn't be entirely wrong to say your daily activities will play a big part," Rem replied coolly.

"I see... So the faster I rake in trust points and affection levels, the quicker the route opens up, huh?" Subaru nodded, putting his hand on his chin.

"I don't understand what you're saying, but I do know it's something unpleasant."

Subaru could almost hear her unhappiness gauge ticking up.

As their conversation trailed off, Holly returned, carrying the prepared black deer over her shoulder.

"Sorry for the wait. The black deer came apart nicely!" she said cheerfully, her wide smile beaming.

Behind her, Kuna followed with a tired expression.

"Why'd I have to do all the work...?" she grumbled.

"Because you're better at it! If the meat we found went to waste, I'd be hungry no matter how much I ate."

"Why? Keep what you eat in your stomach like a normal person!" Kuna snapped, her irritation evident.

Holly shrugged off the outburst with her usual grin, then noticed Subaru's bundle of sticks.

"Oh, you gathered some wood. Wow," she said.

"I can at least handle this much. As for lighting it, may I study your excellent example?" Subaru asked.

"What are you saying?" Holly cocked her head.

"He means he wants to learn," Kuna clarified, sighing.

"Really?" Holly asked, her smile widening. She pulled a black rock from her bag and struck it against another stone. Sparks flew, catching on the dried twigs, and a small flame took hold.

"Whoa, so cool! You're, like, an artisan!" Subaru exclaimed, clapping.

"It's super easy once you know how," Holly said, clearly pleased. "Now we can cook up the meat quickly."

As the black deer roasted over the fire, a rich, mouthwatering smell filled the air.

"Still, Holly, that was incredible, how fast you were. The moment you spotted the herd, you moved almost instantly," Subaru commented.

"It's because Kuna spotted the herd first. Thanks to her, we can keep having fresh meat."

"I just found the herd… While they might not be as fast as Holly, every one of the Shudrak can use a bow and arrow," Kuna said matter-of-factly.

"Except Kuna," Holly teased.

Kuna groaned, clearly annoyed.

"Really?" Rem asked, her eyes widening. "That's surprising. Mizelda said you have amazing eyesight…"

"…Even with good eyes, it's useless if your arms aren't strong enough," Kuna muttered, frowning.

"When it comes to bows, Kuna even loses to Utakata. So cute," Holly added.

"No one asked you!" Kuna snapped, delivering a knife-hand jab to Holly's stomach. Holly's plump frame absorbed the blow, and her cheerful demeanor remained unchanged.

Rem watched their exchange with an amused smile. The mention of Utakata's archery skills, however, made Subaru grimace. After all, he had once been killed by one of her poison arrows.

"Also, when it comes to bows and arrows…," Subaru murmured, placing a finger to his lips as he thought.

He remembered the hunter who had attacked him and Rem before they were captured by the imperial soldiers. That same hunter had protected them from a demon beast—and had also killed Subaru once.

He still didn't know who the hunter was.

So when he had seen Holly take down that black deer, Subaru had gone pale. But from what Kuna said about the Shudrak…

"…It could be any of them. Thinking about it more than that is probably pointless," he muttered to himself.

At the time, Subaru and Rem had been suspicious outsiders, stomping loudly through the jungle. It wasn't unreasonable for the Shudrak to assume they were enemies. But later, that same hunter had saved him during that encounter with the demon beast.

Not every encounter had been hostile.

"The two of you seem to get along nicely," Rem said, addressing Holly and Kuna.

Holly grinned, but Kuna stuck out her tongue in distaste.

"Ugh."

"What's with that face? It's not a great look for such a pretty lady," Holly teased.

"I was just reminded of a certain annoyance I can never seem to escape. I'm always the one doing all the work…," Kuna complained.

"Ah-ha-ha-ha, you're always such a worrier, Kuna."

"And whose fault is that?!" Kuna shot back.

Kuna angrily grabbed Holly's shoulders and shook them with all her might. However, the sheer size difference made it futile. Holly was more than twice Kuna's size, after all.

"Kuna and I were born on the same day. We're neighbors, and sort of like sisters."

"I'm not interested in being like you or being your sister, older or younger…"

"Ah, it's just about cooked up," Holly interrupted.

"Listen to me!" Kuna snapped.

Holly, as always, moved at her own pace, and Kuna was constantly being dragged along. Watching their dynamic, Subaru couldn't help but think of a certain hardworking adviser.

"Kuna's hair is dyed green, too, so their theme colors even match.

That dude's always making his presence known, even when he's not around," Subaru mused.

If the adviser heard that, Subaru imagined the reaction would be a loud, indignant, *That is an entirely ungrounded accusation!* But since the person in question wasn't there, Subaru dismissed him as a figment of his imagination.

Meanwhile, Holly and Kuna continued bickering over the readiness of the meat. Watching them, Rem's eyes softened slightly.

"It must be nice," she murmured, "having someone you can argue with so frankly..."

Subaru noticed the faint envy in her voice. To Rem, who had lost her memories, everyone around her—Subaru included—must have felt like a stranger, an invader emerging from the darkness. She had no one she could truly relax around, no one she could let her guard down with.

I don't know if it'll be a balm for her overworked heart, but...

"...Um, Rem, mind if I say one thing?" Subaru asked gently.

"What is it?"

"I know I said I'd wait until you wanted to ask me questions, but I'm going to let one thing slip out."

"Eh..."

"You have an older sister. An older twin who loves you from the bottom of her heart. So...no matter where you are, you're not alone."

Rem's blue eyes widened in surprise. Subaru had just gone back on his promise to wait, but he hadn't been able to help himself. Both he and Rem had their limits.

At the very least, he thought it would be okay to tell her about Ram—her twin sister, who was undoubtedly worrying about her even now, somewhere in Lugunica.

"I don't know if it'll work, but if you close your eyes and think about her, maybe you'll feel her. It's a shared consciousness you two have as twins."

"'Shared consciousness'...," Rem repeated, her voice uncertain.

After a moment of hesitation, she placed her hand over her chest and closed her eyes. Subaru watched silently as she reached into the darkness of her mind, searching for the other half of her soul—her twin, born on the same day, from the same mother.

However...

"...I...cannot feel anything," Rem said softly, shaking her head.

"I see...," Subaru muttered. "...I guess it's hard without an image in mind."

For a fleeting moment, worry crept into Subaru's thoughts. Could something have happened inside Rem that prevented her from connecting with Ram? But he quickly reasoned that the distance—both physical and emotional—was simply too great for now.

If it had worked, it would have solved so many problems. The failure was disappointing, and no one was more disappointed than Rem herself.

"Ah."

"Uuu?"

Subaru flinched as a soft breath escaped Rem's lips.

Louis, who had been resting her head on Rem's lap, had placed her small hand over Rem's hand on her chest. It was a simple, instinctive gesture, as if Louis was trying to comfort her.

Rem's lips softened, and she flashed a brave smile. "Thank you. I am all right."

Her words brought a bright smile to Louis's face, and the mood between them turned warm and tender.

Subaru, however, gritted his teeth, annoyed at having been beaten to the punch.

"Damn it... You really are my enemy...!" he muttered, glaring at Louis.

Rem, noticing his expression, misunderstood.

"Why would that be? Don't you think that's an immature reaction?" she scolded.

Louis, entirely oblivious to Subaru's frustration, kicked her legs and flailed her arms happily in Rem's lap.

Meanwhile...

"It's done!" Holly declared triumphantly.

"It's still raw!!!" Kuna shouted.

...The only two there who didn't have a half-baked relationship continued arguing about the meat.

6

—It took four days, but the group finally arrived safely at Guaral.

"So that's Guaral... It's got a nice wall protecting it," Subaru said, marveling at the fortified city visible in the distance.

The towering walls encircling the city were far more imposing than anything Subaru had imagined when he heard "nearest town." Seeing its size, he felt both surprised and fortunate—it was an unexpected stroke of luck.

"That's a pretty imposing aura... Are there giants here or something?" he mused aloud.

"Giants? I heard they were almost wiped out a long time ago," Kuna responded earnestly.

"Really? Then maybe the old man I know is the last giant...," Subaru muttered, thinking of Old Man Rom. To think he might actually be that rare.

He was reminded of Rem mentioning that the oni were also on the verge of extinction. The struggle for survival in this world seemed brutal.

"Now that I think about it, I haven't met any elves other than Emilia-tan. Maybe there aren't a lot of elves around, either," Subaru added, his thoughts drifting.

It fit the classic fantasy trope—long-lived races that reproduced slowly becoming scarce over time. Add the deep-rooted fear of the Witch of Envy, and it wasn't hard to imagine why elves or half-elves might struggle to find acceptance in many lands.

"Without Emilia-tan around, I end up thinking about her. Damn it, it's been ages since I've seen Beako, too. I'm probably running critically low on emiliase and beatrimin," Subaru lamented.

The only cure for those deficiencies was spending time with Emilia and Beatrice. More seriously, even hearing their voices would ease the constant worry and tension he felt.

"I miss Ram, Petra, and Frederica's voices... At this point, I'd even settle for Roswaal's," he said with a sigh.

"Umm, is there a point to this?" Rem's sharp question cut through his rambling.

Subaru had managed to carry her the entire trip without needing help from anyone else. The first couple of days had been rough—he'd wasted stamina figuring out how to balance the frame—but by the third day, he had settled into a comfortable pace and technique.

"There's no one better than me at carrying Rem."

"Please don't strive for a title so disgraceful. Also, Holly and Kuna are here," Rem pointed out.

Subaru turned to see Holly and Kuna behind him. Kuna scratched her head, looking bored, while Holly smiled cheerfully as always.

"All right, you made it safely, so this is goodbye," Holly announced.

"Ah... You're not coming into the town?" Subaru asked.

"There's no point. Our role was to deliver you here."

"I see... You two were a huge help," Subaru said, his tone heavy with gratitude.

It had been easy to forget their presence was merely a Shudrak courtesy because Holly and Kuna had been invaluable. Holly's cheerfulness and skill, along with Kuna's knowledge and practicality, had made the journey far smoother.

Now it was really just him, Rem...and Louis.

"...Sheesh, stop looking so pathetic," Kuna said.

"Sorry. Wait, 'pathetic'—whoa?!"

Before he could finish, Kuna thrust a long white bundle into his hands. The unexpected weight made Subaru stagger forward. It was the item Holly had been carrying on her back the entire trip.

"Huh. I assumed it was a weapon, but I never saw you open it. What is this?"

"It's yours. The chief said to give it to you when we reached town," Kuna explained.

"Mine? And only once we got here...?" Subaru's brow furrowed in confusion.

"Just open it already," Kuna urged.

Subaru set the frame down and unwrapped the white bundle. Inside was a large white animal horn.

"This is...a horn?" Rem murmured.

Subaru recognized it immediately—it was the horn of the elgina, the demon beast from the ritual of blood. It was the same horn he had shattered during the ritual.

"Is this...the elgina horn?"

"That's right. You broke it, so it's yours," Kuna replied matter-of-factly.

"It's valuable. With that size, it'll sell for a high price," Holly added.

"—gh!"

Subaru inhaled sharply, realizing their intent. The horn would pay for his journey back to Lugunica. They had carried it all this way without mentioning it once.

"This is pretty heavy to carry..."

"You carried Rem the whole time," Kuna said with a shrug.

"And I'm really strong, so it was fine," Holly added, smiling.

Their casual remarks only deepened Subaru's appreciation. They had not only protected him during the journey but had also ensured he had a way to fund his travels. And after he left them to go home, they would return to join the Shudrak in Abel's battle to reclaim the capital.

Who knew how many would die along the way?

"I..."

Subaru opened his mouth, but before he could speak, Kuna cut him off sharply.

"Quit thinking stupid things."

"..."

"Fight to protect what you want to protect. That's what we're doing, too," Kuna said, glaring at him with her usual bored expression.

Despite her complaints and frustrations, Kuna's loyalty to the Shudrak—and even to Holly—was unwavering. She knew what was important to her and stood firm in that belief.

"Don't be lazy. I've got good eyes. If you do something stupid, I'll be the first to see it."

"And if Kuna tells me, I'll bring the boom with my bow!" Holly chimed in.

"...Yeah, that's a scary thought," Subaru replied, feeling the weight of their words.

Understanding their intent, Subaru swallowed the emotions swelling inside him and said, "Thank you. I'll use this for the road. You've both been a huge help."

Both Holly and Kuna nodded in acknowledgment.

"Holly, Kuna, thank you for everything during the journey. I won't forget my gratitude to you and all the Shudrak," Rem said, dismounting from the frame to bid them farewell properly.

"Please don't forget. Since you apparently forget a lot of things."

"I think that's going a bit far, Kuna," Holly murmured.

Even Louis seemed reluctant to leave. She had gotten especially attached to Holly, who was always open with others. Louis clung to her waist for a while, refusing to let go.

"See you, Subaru. Don't forget, I'm watching you," Kuna said.

"That's right!" Holly added with a wave.

"Yeah! I'm really grateful. Thank you!" Subaru called back as the three of them set out toward Guaral.

Subaru placed the horn back into its bundle and handed it to Louis to carry. It was a tough decision, but he needed to keep his hands free. Surprisingly, Louis carried it carefully, perhaps inspired by Holly and Kuna's encouragement.

"She's seeing all sorts of things," Rem murmured softly.

"...I know full well she's a bundle of curiosity," Subaru replied bitterly.

Louis Arneb, the Archbishop of Gluttony, consumed every life she could get her hands on in search of the optimal life for herself. Put generously, she was a researcher, or, less generously, she was an omnivore. So her showing a mildly admirable quality was not enough to change Subaru's perception of her.

And it shouldn't.

"Let's go," Subaru said, stepping forward.

Rem sighed but followed, and Louis's small steps trailed after them.

Just like when they first arrived in Volakia, the three of them were together, and now they were finally moving in the same direction.

Passing under the great gate, they entered the fortified city of Guaral.

CHAPTER 2
CREEPING MALIGNANCY

1

—The fortified city of Guaral.

It was the first developed place in Volakia that Subaru and company had reached. Having spent all their time in an imperial army field camp and the Shudrak village—which was not much different from camping out in the wilderness—they were especially moved by the sight of civilization.

However, there was a reason not to get too excited about this semblance of civilization: inspections.

Guaral was enclosed by walls on all four sides, with entry limited to the main gates on the east and west of the city. From afar, the guards looked imposing, and a strict inspection point was clearly in place.

"Right now, we're foreign Lugunicans with no backing... Even I, someone known for my inability to read the mood, can tell that this isn't exactly a situation where the empire will just welcome us in," Subaru muttered.

If they honestly revealed their identities, they would undoubtedly draw the ire of the gatekeepers. Being turned back at the gate would be frustrating but manageable. However, being arrested would be another story entirely. This inspection would be a litmus test for how well they could manage in Volakia.

"What will you do? Just getting into the line isn't an option, right?" Rem asked from atop her seat, her gaze fixed on the line of people awaiting inspection.

"I know." Subaru nodded. "I'm not just staring at the line without a plan here. I do have something in mind."

"Are you not embarrassed to lie so easily?"

"Try having just a little faith in me! Isn't it a bit soon to assume I'm lying?!"

Subaru's attempt to explain his secret plan was met with Rem's staggering lack of faith.

The key point was that the three of them alone would not pass the inspection.

"In other words, it's time for Subaru Natsuki's one-hundred-and-eighth special technique: *relying on others*. This is its time to shine."

Even though he couldn't see her face, and she shouldn't be able to see his, he somehow knew her face was twisted into a scowl.

Either way…

"We made it!"

"Aauuu!"

As they entered the city and took in the townscape, Subaru raised both hands in triumph. Beside him, Louis mimicked the gesture and laughed. This made them seem like comrades, but Subaru's joy at successfully entering the city outweighed any annoyance. To his chagrin, Louis's presence had been a big help in getting past the inspection.

"Still, it really is different from Lugunica," Subaru remarked as he looked around the town, comparing it to his memories of the neighboring kingdom.

The most prominent cities in Lugunica were the capital, Lugunica; the Water Gate City, Pristella; and the industrial city of Castour near Roswaal's manor. Guaral bore little resemblance to any of them.

Compared to the kingdom with its standard fantasy aesthetic, the empire's city had a more utilitarian and unrefined look and less vibrant colors. Function seemed to take precedence over decoration.

"In Lugunica, the roads would be paved with stone, but here the ground is unpaved. I wonder if that's just normal here?"

"Umm, could you let me down now?"

"Sorry, sorry," Subaru apologized, gently setting the frame down.

"This is..."

Getting off her seat, Rem stood on her own two feet on the road, her eyes widening as she took in the scene. A mix of surprise and faint excitement flickered in her light-blue eyes, softening Subaru's expression.

"How is it, seeing your first city?" he asked.

"...I'm surprised. There were many people in the line, but to think there are so many more here."

Up until now, Rem had only experienced isolated places and exceptional circumstances. With no memories, she couldn't recall ever living among others. Her time with Subaru, Louis, and the Shudrak was the extent of her experience.

As cities went, Guaral was not exactly bustling with activity.

A long line at the gate, a cityscape that was rough around the edges and not a particularly bright palette—it didn't leave a particularly vivid impression. The city probably housed only a few thousand people. Even so, it was enough to evoke genuine emotion in Rem's eyes.

"In that case, do you want to walk around and take a look?" Subaru offered.

"...No, there's no need. I don't want to waste more time than necessary."

"I wouldn't call it a waste if it's for you," Subaru said, scratching his cheek. "If it weren't for you, things wouldn't have gone so smoothly with Flop and the others. You can be a little selfish if you want."

"...I'm saying it wouldn't be good to keep those very same people waiting. You've already relied so much on them, and now you'd put yourself even further in their debt?"

"Ugh... When you put it that way, yeah, sorry..."

Rem's sharp gaze pierced Subaru's chest.

Behind them, a cart drawn by a farrow creaked heavily as it passed through the gate. Farrows were domesticated animals, like land dragons and ligers. Lacking wind-blocking blessings like land dragons, farrows were slower and primarily used for transport within towns.

And...

"Hey, hey, hey, kept you waiting! They took their time checking the load! Sheesh, talk about a hassle!"

A young man with long forelocks sat in the coachman's seat, shrugging dramatically as his cart approached. His dazzling blond hair, fair skin, and loose-fitting clothes over a slender frame gave him a relaxed, gentle air that put others at ease.

Seeing him, Subaru bowed his head.

"Sorry about that, Flop. You even let us go ahead of you."

"Nah, don't worry about it! Cargo inspections are boring work. There's nothing to gain sticking around for that!"

The man, Flop, shook his head gently, dismissing Subaru's apology. His long hair swayed like a tail in an elegant gesture, almost sparkling alongside his soft smile. His energetic manner of speaking created an intriguing contrast with his gentle appearance.

Flop casually touched his forelocks.

"Yeah, it's a boring job. So just leave that to m...y sister!"

"Hey, Brother, I heard that, you know!"

"Ha-ha-ha, I wasn't trying to hide it, Little Sis! Don't underestimate your brother's voice control."

Flop's response was painfully vague. The person who'd answered was a tall woman walking beside the slow-moving cart. She had the same blond hair as Flop, a similar facial structure, and a remarkable height—she was easily taller than any woman Subaru had encountered in this world.

Her clothes left her shoulders and legs mostly bare, and her voluminous hair was divided into countless intricate locks and arranged into a striking style.

While the rest of her appearance was eye-catching, her most notable feature was the pair of swords at her hips. Judging by their well-worn condition, they were clearly not decorative.

She introduced herself as Medium. She and her brother, Flop, had been traveling together. The O'Connell siblings were the ones who had helped Subaru and his party pass through the inspection point.

When Subaru implemented Operation: Rely on the Kindness of Others, he'd carefully observed the line to identify whom to approach—and ultimately settled on Flop and Medium.

The reason for choosing them was...

"Whooooa! You saw through everything and knew what I was thinking?!" Medium asked, amazed.

"Of course. If you can't see into the future, you'll never succeed as a merchant. Our O'Connell Company is built on my brain and your brawn, after all!"

"That's my bro for you! I don't have a clue what you're talking about!"

"Ha-ha-ha-ha, as long as you're enjoying yourself!"

The siblings exchanged loud laughter. Their easygoing rapport and vibrant personalities were what had drawn Subaru to them. Flop managed the business aspect of their traveling company, while Medium protected her brother and their goods on the road.

"I used what I learned from talking with Otto and Anastasia...," Subaru muttered to himself.

Both Otto, his ally, and Anastasia, whom he had traveled with extensively, were merchants. While Anastasia had been Echidna in disguise, her knowledge had been no less impressive than Otto's. Thanks to them, Subaru had developed a certain trust in merchants.

Even in a foreign land, he believed he could negotiate with merchants, which had ultimately led him to the O'Connell siblings. Subaru had successfully persuaded this eccentric duo to help them through the inspection point.

As for the cost of their assistance, what had caught the siblings' attention most was...

"Still, is this frame really enough compensation? It's got some clever design elements, but it's clearly handmade."

"I won't deny it's a bit simple! But I'm interested in its practicality and the extra features for carrying things. It'll be great for transporting heavy loads, right?"

"...Well, if you're satisfied with that, then I'm good with it," Subaru said.

The O'Connell siblings had bartered for the carrying frame Subaru had made for Rem. After disassembling it, Medium loaded it into their cart.

"I was planning to make a new one when we got to town anyway. Besides, you might not even use it again," Subaru said.

"That's true. I'd prefer to walk on my own feet if possible. When I rode it, the breeze carried your horrible stench," Rem quietly retorted, leaning on her staff.

"My bad...," Subaru muttered, wincing at her bluntness about the miasma that clung to him. She had endured it throughout the journey, so her bringing it up only after they'd arrived showed a surprising bit of compassion.

Watching their interaction, Flop shrugged lamentably.

"That's no good. You two should get along better! A husband and wife should support each other—it was beautiful how you literally supported each other before!"

"But you're the one who took their carrying frame, Brother!"

"Ah, you're right! What right do I have to talk!" Flop exclaimed, pressing his palm to his forehead as Medium burst into laughter.

Their silly exchange brought a smile to Subaru's face. However, when he glanced at Rem, she wasn't smiling.

"Umm," Subaru began hesitantly. "Ms. Rem? Are you upset?"

"Huh? Why would I be upset? I can't imagine why you'd think that."

"It's just..." Subaru fidgeted, poking his fingers together. "Even if it's just a story, the whole thing about us being married might not have been something you liked..."

As far as Flop and Medium were concerned, Subaru and Rem were husband and wife.

When Subaru had approached the O'Connell siblings for help

with the inspection, they'd naturally asked about his relationship with Rem and Louis. Caught off guard, Subaru had been pressed for an answer on the spot.

—No, that wasn't entirely it. He *had* an answer prepared. It just wasn't believed, leaving him with no other choice.

"I didn't think they wouldn't buy the traveling-siblings setup...," Subaru muttered.

"Flop and Medium are siblings themselves, and they resemble each other strongly. It wasn't a believable lie for you, me, and that child," Rem pointed out.

Subaru could only concede the truth. His attempt to deceive Flop, a merchant who made a living discerning lies from truth, had failed spectacularly. However, it wasn't Flop who poked holes in the story—it was Medium, loudly exclaiming from the back, "They don't look anything like each other, Brother!"

With the sibling lie exposed, Subaru had panicked and pivoted to a convoluted tale about journeying to a distant mountain to dispose of a cursed ring. Unfortunately, the story became so complicated and incoherent that it spiraled out of control.

What ultimately saved them was Rem's simple declaration: "I'm his wife."

"You and I are married, and she's your older sister's kid, who was left in our care..."

"You were the one who decided I have an older sister. We're twins, so it's unlikely she'd have a child this old...but I'll set that aside," Rem said, patting Louis on the head.

"Uuu?" Louis made a soft sound, seemingly tickled by Rem's hand.

Louis's innocent behavior had played a big role in convincing Flop and Medium about their story. At the very least, the siblings seemed assured that Subaru and company weren't troublemakers.

"Why did you struggle so much back there? Normally you're quick to say whatever's most convenient."

"You almost made that sound like a compliment, but it's really just a complaint...," Subaru replied, scratching his cheek.

Still, he had to admit that his lackluster response had endangered

Rem. There was only so much he could gloss over with small talk. He swore to himself that he wouldn't let her down again, especially after seeing the way she'd groaned and looked at him.

"Yeah, I was surprised, too. When they saw through my lie, my mind just blanked. Maybe...maybe getting stabbed in the shoulder for talking carelessly was a bit traumatic."

"Ah..."

"I was just afraid of things going south because of a bad response. I know it's pathetic, but my brain just froze up. I'm sorry," Subaru said, lowering his head apologetically.

The memory of Todd's sudden betrayal at the army camp, right after Subaru had Returned by Death, haunted him. That experience had etched fear into his heart, leaving him hesitant to lie. His failure had put Rem's life at risk—a mistake he couldn't afford.

"...I understand. You did the best you could in that situation."

"...Really? Even with that big of a screwup?"

"Everyone's body freezes up at painful memories. That's what I think, at least."

He had expected a cold rebuke and was taken aback by her unexpected kindness. While he knew Rem had a gentle heart capable of empathy, he hadn't expected her to direct that understanding toward him.

"...You're not mad?"

"I am not. But I can't think up a good excuse every time, so talk to me first," Rem replied.

"Y-yeah, I got it... You're really not mad?"

"I am not mad."

"Really, really?"

"I *said* I'm not mad, didn't I?!"

Despite her earlier patience, Subaru's persistent questioning eventually made her angry.

Shrinking under her sharp gaze, Subaru could only beg forgiveness.

And with that small scene, the three of them finally managed to enter Guaral.

2

"I finally feel alive again!"

Subaru flung himself onto the bed in the inn, stretching out his arms and legs with exaggerated satisfaction.

The bed and sheets were of decent quality, and the room was clean enough—upper mid-tier for lodging and reasonably priced. Considering their circumstances, it wasn't wise to indulge in luxury, but it was a practical expense for safety.

More importantly…

"We had a pretty big fight over the rooms…," Subaru muttered, rolling onto his side to stare at the wall.

Rem and Louis were in the room next door. When they'd arranged their stay in Guaral, they'd decided on a male/female room split, but Subaru hadn't been happy about it.

Even now, Subaru remained suspicious of Louis and couldn't fully let his guard down around her. The idea of Rem and Louis being alone together in a separate room made him uneasy.

"Wow, you must really love kicking back and relaxing, huh? That's great, buddy!" Flop said as he strolled into the room.

Flop entered without hesitation—it wasn't like he was intruding. The room had been arranged with the expectation that he and Subaru would share it, just as Medium was sharing the other room with Rem and Louis.

"I'm really sorry, relying on you for everything like this…," Subaru said apologetically.

"It's fine! You used your wit to survive. Strength isn't just about combat for citizens of the empire, after all!"

"…Hearing you say that is a relief," Subaru replied with an awkward smile, sitting cross-legged on the bed.

Even after they'd passed the inspection, Flop and Medium had been a huge help. Beyond the introduction to a safe and affordable lodging, the biggest help had been their assistance in selling the demon beast horn.

The horn Louis had carried on her back was now gone. Following Kuna's advice, they'd sold it to a merchant in Guaral. Flop had come along for some reason and handled the price negotiations. The heated exchange between Flop and the merchant had sounded almost like a courtroom battle to Subaru, who lacked knowledge of imperial trade laws.

"I can't imagine how much that merchant would've taken advantage of us without you," Subaru admitted.

Thanks to Flop, they'd safely converted the demon beast horn into imperial currency—a hefty bag of gold coins that would serve as their war chest for their time in the empire. It had to cover all their travel expenses, so Subaru knew he had to be careful with it.

"I can't let someone eat my lunch like that!"

"Ha-ha-ha-ha! Boldness is always a good first step. As long as you stand tall and proud, no one will assume you're easy prey. Given enough time, that baseless confidence might just become the real thing—and that'd be a steal, right?"

"Hmmm, that actually sounds convincing coming from someone like you…," Subaru said.

For better or worse, Flop exuded confidence. Subaru had benefited from that multiple times, which had left him quietly appreciative.

"Still, carrying your wife all that way must've been rough. You should get some good rest—we can talk more tomorrow," Flop suggested.

"That's a tempting offer, but I can't afford to waste time," Subaru replied, reluctantly peeling himself off the bed.

"Excellent!" Flop said, puffing out his chest with pride. "That's the spirit! Sometimes you've gotta push through for someone precious. My sister in my case, your wife in yours!"

"That's a bit embarrassing when you say it so directly! …So can I ask you to guide me?"

"Of course! I'm the one who suggested it!" Flop replied cheerfully, thumping his chest.

Subaru summoned his energy, shaking off the lure of the soft bed, and followed Flop to the other room. Knocking on the door, he called out to Rem.

"Rem, everything okay in there?"

"Yes, it's fine. We're just deciding which bed Louis will sleep in."

"...I see."

"You just made a face like you wanted to suggest she sleep on the floor, didn't you?"

"I didn't say it because I knew you'd get angry...," Subaru muttered.

Considering the potential danger Louis represented, Subaru didn't like the idea of her sleeping near Medium. Still, given the situation, he had no choice but to rely on the fact that Louis hadn't caused any problems over the past ten days.

—*Trusting an Archbishop is still incredibly stupid...*

"I mentioned it earlier, but I'm going out with Flop. Let's grab dinner outside later," Subaru said.

"Understood... Although, with so many people here, maybe I don't need to depend on you as much anymore," Rem replied.

"Why'd you have to say something like that? Now it's hard for me to leave!" Subaru exclaimed, visibly conflicted.

Her comment tugged at Subaru's thoughts, but he pushed it aside, focusing on his original plan. Inside the room, Medium was playing with Louis, who was tugging at her hair. Subaru gave a small wave and said, "Medium, please take care of them. If she gives you any trouble, feel free to give her a good smack."

"You sure? My smacks really, really hurt."

"Yeah, she won't learn if it doesn't hurt."

With that, he and Flop left the inn, though Subaru could only pray that nothing would happen in their absence.

We're finally in a city; I'd like to relax a little.

"It seems you've had quite the rough road, buddy," Flop said, patting Subaru on the shoulder as they walked through the bustling streets.

Hearing that, Subaru felt the weight of exhaustion press down on him. He wanted to slump to the ground and wallow, but doing so would only burden Flop further.

"Even if relying on others is my one-hundred-and-eighth special technique, I can't keep causing trouble," Subaru admitted.

"Hey, there's nothing wrong with relying on people. Without covering for each other's weaknesses, my sister and I wouldn't have lasted long on the road. That's part of the imperial way, too, isn't it?"

"The imperial way…," Subaru echoed, the phrase weighing heavily on him.

Flop's words were unexpectedly thoughtful, though they clashed with Subaru's impression of Volakia's harsh values. Flop's perspective felt more relatable and grounded, contrasting sharply with Subaru's fears about imperial culture.

"Not everyone's cut out for the soldier's life. What matters is understanding yourself and finding your place. That's what I think," Flop continued.

"Understanding yourself?" Subaru asked.

"Exactly. My sister and I both have our weaknesses, but we make up for each other. Together we can do things neither of us could manage alone. You could say that's our secret to survival."

"…"

"Remember this, buddy: You, your wife, me, my sister—we're all alive today because we've won every battle we've faced… See, I'm a man of the empire, too." Flop smiled warmly as he paused for effect like he was waiting for applause.

Staring at Flop's face, Subaru felt as though he'd stumbled onto an unexpected revelation. The idea of two people compensating for each other's weaknesses resonated deeply with him after his fear that it wouldn't translate well here in the empire.

"So it's not hopeless after all…," Subaru murmured.

"To be clear, when most people here talk about the imperial way, they *are* talking about brute force! Plenty have laughed at me for my ideas, calling them the buzzing of a little gnat. I wouldn't say I'm exactly normal," Flop admitted, laughing.

After issuing a warning about treating his general advice as a hard and fast rule, Flop continued. "And that's why sometimes you can put a price on strength— and places like the one I'm taking you to now is where you can buy it."

"Makes sense." Subaru nodded. "I appreciate it."

He was grateful once again for Flop's assistance. In addition to helping them through the inspection and securing them lodging, Flop was now leading Subaru to a bar where mercenaries and adventurers gathered.

The purpose was clear: to recruit reliable escorts and transport for their journey ahead. Just as Kuna and Holly had protected them en route to Guaral, Subaru knew they would need skilled help.

There was also a limit to how much they could do with Subaru carrying Rem on his back. A ground dragon would be ideal, but if that was too difficult, an ox or liger would do.

He would have to recruit both of those things on their limited war chest.

"It's a huge help having you point me in the right direction," Subaru said.

"It's no problem. Though really, it's just knowing a bar where these folks hang out. As for pack animals, I'm a bit more useful—how about a farrow cart?" Flop suggested enthusiastically.

"You really like farrows, huh...?" Subaru said, slightly exasperated.

"It's no exaggeration to say I was raised on farrow's milk. I'm something of a farrowphile!" Flop proclaimed, launching into an impassioned rant about the virtues of farrows.

While farrows were reliable for moving heavy loads, they were slow, making them less than ideal for long journeys. Subaru listened politely but wasn't convinced they were the right choice.

"It's always better to play it safe while you're on the road," Flop advised. "Just between you and me, things seem to be heating up in the capital. There's no guarantee the sparks won't spread."

"Trouble in the capital?" Subaru asked, raising an eyebrow.

Flop didn't seem to notice Subaru's reaction as he folded his arms and continued. "That's right. It wouldn't be the empire without some smoldering uproar. But the worry is whether those flames will spread. Keep this between us, though—no need to worry the missus."

"Thanks for the concern... Incidentally, does the emperor have anything to do with those sparks?" Subaru asked.

"His Highness Emperor Vincent Volakia?" Flop's eyes widened in surprise. "No way, not at all. I haven't heard anything about His Highness stirring up trouble. If anything, he's done an incredible job restoring order."

"But you said the flames were smoldering," Subaru pointed out.

"That they're just smoldering is thanks to His Highness. It's been seven or eight years since he ascended to the throne. Things were a lot rougher before then."

"..."

"His Highness is directly taking charge to deal with the current turmoil. Our homeland with its smoldering sparks will be back to normal in no time," Flop said confidently.

"Huh?" Subaru murmured, unable to hide his unease.

Flop spoke as if the smoldering sparks were simply part of what made the empire feel like home. Yet one thing caught Subaru's attention—the claim that the emperor was taking direct command of the situation.

"The emperor is personally involved in this back-and-forth at the capital?" Subaru asked.

"It's not typical, but when the sparks start flying around your own home…and in this case, it really is his home…even the emperor has to act. The proclamation said there'd be no mercy for those taking advantage of the situation!" Flop replied enthusiastically.

"The proclamation…," Subaru repeated, letting the words sink in.

Flop's excitement didn't seem deceptive; there was no reason for him to lie. At the very least, he genuinely believed what he was saying. But for Subaru, that last detail raised a significant concern.

"If Abel really is the emperor, would he have issued a declaration…? The timing doesn't add up," Subaru murmured to himself.

Even without the emperor's direct involvement, someone else could issue a statement by proxy—like a secretary or official using his name. According to Abel's story, those remaining in the capital were rebels who had ousted him. They wouldn't hesitate to exploit his title.

"But there's always the chance Abel is just a madman…," Subaru admitted grimly.

If you swallow everything without thinking, you won't last long in a stormy sea.

The uncertain situation in Volakia required a healthy dose of skepticism. While Abel's actions didn't convince Subaru that the man was a mere self-proclaimed emperor, he couldn't dismiss the possibility entirely.

"Buddy, you've gotta work on those wrinkles," Flop said, stepping in front of Subaru and pointing at his brow.

Subaru stopped walking and blinked at him, puzzled.

"Good fortune won't come to those who can't smile and don't have any room in their hearts. You're about to look for someone to join you on your journey, right? You need to find a good match."

"That's…"

"In that case, smooth out those wrinkles, relax your face, and act like you've got it all together. That's the look of a capable man."

Flop ran a finger along his own brow and used his hands to gently massage his cheeks, demonstrating his point. Subaru, caught off guard, let out a small breath before reluctantly following suit.

"…Ah, I forgot. My expression is already bad enough with my eyes as it is. I need to work on making my overall vibe friendlier," Subaru admitted.

"Sorry! Even with all my power, I can't fix that!"

"You don't have to take it so seriously! I got this face from my parents—it doesn't bother me that much!"

Their exaggerated banter eased the tension that had been weighing on Subaru's thoughts. Spirits lifted, they turned down an alley and arrived at their destination—a hole-in-the-wall bar.

"If you had a big group, you'd want to hire a bunch of guards," Flop explained. "But since it's just you, the missus, and your niece, you don't need a whole army. Just remember me and my sister won't be able to leave Guaral with you."

"But if I played my cards right, I feel like I could convince Medium to come with us…," Subaru mused.

"If you take my sister away, I'll lose my other half, and I'll just lay down and die!" Flop declared dramatically.

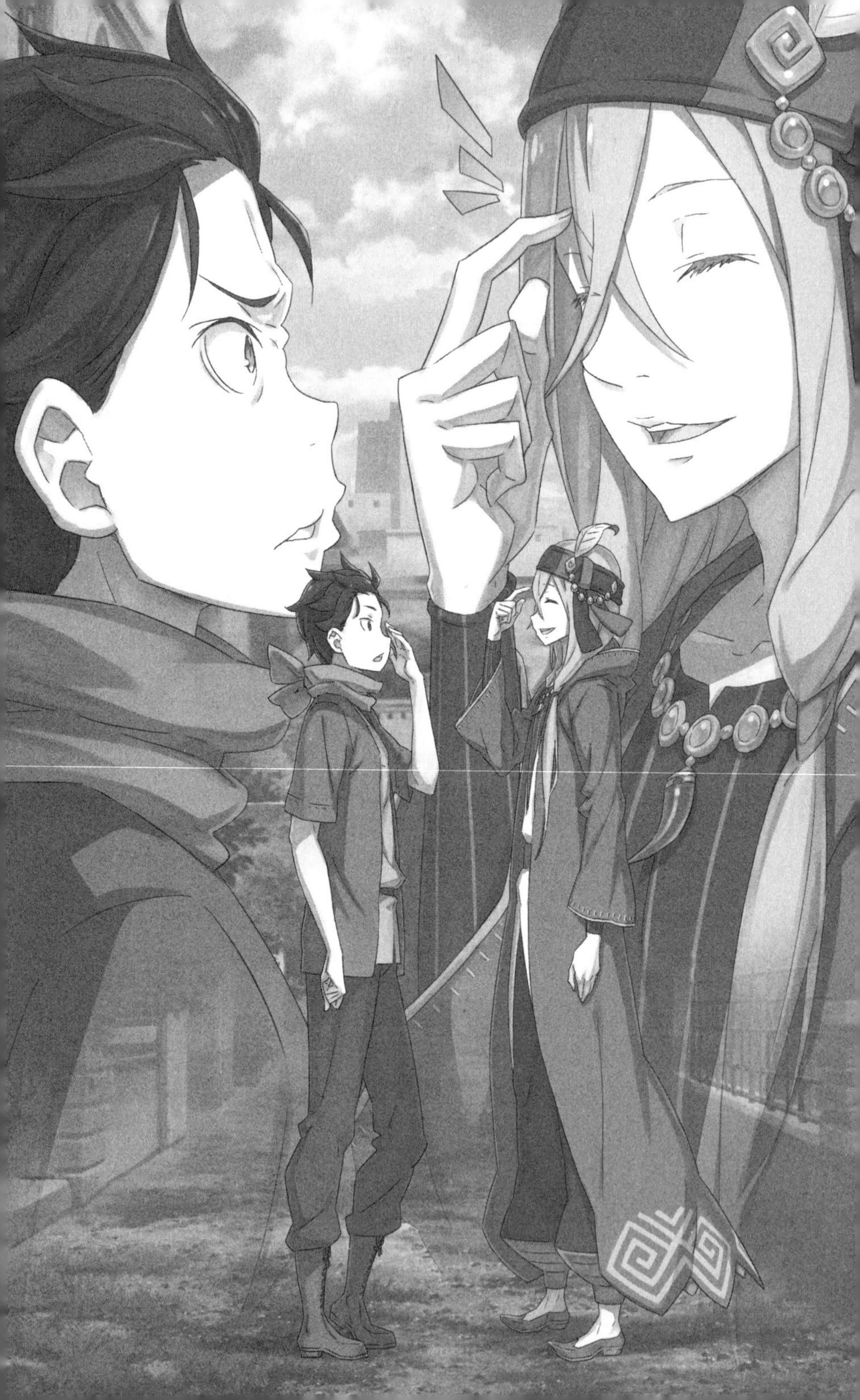

Subaru chuckled at the exaggeration, but he knew Flop and Medium would be an excellent choice in terms of balancing trust and safety. Still, he didn't want to burden them further.

"Worst case, we could bring the two of them back to Lugunica with us. They could help Otto build his merchant network...," Subaru thought aloud, his mind drifting.

"Hey, buddy? You all right?" Flop waved a hand in front of Subaru's face, snapping him back to reality.

"Sorry," Subaru said, scratching his head sheepishly. It was just a passing thought, but not necessarily a bad idea. Still, he had something else to focus on now.

"Hey, Flop, there's something I was thinking of asking you—," Subaru began.

Just as he spoke—

—there was a faint, dissonant sound.

3

"Buddy, you gotta work on those wrinkles."

"...Huh?"

Suddenly the world shifted, as if he had blinked, and Subaru's consciousness went blank.

When he came to, Flop was standing in front of him, pointing to the space between his own eyes. Flop began massaging the spot, demonstrating for Subaru.

"Good fortune won't come to those who can't smile and don't have any room in their hearts. You're about to look for someone to join you on your journey, right? You need to find a good match," Flop said, smiling.

"..."

"In that case, smooth out those wrinkles, relax your face, and act like you've got it all together. That's the look of a capable man."

Flop then began stretching and kneading his cheeks.

The gesture felt eerily familiar. *Too* familiar. Subaru stiffened, realizing it was the exact same conversation they'd had a few minutes ago.

"Hey, whoa now, wait just a minute…"

Subaru broke out in a cold sweat, and he covered his face with his hands.

"Not hide, *relax*!" Flop said in a loud voice, misunderstanding Subaru's reaction.

But Subaru wasn't composed enough to respond.

When he looked around, the street and surroundings seemed disturbingly familiar. It was his first time in Guaral, so he shouldn't have been intimately familiar with the city. Still, his memory wasn't bad enough that he didn't recognize a place he'd just been.

In other words…

"…I Returned by Death?"

For an entirely different reason from last time, Subaru's face tensed. He had no idea what had even happened.

Trying to process the incomprehensible situation, Subaru felt the cold sweat soak through his clothes. This was one of the most terrifying scenarios imaginable—a moment he had lived through repeating itself. It wasn't simply déjà vu. It was something that had truly happened, playing out again.

And that could mean only one thing: Subaru had died and come back to life.

"But…why?"

There had been no warning signs. It was as if the world had simply cut out in an instant, like a light switch flipping off. The abruptness felt so unreal that Subaru briefly wondered if his ability had malfunctioned—as if Return by Death had forgotten the "death" part and simply rewound time.

"What am I, stupid? No, I'm an idiot," Subaru muttered, correcting himself.

As ridiculous as it sounded, he had to trust Return by Death. In all the time he'd had this power, it had never activated without him dying first. If time had rewound, then Subaru had died. That much was certain.

"...Okay, I've accepted it's true. Now figure out what to do next, me," Subaru muttered, pressing a fist to his forehead in an effort to steady himself.

If he accepted that he'd died, the next step was identifying *what* had killed him. He replayed the moments leading up to his presumed death, trying to piece it together.

"...There's nothing..."

When he thought back, there was nothing obvious to suggest a threat. They'd been heading to a bar. Flop had been talking. He had heard the sounds of the main street in the distance. The shady alley smelled ever so slightly. Then there had been a faint, dissonant sound he'd barely registered.

None of these things pointed to anything that should have been life-threatening.

"Damn it, why am I always like this...!"

He cursed his lack of caution. If he had been more attuned to changes in his surroundings, perhaps he wouldn't feel so powerless now. Even so, he forced himself to keep thinking.

"...It's sort of like the first time Shaula killed me," Subaru muttered.

He remembered the first time they had crossed the Auguria Dunes on the road to the Pleiades Watchtower. Shaula, defending the tower, had killed him with a single shot—a beam of white light that obliterated him before he could react.

The experience had been horrifying. Not knowing what had happened, not knowing what had killed him, only knowing that he had died.

In that sense, this was eerily similar to that first death in the desert.

However, unlike that time in the Auguria Dunes, Subaru was inside a city—a completely different setting. This wasn't a place where it felt like his life was on the line every second.

"What's taking my life in this situation...?"

When he thought of sudden, unannounced death, Shaula's sniping immediately came to mind. But that scenario clashed with where he had died: an alley. The buildings on either side weren't particularly tall, and the location wasn't open enough for a sniper to have a clean shot.

"...Buddy? Why are your wrinkles getting worse again?" Flop asked.

"Ah..."

"Didn't I just tell you? Furrowed brows scare away good fortune! And it's really hard to chase it down once it's gone, especially since I'm usually riding a cart!" Flop gestured dramatically, trying to lighten the mood.

Subaru froze, not because of Flop's antics but because of the implications of his current train of thought. If Subaru had died, the most logical way to start was by questioning the person who had been with him.

If he hadn't been killed by a sniper, then the next prime suspect was Flop.

Flop had been with him and was the closest at the time of his death. However, when Subaru thought back, there hadn't been any indication that Flop had tried to attack him. While there were plenty of people in this world capable of killing Subaru in an instant without him noticing, Flop didn't seem to be one of them.

"First of all, would he even have a reason to kill me?"

The most plausible explanation was that Flop had been feigning kindness to rob him. But that didn't make sense, either. They'd met in the line outside the city gate—Flop could have lured Subaru away and finished him off in a less conspicuous location.

The timing, method, and motive didn't line up.

Every time someone or something had killed Subaru, there had been a reason for it. Even demon beasts acted on instinct or purpose, following a kind of twisted logic.

"Flop, why are you being so kind to us?" Subaru asked suddenly.

"Hmm?" Flop raised his eyebrows. "What brought that on?"

"Ah, sorry for the sudden question. I've just been feeling a little nervous," Subaru replied, forcing an awkward smile while his heart pounded in his chest.

I don't have a logical reason to doubt him. So it all comes down to whether I can believe his answer.

He wanted to believe that the O'Connell siblings, who had been so kind and helpful, did not have any ulterior motives.

Flop nodded, seemingly deep in thought. "It's nothing too complicated. Me and my sister doing right by you, your wife, and your little niece is just…"

"'Is just'…?"

"Revenge!" Flop declared, spreading his arms wide.

Subaru blinked, stunned by the cheerful tone that clashed so starkly with the unexpected answer.

"Listen here," Flop continued, touching his forelocks. "Way back, my sister and I lived every day not knowing if it would be our last. Abandoned by our parents, raised in an orphanage… It was a rough place, let me tell you!"

Subaru vaguely imagined a run-down facility, far worse than anything he could picture from his own world.

"Every night, the kids would dream about escaping. And one night, me and my sister managed it. That first night without a beating, I swore I'd get revenge," Flop said, clenching a fist.

"Revenge…on the people at the orphanage?"

"No, not them. On the world."

Flop's fist tightened as he leaned forward with a passionate look in his eyes.

"Those adults who beat us—they weren't happy, either. They were miserable people taking out their frustrations on us unhappy children. Could there be anything more pointless?"

"…"

"So me and my sister decided to break that cycle. I became a merchant, and we set out to bring as many people as we could out of misfortune, just like the person who helped us escape that night."

"…That's your revenge on the world?" Subaru asked quietly.

"That's right. Helping you and your family is just another step in our fight against the world's unfairness."

After finishing, Flop scratched his nose, looking a little embarrassed.

Subaru was speechless. The raw honesty of Flop's words struck him deeply, and for a moment, all his doubts faded.

"Thank you, Flop. I'm glad it was you and Medium who we met in that line," Subaru said.

He had planned to decide whether or not to trust Flop based on his answer. But the response he got went far beyond what he'd expected.

He decided to trust in Flop O'Connell's righteous vengeance against an unfair world.

With that resolve, Subaru turned his attention to the looming threat.

"Flop, I've got a bad feeling about this alley. The feng shui's no good. The hexagram we'd pull would be awful. Can we take a different route?"

"'Feng shui'? What's that? Is that why your brows are so furrowed and your eyes are like that?"

"It's an ancient practice that's got nothing to do with my eyes! I'm serious. This alley's no good. We can take a detour, so please."

While relying on Flop's goodwill, Subaru rather forcefully moved the conversation along.

If he trusted that Flop was not the culprit, then the next priority was avoiding the death that was approaching. Whether from a sniper or something else, there would be an attack of some kind. He needed to evade that attack and escape an unwelcome death.

"Not that there were any welcome ones… Maybe once or twice."

And those instances had been welcome only because of looming situations and nothing else. Unless there was something that could only be fixed by dying, Subaru would never choose death. As he thought about those sorts of moments, Subaru began to understand Flop's desire to get revenge on the world.

"Huh, all right. If you're feeling that strongly about it, why not? It'll be a bit of a detour, but we can take another route," Flop agreed easily.

"I appreciate it! Ideally one with lots of people. Let's take a main street."

"Got it!"

Grateful, Subaru followed as Flop led them back to the main streets, avoiding the shady alleys as much as possible.

Subaru felt a flicker of relief. Whatever had killed him before, he was taking precautions now.

"All right, buddy, from here—," Flop began, turning to point to a new road.

But then, his eyes widened in alarm.

"...Ooo."

Subaru opened his mouth to ask what was wrong, but before he could speak, blood spilled from his lips.

"Gah...?!"

In the blink of an eye, something hot and sharp sliced across Subaru's neck.

He felt his head forcibly jerked back as his throat was slit, blood pouring from the gaping wound.

"Guh...!" Subaru choked, pressing both hands against his neck in a futile attempt to stanch the bleeding.

The wound was too wide, too deep. He could feel his life draining away.

Take off my clothes, stop the blood... No, first escape. Find the enemy...

His thoughts blurred as his strength faded.

Flop is here. Sorry for doubting you. I believed you after, though that might not make up for it. But Flop is here...

"...eemmm..."

...Rem is back at the inn... I have to get back to her, even bleeding out. Get back and take her away. It's dangerous. Take her by the hand and drag her away, even if she hates me. As long as she lives. If she doesn't... So I have to stop this blood.

Stop, stop, st-st-st-stop, stop it, stop...

"Ugh."

-op.

4

"Buddy, you gotta work on those wrinkles."

"..."

Right in front of him, Flop started massaging his own brow, emphasizing his point.

Subaru instinctively raised his hands to his neck, feeling for the warmth of life spilling out of him. The feeling of blood escaping with each heartbeat. The terrifying pulse of his life escaping and his death approaching.

"In which case, get rid of those wrinkles... What is it, buddy? You're deathly pale."

Seeing Subaru silent, Flop seemed shocked and concerned.

That earnest look made Subaru remember the moment his throat had been slit moments ago.

Right, my throat was cut.

He remembered it clearly—blood spurting out, the primal desperation and wanting to escape, and then...nothing. Now he was back here, standing with Flop, his instincts eerily silent again.

I died. I died and came back. But this time, there's a clearer sense of an enemy.

"...Bhwah..."

Still clutching his neck, Subaru let out a ragged breath, the sensation of survival washing over him like a wave.

"Are you all right?" Flop asked, his voice filled with concern as he touched Subaru's shoulder.

Subaru couldn't answer immediately. His thoughts were a chaotic swirl of confusion and fear.

"F-Flop, t-today is a bad day according to feng shui! Let's go back for the day...!" Subaru stammered, his panic spilling out.

"'Feng shui'? Well, judging by how you look, maybe you should rest...," Flop said, his tone skeptical but still good-natured.

"No, resting won't work! It's...it's a spasm that only holding Rem's hand can cure!" Subaru blurted out, grasping for any excuse to retreat.

"R-really? That sounds...troublesome!" Flop replied, his expression caught between genuine concern and disbelief.

Despite the nonsensical explanation, Flop didn't press further. Subaru grabbed his arm and urged him to move. He didn't care if they went forward or back; all he wanted was to escape the danger.

They quickly navigated a side street, emerging onto a busier main road. The relative safety of a crowd was preferable to the isolation of an alley.

"Buddy! Your hand is freezing! We should hurry up and get to your wife!" Flop said, trying to keep things light.

"Yeah, I want to see her, too...but...no."

Even if it means getting an earful about coming back without doing what I left to do, I need to get back...

"...No."

Was it really right to go back? If he returned to the inn now, still clueless about who or what was after him, he might just lead the danger straight to Rem. That thought was unbearable.

Just stumbling on back to the inn in this situation when he didn't even know who was out to get him? Would that not just be inviting the enemy back to their base, back to Rem?

Cursing his lack of foresight, Subaru bit his lip right as they emerged from the alley. He and Flop had reached the main street of the city. The number of people passing on either side were fewer than in a major city, but it was at least better than the sort of back alley with a hole-in-the-wall bar where they had been headed.

Nonetheless, it still took courage to go out into a crowd. Subaru needed to decide his next course of action.

"From here, the inn should be that way. So, we should go—"

"No, Flop! We can't go back to the inn. Going to Rem is out of the question!"

"Didn't you just say that's where we should go?!" Flop asked, baffled.

Subaru's erratic behavior was becoming harder to explain. He couldn't keep dragging Flop along without an explanation.

But what do I say to get him to understand?

"Damn it...!" Subaru muttered, his nerves fraying as he scanned the street. He was far away from Rem and being attacked in a town he did not know. The only person with him was the good-natured Flop, but he could not be counted on in a fight. And Subaru himself did not have any strength he could wield, either.

He did not know who was after him or whom to be wary of.

"Buddy? Are you all right? What's bothering you? If there's anything I can help with, try talking it over," Flop offered, placing a reassuring hand on Subaru's shoulder.

"Flop..."

The merchant's earnestness struck a chord. Subaru hesitated, wondering if he should gamble on Flop's kindness. Maybe he would understand and offer his help once more.

"Sorry for being so pathetic and relying on you so much, but... would you mind hearing me out?"

"Of course! Even if I can't help, maybe my sister can. We cover for each other's weaknesses."

Subaru felt a flicker of hope. If the situation called for strength, Medium was undoubtedly the best option.

Subaru started to explain the situation. He didn't mention the Return by Death part, of course, but said that someone was hunting him.

"The truth is, someone's been following me—"

"...What's that?"

"Huh?"

Making up his mind, and careful to avoid triggering the penalty for talking about his ability, he tried to explain the situation to Flop. But before Subaru could finish, Flop's gaze shifted down the street. Subaru followed his line of sight and froze.

Screams erupted as a massive shadow barreled toward them—a large, out-of-control vehicle was hurtling down the road, heading straight for Subaru and Flop.

"Wh—?!"

"Buddy, watch—!" Flop shouted, but it was too late.

Something slammed into Subaru with brutal force, sending him flying. His body bounced off the hard ground before crashing into a wall.

The collision left Subaru dazed, but before he could recover, a second impact struck him. He was launched through the air again, tumbling and rolling across the ground.

"...Aakh..."

Somersaulting, Subaru came to a stop, his body broken and battered. His vision blurred, darkness creeping in at the edges.

It wasn't as if the sky had suddenly darkened with clouds. What obscured Subaru's vision was something far more visceral, far more immediate. He didn't know the exact cause, and instinct told him there was no point in trying to figure it out.

But what he could say was…

"D-d…"

Dying. Every cell in his body screamed the truth.

Subaru Natsuki, having experienced more than forty deaths, had developed a keen sense of where the threshold lay between life and death. This time, his body was far beyond that line.

An overwhelming, all-encompassing pain radiated through him.

It wasn't isolated to one specific part of his body; it was everywhere, all at once. Every fiber of his being screamed in agony, his entire existence reduced to raw, searing torment.

He was in pain, so of course it hurt. Everything hurt. The pain refused to go away.

Somewhere in the distance, a sound reached him—a whistle, like that of a steam engine. It echoed faintly, reverberating in the chaos of his mind.

What he could faintly hear was the shouts of joy and sorrow— *No, not joy. It's pandemonium. Pandemonium. What a joke. What is that, even?*

In contrast to the sound of it, what actually happened was heavy, unyielding.

"—ande…oni…m…"

He tried to speak, but his lips wouldn't form the words. They were in tatters. His teeth were missing, and his mouth gaped, making an unintended way for air to escape.

His body was torn open. Blood mixed with air, pain with sound. It was impossible to separate one sensation from another.

Something…something had…something had…

"…ats…"

Something had killed Subaru Natsuki.

5

"Buddy, you gotta work on those wrinkles."

"..."

Flop was using his fingers to massage and loosen the skin around his brow, performing his usual exaggerated demonstration.

Watching him, Subaru clutched his own shoulders, his mind racing as he tried to process what had happened. He thought of his formerly "ventilated" mouth and the pain that had vanished.

—I died again.

"And…this time…it was a dragon carriage…?"

The memory hit like a hammer. Subaru had been broken by the carriage's impact, his body sent tumbling, unable to move. Pain enveloped him, overwhelming every fiber of his being until the flame of his life weakened and faded.

"..."

His shoulders trembled, and his knees quaked.

Even though the pain and injuries were gone, his soul still bore the scars. The terror of his violent death clung to him, eating away at his resolve.

Subaru could no longer mask his fear of the unknown menace stalking him.

The first time, it had been an instantaneous death. The second, his throat had been slit. The third, he had been run down by a carriage. None of these could be coincidences. Someone or something was deliberately and mercilessly trying to kill Subaru Natsuki.

The most horrifying part was that despite this being his fourth cycle, he still knew nothing about his killer besides the fact that they were out there somewhere.

"In which case, get rid of those wrinkles… What is it, buddy? You're deathly pale," Flop said, looking genuinely concerned.

"Flop…"

Once again, Flop's concern was plain to see. Subaru's disheveled appearance and his lingering reaction to the pandemonium from earlier clearly worried him.

Subaru vividly recalled the moment of impact with the carriage. Flop had reached out to help him, trying to pull him to safety. But he hadn't made it in time. Subaru had died from the impact, and Flop had been standing right next to him.

He must have been caught up in it, too.

"And not just that, either...," Subaru whispered to himself.

There was no guarantee the killer would stop with just Subaru. It was entirely possible that Flop had been caught in the collateral damage of the previous deaths—or, worse, deliberately targeted as well.

Grinding his teeth, Subaru forced himself to suppress his rising panic.

"Gh! Flop!"

"Wh-what?!"

Subaru turned toward Flop, biting down hard to keep his fear in check. Without hesitation, he grabbed Flop's hand, startling the man.

But Subaru didn't have the luxury of explaining everything. The countdown to death had already begun.

Forward is hell. Back is hell. Dodging is hell.

If every option led to disaster, Subaru had to create a new path to survival—not just for himself, but for Rem and for Flop, the kind-hearted man who had helped him.

"Let's run, Flop."

"What?! Why?!"

"There's only so many hours in a day! We can't waste a second!" Subaru said, his voice sharp and urgent.

Stopping to explain would be a losing move. Subaru relied on momentum to overpower Flop's resistance, forcing him to follow.

"That's true!" Flop nodded, caught up in the moment. "Life is short! And for me and my sister's goal, it's important not to waste time!"

"Let's run! We'll run straight into the bar! We'll worry about the details later!" Subaru shouted.

"G-got it! I got it! But you don't have to pull me—you're messing up my hair!" Flop yelled, stumbling as Subaru dragged him along by the arm.

Subaru charged down the road he'd taken before, sprinting toward the alley and the bar where they had originally planned to recruit protection.

But this time, his goal wasn't just hiring guards for the road ahead. He needed immediate support—someone or something that could help him break free of this unending cycle of deaths.

6

"—You want to hire the best person here?"

The bartender raised an eyebrow, looking Subaru up and down with a skeptical expression.

Subaru and Flop had arrived at the bar, both out of breath. The older man behind the bar, his hair showing streaks of white, had glanced at them dubiously.

At present, they were inside the bar they'd originally set out to visit. It was quite a gamble coming here, especially since he had been killed right outside the bar on the first try. This time, their hurried pace seemed to have thrown off the timing of whatever threat had targeted him.

Still, Subaru knew it was too soon to think they were out of danger.

"Like I said, I need to borrow the strength of the best person you've got," Subaru repeated.

"...If you're asking for the best one here, that'd be Louann, over there in the corner," the bartender replied, jerking his chin toward the far end of the bar.

Subaru turned his gaze past a cluster of patrons lost in their cups. Near the edge of the room, a man was sprawled across a table, completely collapsed.

The man appeared to be in his fifties, with long, unkempt hair loosely tied back and a katana at his hip. Several empty glasses were scattered on the table, evidence of a long, ongoing binge.

"Ho-ho, so he's skilled? You can't judge someone by appearances!" Flop exclaimed.

"He's got a bad drinking habit, but yeah, he's good. Real bad drunk, though," the bartender warned.

"Not exactly reassuring when you feel the need to say it twice," Subaru muttered.

Still, appearances and habits weren't the priorities here. What Subaru needed wasn't charisma or a strong liver but raw strength—someone capable of getting them out of this nightmare.

"Hey, Louann, willing to listen to a proposition?" Subaru called as he approached the table with Flop.

"Nnnaa?"

The man groaned as Subaru shook his shoulder, slowly lifting his head. His face was flushed red, his eyes unfocused and sleepy. Though his features weren't unpleasant, the bright red nose and disheveled appearance ruined any impression of composure.

"What's that, kid? You need somethin' from meee…?" Louann slurred.

"Yeesh, you're falling-over drunk… Anyway, just listen. I've got a job—ugh, that smell!" Subaru gagged, recoiling from the strong stench of alcohol.

"Oi, mind your manners," Louann grumbled, sitting up unsteadily. He let out a long sigh that sent another wave of booze-laden air straight into Subaru's face.

That booze stench is so bad I almost got drunk off his breath. He's been going at it for a lot longer than a few hours. There should be a limit to getting drunk, right?

"Looking back, maybe I should've handled Otto better when he got drunk instead of tossing him outside…!"

"Ugh…" Louann hiccupped and groaned, flipping an empty glass upside down over his mouth in a futile attempt to extract a last drop of beer.

"Tch, not enough booze. Hey kid, buy me a drink," Louann demanded, his voice sluggish.

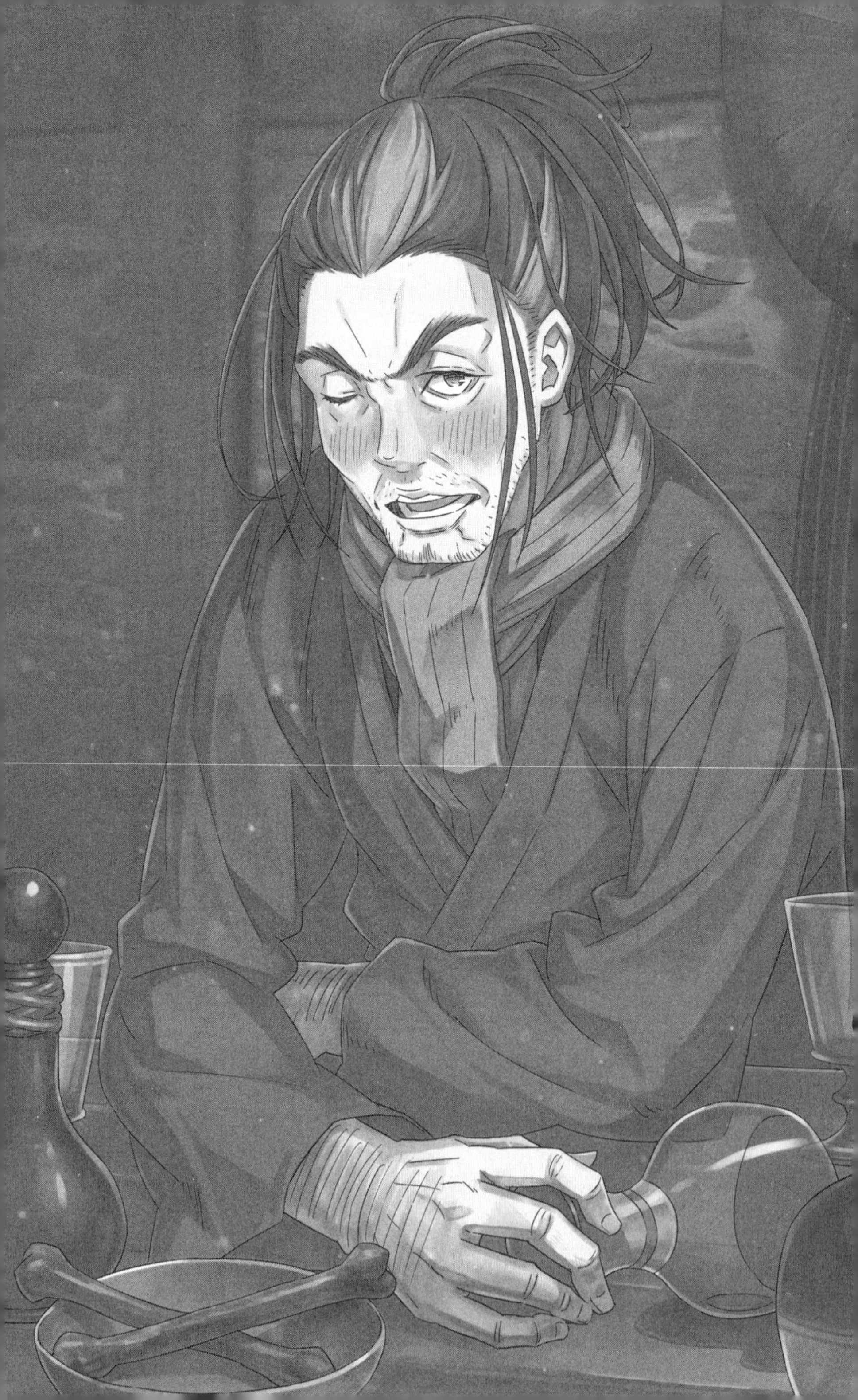

"Mm, you want a drink? All right, bartender, a drink for—"

"Wait, Flop! Hold on a second!" Subaru interrupted, stepping in front of Flop before he could finish the request. "I know it's not my place to criticize your kindness after all you've done, but maybe save it for later!"

Flop blinked, surprised, but relented. Subaru turned to Louann, planting a hand on the table with a thud.

"Louann, I'll get straight to the point. We're not buying you a drink. But we *will* pay you a reward that'll let you buy as much as you want. I want to hire you."

"Ahh, a job, you saaay…?"

"That's right. I want to hire you for protection. Starting right now."

Subaru endured the overwhelming stench of alcohol as he laid out his terms, meeting Louann's sleepy gaze head-on.

"…That's a pretty forceful tone. You boys must be in a tight spot."

"Yeah, no joke. So, how about it? This here's as much as I can pay."

"Buddy, that's—!" Flop started, his eyes wide in alarm.

Subaru raised a hand to stop him and locked eyes with Louann as he pulled out the bag of money he'd earned from selling the demon beast horn and slammed it onto the table.

"This is everything I've got. Will you take the job?"

"…"

Louann opened the bag, peering inside. His flushed face and drunken demeanor vanished as a sharp, calculating expression took over.

I don't know the prices here in the empire, but he should be able to drink his ass off for a few months with that much money.

"I was gonna say I don't come cheap…but you came at me with this much on a first offer."

"Fair warning, I'm not taking any upselling," Subaru replied.

"I don't doubt it. Looks like you're serious," Louann said, rubbing his red nose. He stood up slowly, pocketing the bag of coins.

"I'm not giving this back, even if you ask."

"As much as it pains me, I won't ask for it back. As long as you do the job," Subaru said.

"Bwa-ha!" Louann let out a boozy laugh and accepted Subaru's job. Hearing that, Subaru felt the tension in his shoulders finally ease. The weight of uncertainty and dread that had been building finally gave way to a flicker of hope.

"Buddy, are you sure about this? That money was..."

"It's fine. You can't put a price on safety. I'm sorry for shocking you, and thank you for showing me this place."

"If you're content, then I am, too," Flop replied. "Fortunately, the inn was paid for up front!"

At least Subaru wouldn't have to worry about lodging expenses—everything had already been covered, including Flop and Medium's share.

"So then, boss. I haven't heard your name yet."

"Ah, right. Sorry. We were just in a rush."

Realizing he had forgotten his manners, Subaru quickly started to introduce himself. "My name is—"

"Wait."

Louann held up a hand, cutting Subaru off mid-sentence. His sharp gaze shifted to the window of the bar, his expression darkening.

"Louann...?"

"...I sense something," Louann said softly, his tone low and measured. "Were you followed, kid?"

Subaru gulped.

"What are you talking about?" Flop asked, looking confused.

But Subaru wasn't confused. It was less of a *What?* and more of a *Just as I thought*. Louann had picked up on the presence Subaru already knew about—the enemy that had attacked and killed him repeatedly. They were still out there, still hunting him.

"Who are you being followed by?"

"...Honestly, I have no idea. But I was sure they'd come after me again if I stayed outside. That's why I hurried to hire you," Subaru explained.

"I see." Louann smirked faintly. "Maybe I should've charged you a little extra."

It was a lighthearted joke, but Subaru didn't have a single coin left to spare, and nothing would come out of his pockets even if he got flipped upside down and shaken.

Despite the tension in his words, Louann's expression remained calm and confident. With the alcohol's haze fading from his eyes, he stood with the air of a seasoned warrior.

"..."

Subaru's eyes were drawn to Louann's weapon: a single katana at his left hip. The sight of the blade caught him off guard. Katanas were rare in this world where western swords were the norm. Between the weapon, Louann's disheveled hair, and his outfit, he resembled a wandering samurai—or, perhaps more fittingly, a ronin.

"Louann, the opponent is..."

"You don't need to get so twitchy. Doesn't matter who it is—if they come at me, they'll be split in two. I've got some booze in me, so my sword's in top form."

"Drunken fist...I mean sword? That's a new one," Subaru muttered.

Louann didn't sound like he was bluffing, and Subaru decided to trust his confidence. Moving away from the window, Subaru tugged on Flop's sleeve, pulling the merchant to the side.

"Flop, let's leave this to Louann."

"If you say so! Not that I really get what's going on. Buddy, what are you and your bodyguard even fighting?"

"I don't—"

Before Subaru could finish, the situation escalated.

A large man suddenly tumbled into the bar, groaning loudly as he fell to the floor.

"Bugh..."

The sound startled Subaru, making him jump. But the bar's patrons barely reacted, as if they were used to such things. Only Flop and the bartender moved toward the man—Flop out of concern, and the bartender with a reluctant expression that screamed, *Don't get my floor dirty.*

"Hey, you! Are you all right? Get yourself together!"

"Hu, hggh, haaah..."

"Hggh Haaah?! Is that your name? Get a hold of yourself, Hggh Haaah!"

"N-no, Flop. This guy is…," Subaru began, but his words trailed off as unease crept over him.

And also, the sort of person who would go into a bar in a situation like this…

"Hgh…"

"Gh! Flop! Get away!" Subaru yelled.

The man on the floor suddenly grabbed Flop's arm, trying to use it for support. But Subaru, sensing danger, yanked Flop backward with all his strength.

The next moment—

"Gh!"

The man's body swelled grotesquely, glowing with an ominous red light. And then, with a deafening roar, he exploded.

"Gaaah?!"

The explosion knocked Subaru and Flop off their feet, sending them sprawling. Flames and smoke filled the bar as chaos erupted.

The man's body had been rigged with a flame magic stone, likely implanted inside him. The resulting blast scattered fire throughout the room, igniting anything flammable.

But the fire wasn't the only danger.

"Geha! Wh-what's this?! My eyes! My eyes!"

As flames spread, one of the drunks screamed, clutching his face. He wasn't alone—other men around him began shouting in agony, covering their eyes and noses as smoke billowed from the epicenter of the explosion.

"G-get out of the bar! Everyone! Quick!"

"Wai—"

A man shouted with a dreadful stream of tears running down his face, and the rest of the men covering their faces followed him to the entrance. Seeing them push and shove, Subaru tried to stop them.

But it was too late.

"—gh?!"

A second explosion tore through the bar, this one even larger than the first. The men rushing the exit were caught in the blast, their bodies thrown like rag dolls as flames engulfed the space.

As the heat and shock wave pummeled him, Subaru froze at the terrible scene. It was like a string of nightmares. It did not feel real.

"This is…"

"Get it together, boss! If you went down here, it'd be a problem for me, too!"

Frozen in shock, Subaru was hauled to his feet by the back of his neck. The one who pulled him up was Louann, covering his face with his sleeve. He gestured to stay low, to avoid breathing the smoke that had gotten the other men.

"Bartender! We're taking the back door! The front's being watched!" Louann barked.

"G-got it! Over here…!" The bartender, bleeding from his forehead, nodded at Louann's directions.

Pointing to the older man crawling along the floor, Louann pushed Subaru forward.

"Go, you and the other kid, too! Move now if you don't want to die!"

"I—I can't die here! Me and my sister are still in the middle of our journey…!" Flop shouted, scrambling to follow Subaru.

"Damn it…!"

Subaru's anger at himself mingled with the fear and chaos.

He was, of course, furious at the enemy orchestrating this nightmare, but he was equally enraged at himself for misjudging the situation so badly. He had known there was an enemy and had still underestimated their ruthlessness. The earlier dragon carriage attack should have made it clear that bystanders were fair game to this unseen adversary.

Because of his miscalculation, the men in the bar—innocent bystanders—had been dragged into this hell.

"…! The back door isn't opening!"

Subaru's self-recrimination was interrupted by the barkeep's despairing shout. The older man was frantically pulling at the door, but it showed no signs of budging. Maybe the door had been broken in the explosion earlier, or else…

"Not good! The front entrance is blocked! At this rate…"

"Outta the way! A door like this can't…," Louann growled, stepping forward.

He placed his hand on the hilt of his katana and drew it in a single fluid motion, slicing through the door.

"All right! It's open! Everyone, keep low!"

Opening the closed door wide, Louann shouted back to the three behind him.

Subaru's heart pounded as he watched Louann take control of the situation. The chaos raging inside the bar seemed manageable now—they could escape through the back door. Louann's judgment and skill were the real deal.

We'll make it out of here, and then…

"…"

Subaru caught his breath. There was a hang-up. *—I can predict this merciless enemy's thoughts.*

Turning someone into a living bomb and throwing them into the bar, driving people out using smoke, blowing them all away with a magic stone set at the entrance. And blocking that entrance and the back door, too. They had broken through that and were coming through the back door anyway, but…

"Louann—"

Subaru tried to say that something was off. If the enemy was that careful, there was no way they would let up on the attack. Subaru called out in order to say something, but there was no reply.

"…"

But before he could finish, Louann leaned out through the exit.

And then…

His body suddenly tilted backward. And collapsed.

Subaru and Flop and the barkeep were stunned seeing him fall. His head was crushed from the forehead up. Eyes dangling out of their sockets.

He was clearly dead.

"Eeep!"

The barkeep screamed at the sight, but his terror was cut short.

From within the flames, something shot forward, piercing the barkeep's chest with lethal precision. His organs splattered, painting the room crimson as he fell into the fire, where his body started to burn almost immediately.

"..."

Subaru's body froze as his wide eyes locked on to the figure emerging from the smoke.

A man, his face obscured by a wet cloth, stepped forward, holding an ax. He was the embodiment of terror—relentless and methodical. This was the one who had crushed Louann's skull and killed the barkeep.

"Wh-who are you? Why are you doing this?" Flop stammered, his voice shaking as he faced the monstrous figure.

"You think you can just—"

Flop's resolve to censure the man ended mid-sentence.

The ax came down on Flop's head with brutal force, splitting it open. Blood and brain matter sprayed across the room, the vibrant red of flames merging with the vibrant red of death. Flop's body dropped to the ground, blood pooling beneath him.

Subaru sat on the floor, paralyzed. Blood soaked into his clothes, but that wasn't the only thing staining him.

He had soiled himself in terror.

The figure loomed closer, ax dripping with fresh blood. Subaru could feel the overwhelming malice, the persistence, the horror that shook his soul.

"Why...?"

It was a stupid question, he realized. Flop had asked the same thing and been mercilessly killed for it.

He did not have the strength to scoot back or the courage to crawl. He could not look away.

It was scary looking at the man, but he was too scared to look away.

"Why...why!"

The man still didn't answer. With his face still hidden, he simply raised his ax, the blade poised directly above Subaru's head.

"Why!"

"I'm not telling you anything. It'd be a problem if you got away again."

At last the man answered Subaru's hoarse shout. His voice sounded familiar, like Subaru had heard it before.

"Bgh."

Before Subaru could process the words, the ax came down.

The blow split his skull, and everything went dark.

There was a faint, dissonant sound.

Was.

Chapter 3
THE BATTLE OF FORTRESS CITY GUARAL

1

—If he closed his eyes, he could see it play out again.

A dense, lush jungle, humid air, and big, brawny men.

A demon beast's roar cut through the air as a furious battle began to unfold. And then the murderous focus fell on Subaru Natsuki, who had orchestrated all of it.

Subaru had willfully, consciously, and intentionally provoked it. He had carefully weighed what was precious to him against what was not and acted. He had made the choice to do harm.

He did not know how people without experience fighting demon beasts would handle such a battle. Maybe they would prevail quickly, or perhaps they would be gravely injured. He dreaded the thought, but it might not end there. Some could die.

—*No, I should assume some did. I should accept it. I justified it to myself, and I did it intentionally.*

Subaru Natsuki had tipped the scales and carried out a plan that might have caused them to die—not Witch Cultists, not Archbishops, not malevolent believers out to harm others. He had attacked people who were merely following orders, doing their jobs to survive, people who could have been reasoned with under other circumstances.

So this was natural, the obvious result.

Subaru Natsuki would have to pay the price for what Subaru Natsuki had done.

"Buddy, you gotta work on those wrinkles."

"..."

"Good fortune won't come to those who can't smile... B-buddy?!"

Right after the ax blade sank into his skull with a dissonant sound, his vision cleared. Leaping into view was Flop, pressing his fingers against his own brow.

The slender, handsome young man with long forelocks stood there. Remembering the moment his skull had been split, just seconds ago, Subaru immediately covered his mouth and knelt down.

Nausea and anguish from the series of murderous events poured over him. His heart raced violently as if it might burst, his insides clenched, and a distracting ringing filled his ears.

Flop's concerned voice was distant, barely registering in Subaru's mind.

"...Todd."

Through the ringing in his ears and the cries of his battered body, Subaru managed to utter that one name. It belonged to someone he had met in Volakia—the first person to ever face Subaru with pure enmity—and also...

...the madman pursuing Subaru who had unleashed that terrible calamity.

"..."

The burning bar, the black smoke rising. Many patrons fell victim to the second blast due to the irritant mixed in the smoke. It was likely a powerful spice repurposed as makeshift tear gas, and its effect was devastating.

Starting the fire with a magic stone, sealing the entrance, and luring survivors to the back door—blocking the door, and, when the strongest survivor broke through and let his guard down, attacking with a surprise blow. Protecting himself from the smoke with a wet cloth. Killing Subaru with chilling precision.

The final words, the voice, and most of all the eyes peering from behind the cloth had revealed his identity.

That was Todd.

…Someone who should have died in the Badheim Jungle.

"No…"

That was unconfirmed. The attack Abel led with the Shudrak had forced the imperial camp to collapse. Subaru had heard of the numerous lives lost but had intentionally shut out further information, unwilling to inflict more pain on himself. That weakness had led to this.

"This is the nearest town to the jungle, so of course any survivors would have fled here."

And yet, Subaru hadn't even considered that possibility. He had walked right into a town where his enemies awaited him—with Rem in tow, no less.

More than anything, this enemy was one Subaru had made through his own actions.

"Gh…"

Subaru gritted his teeth audibly. Biting the inside of his cheek, he used the sharp pain and the taste of blood to forcibly drag his consciousness back to reality. If that wasn't enough, he was ready to tear up his entire mouth.

I can't just sit here terrified and overwhelmed.

"Get yourself together, buddy! Can you drink some water?"

"…Gh, I'm all right. Sorry to worry you, Flop…!"

His face and voice betrayed his words, but Subaru tried to will them into reality as he slowly stood. His knees trembled, and the unpleasant feeling in his gut lingered. But he couldn't stay curled up in a ball. Time was still moving, even as he indulged in weakness.

Todd was surely advancing his plan even now.

"Hey, I've got a favor to ask, Flop. Could you go back to the inn and get the medicine for my chronic disease from Rem?"

"Medicine? Do you have some sort of bad sickness?"

"Yeah, I've got a pretty bad case of glossy ankle."

"Ohh! That's a disease I've never heard of!"

Flop's eyes widened at the half-assed made-up name Subaru had produced.

I don't feel good taking advantage of his kindness, but it has to be done. I need him away from me as soon as possible.

If Todd's goal was revenge, Flop would be safe as long as he wasn't near Subaru. By isolating himself, Subaru could focus solely on protecting himself. It was a gamble, a desperate hope that separating them would spare Flop harm.

But the uncertainty gnawed at him.

"Link up with Louann at the bar, and then leave immediately to avoid the surprise attack. After that…"

He had no clear plan, just a patchwork of ideas hastily thrown together. There was no time to strategize. He had to act now and hope for the best.

"If it's Rem…"

If Flop returned to Rem with the story about Subaru's supposed illness, Subaru hoped she would sense that something was wrong. He prayed that she would stop Flop from coming back into the chaos. It was wishful thinking, but it was all Subaru had to cling to.

"Please, Flop!"

"G-got it! You just wait here! Keep your head up and wait for me, buddy!"

Moved by Subaru's urgency, Flop nodded and hurried back up the road toward the inn. Watching him leave, Subaru turned and ran toward the bar.

But just as he began to move—

"Ugaaaaa!!!"

Just as he was about to run, the sound of Flop's scream broke his heart.

Spinning around, he saw Flop collapse up ahead. He was lying on his back, clutching his right leg. A small knife was embedded deep in his thigh, rendering him immobile.

"Flop!"

Subaru's heart sank as he abandoned his run and dashed toward Flop. His foot slipped slightly on the dirt as he pushed himself forward, biting his lip in frustration.

The sight before him filled him with regret. He had miscalculated. He'd thought the enemy would prioritize him if they split up, but Flop had been targeted instead. The attack had come far sooner than Subaru had anticipated.

"Flop! I'll take you someplace to get it looked at!"

Consumed by regret and self-recrimination, Subaru reached Flop. He writhed in pain, but there was no time for proper care.

Lend him a shoulder and get somewhere with more people... No, it'll just end up like when we were run down on the street. Should I try to force it and drag him to the bar?

"..."

And then a thought struck him.

The wound wasn't fatal. Why?

Judging by the precision of the murders at the bar, the enemy clearly had the skill to kill. Yet the knife in Flop's leg had only incapacitated him. Why?

"Shi—"

Before he could finish the thought, a dark flash came from the alley beside where Flop had fallen. Subaru barely had time to raise his arms before a heavy blow sent him flying.

"Gaaah?!"

The impact drove Subaru to the ground, his head hitting hard as his vision went white. The ringing in his ears returned as he rolled over, trying to create distance from the attacker. He reached up to touch his forehead, which was still burning from the force of the blow he had not managed to completely dampen. Most likely the hard blow had cut his forehead...

"...Ah?"

When he tried to touch his forehead with his right hand, he realized the forearm had been severed partway down from the elbow.

"Gyaaaaaaaa!!!"

Subaru's scream echoed as he stared at the grotesque sight of white bone and pink muscle fibers exposed beneath a torrent of blood. Panicked, he tried to stanch the bleeding, but his left hand was mangled—fingers split and pointing in unnatural directions.

He had failed. Miserably. Recklessly rushing to Flop had been a mistake, and now he was paying for it.

Wrong, wrong, wrong, wrong, wrong...

Subaru put pressure on his wounds, overwhelmed by the pain and emptiness.

"...Hmm."

A small grunt came from the alley.

A man emerged, ax in hand. His orange hair was tied back with a bandanna, and his face, now unmasked, was unmistakable. Todd.

The crazed eyes Subaru had seen in the bar belonged to this man. He stood before Subaru, his gaze cold and detached.

"Ugggyaaaa...!"

Subaru gritted his teeth so hard they threatened to crack. Bloodshot eyes filled with a mix of rage, hatred, and desperate fear glared at Todd.

But Todd remained calm, emotionless. Slowly he ran his finger over the blade of his ax, the very weapon that had left Subaru's arms useless, with an expression that betrayed no emotion.

"I need to sharpen this more. My mistake," Todd calmly muttered to himself as he examined the ax. "Now then."

Subaru's eyes widened, and he tried to speak, his tongue trembling from fear.

But Todd seemed to have no interest at all in Subaru's words or his identity. He raised his ax.

"Uwaaaa!!!"

"Whoa."

Before Todd could bring the ax down, someone latched on to him. It wasn't Subaru, whose arms were destroyed and who could do nothing but groan in pain. It was Flop—despite the knife embedded in his leg, the good merchant had fought through the agony to shield Subaru.

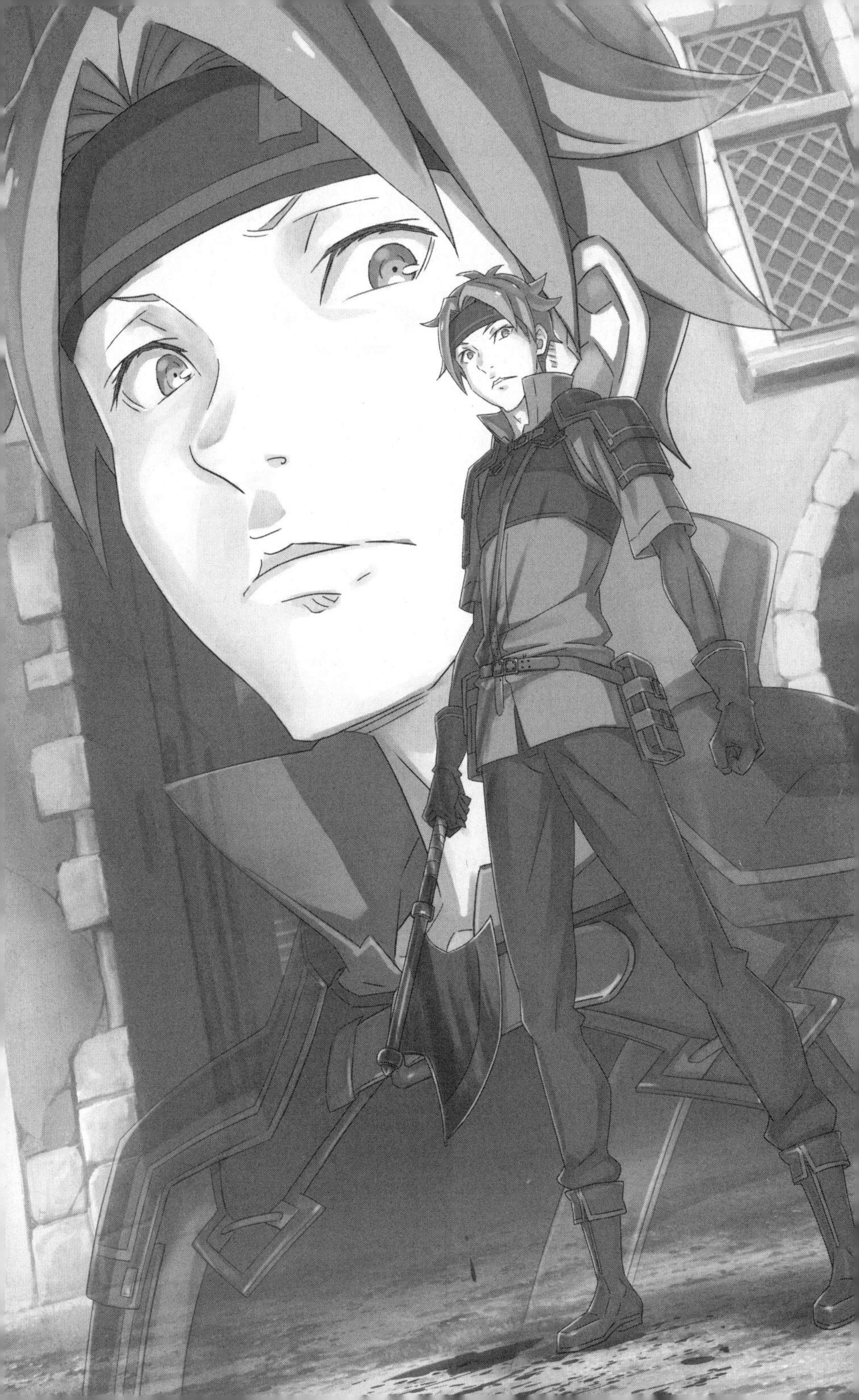

Flop clung to Todd from behind, his expression fierce despite the pain. Over Todd's shoulder, his eyes locked on to Subaru.

"Buddy! Run! Ru—!"

But Flop's desperate cry was cut short. Todd struck him with an elbow, effortlessly knocking him away. Inexperienced in combat, Flop couldn't resist and was easily thrown off.

Todd turned toward Flop, raising his ax once more.

"Stop…"

"Heave…ho!"

A sickening, wet sound followed.

The blade split Flop's face and skull in one clean strike. His slender, earnest face was cleaved apart, blood spilling as his brain matter dripped onto the ground. Flop's body twitched as life left him, his limbs spasming as he died.

The crimson pool spread across the road, and Subaru could only stare, his mouth moving without sound. Panic and terror welled up, robbing him of coherent thought.

Who the hell is he?

Todd, stepping carefully to avoid Flop's blood, turned his attention back to Subaru.

"I…"

"Hmm?"

"I can understand…having a grudge…," Subaru stammered, his body trembling as tears, snot, and blood mingled on his face. His right arm was a bloody ruin, and his entire being ached. But the worst pain was the knowledge that Flop had died because of him—again.

"But people… Gh! Don't get others involved…!"

He could understand Todd wanting revenge on him. But dragging others into it? That crossed the line. It was cowardly. It was unfair. It was just wrong.

"Huh," Todd uttered, his tone nonchalant. "What are you talking about, a grudge?"

Standing amid the carnage, Todd cocked his head in genuine confusion as he wiped specks of blood from his cheek.

Subaru swallowed hard, stunned by the absurdity of Todd's response. His confusion quickly turned to fury.

"Don't fuck with me!" Subaru screamed. "Lying in wait, setting traps…constantly following me!"

Persistent, relentless, unwavering. No matter what Subaru did, Todd always seemed one step ahead, ready to kill him without hesitation. Yet now Todd was acting as though he had no vendetta.

"You…"

"I don't know what you think this is, but killing you isn't about a grudge," Todd replied, his voice cool and measured. "If you see a dangerous person in town, you kill them without question. That's the obvious thing to do."

"…"

"You don't kill a venomous snake because of a grudge. You kill it out of fear. You use whatever means necessary to eliminate the threat. Nothing more, nothing less."

Todd carefully picked away the hair and chunks of flesh that had stuck to his ax, and fragments of Flop's broken skull, too. Subaru could only stare, dumbfounded.

There was no deception in Todd's words, no hidden motive. In fact, every single one of his attacks on Subaru up to this point fit the pattern. Todd had judged Subaru dangerous and intended only to kill him. That was why he did not ask anything, did not let Subaru do anything, and did not let him say anything.

He did not even hate Subaru for what he had done in the jungle. The only thing he felt was confidence that Subaru was dangerous.

And so Todd calmly tried to kill Subaru, without getting emotional about it.

"You're like me. I won't give you time."

With that, he placed a boot against Subaru's chest, forcing him down. Subaru, unable to resist, fell onto his back as Todd straddled him. The ax rose high, gleaming with Flop's blood.

Desperately, Subaru searched for the right words, anything that might buy him time. His best chance of victory—Return by Death—relied on finding hidden possibilities and uncovering truths. It had worked against even the most formidable enemies, like the Archbishops.

But there were situations where even Return by Death could not save him.

"...Wai—"

"I won't wait."

—Such as when the opponent was a merciless killing machine.

2

"Buddy, you gotta work on those wrinkles."

"..."

"Good fortune won't come to those who can't smile... Wh-what is it? You suddenly went deathly pale!"

Most people would go pale after watching an ax swing straight into their face. Subaru was no exception.

He raised his hands to his face, feeling the cold sweat on his skin and the reassurance that his arms were intact. Relief and terror mixed in his chest.

Only twenty minutes had passed. In that brief span, Subaru had already died five times.

At the Pleiades Watchtower, during the final push, Subaru had experienced more than a dozen deaths trying to find a winning strategy. But at least there, he'd felt like he was making progress.

Here there was no progress. No breakthrough.

The corpses of Subaru Natsuki piling up behind him felt like they contributed nothing to any future success.

The one thing he could say was...

"He's watching, right now."

Todd was already observing Subaru and Flop. That was why Todd had not hesitated to use Flop as bait the last time they split up. If Subaru had the ruthlessness to use Flop as a decoy, it might have been different. But he didn't.

Splitting up was no longer an option.

Returning to the inn was off the table as well. It wasn't clear when

Todd had picked up Subaru's trail, but if it had been on the way to the inn, then Todd didn't know where Rem was.

Right—Rem's location isn't known yet. That's...pretty likely.

If Todd knew where Rem was, he would use her. Use her to kill Subaru in a more systematic way. Subaru found it grimly ironic that he had to rely on Todd's cunning as proof that Rem was still safe.

"Anyway..."

Biting his lip, Subaru pressed a hand to his face and desperately tried to think.

Time. I don't have enough time.

If he and Flop split up again, Todd would attack immediately. Waiting for Todd to make the first move and countering wasn't viable, either. Todd was too skilled, and Subaru couldn't hope to beat him by dodging a single strike.

Subaru was unarmed. To defeat Todd, he'd have to disable him with one blow—a hopeless proposition.

If I run to a major street, he'll use a dragon carriage to run me down. Even if I dodge the carriage, he'll have another move ready in the chaos. And too many bystanders will get caught up in that. No.

If I take a different route, every alleyway becomes his hunting ground. I can't keep watch in all directions. Even if I avoid the first attack, it'll be the same as the counterplan. I don't have the strength to fight back. It won't work.

Is it the best I can do to get to the bar with Flop as fast as possible and regroup?

Hard to say how serious that drunkard Louann can get, but this is the best idea I can come up with right now. I think. I can't think of anything better right now.

"Damn it..."

How dangerous an enemy did I have to make?

If Todd had been an Archbishop, Subaru could have exploited his reliance on his authority. Solve the trick behind their power, and their strength became a glaring weakness.

But Todd had no such vulnerability. He used whatever tools and tactics were available to him at any given moment. Just as he'd said.

Given how prepared Todd already was, Subaru's only advantage was that Todd might believe Subaru was still unaware of him.

I can't let him realize I've noticed...

"...Wait."

Suddenly, a realization struck Subaru.

Todd wasn't attached to any particular method, nor did he mind if bystanders got caught in the crossfire. But that only applied to others—not to himself.

Todd was exceptionally cautious when it came to his own safety, which was why he relied so heavily on surprise attacks. He had said it himself:

"You don't kill a venomous snake because of a grudge. You kill it out of fear."

In which case...

Fueled by a burst of insight, Subaru raised his voice.

"...Todd! I know you're there!"

"Wah?!" Flop jumped back in surprise at the sudden outburst. But Subaru wasn't trying to surprise Flop—he was aiming for Todd, who was undoubtedly shadowing them.

Subaru sharpened his gaze, twisted his expression into something wicked, and turned around to glare at the alleys. He poured every ounce of menace he could muster into his words.

"You're awfully stubborn! I thought you'd bit the dust after everything that happened, but I guess you've got the devil's luck! You're not getting away this time, though! I'll murder you!"

He made his voice as threatening and malicious as he could, ensuring Todd could hear him no matter where he was hiding. He wanted Todd to know that Subaru Natsuki had noticed him.

"You think you can win against me? That's a good joke! Ha-ha-ha! I needed a good laugh! I'd love to see you scurrying around like a rat again!"

With ridicule and provocation as his weapons, Subaru stood in the middle of the alley, his scornful laughter ringing out.

For once, Subaru was genuinely grateful for his natural stage presence and cheeky temperament. Without them, his voice would have been shaky, his face and eyes betraying his terror. But he managed to keep his fear hidden behind a veil of defiance and nastiness.

"B-buddy…?" Flop stammered, his voice uncertain.

"Shh, please be quiet for a bit, Flop," Subaru whispered, silencing him. He grabbed Flop's arm and began walking.

There was no going back. Todd was almost certainly lurking behind them. Instead, Subaru stopped after a few steps, turning just his head back.

"If you're gonna do it, then do it. I'll gladly rip you to shreds whenever you want," he taunted, adding a middle finger for good measure.

His heart pounded so hard it felt like it might explode, but he forced an indomitable smile and walked down the alley, Flop in tow.

It was a complete gamble.

There was a real chance Todd might snap and rush at him, ax swinging. But Subaru believed Todd wouldn't do that. Todd wasn't the type to lose his cool. He was calculating, always searching for the optimal move. That was why Subaru thought the bluff might work.

If Todd had truly stumbled across Subaru by chance, the failure of his surprise attack would force him to change tactics and formulate a new plan.

Todd wasn't rigid like an Archbishop. He didn't cling to a single method. His adaptability, which made him dangerous, could also be turned against him.

"Next is…"

He had pulled off the first step of his plan, but what came next was uncertain.

If Todd became more cautious, there would be a brief window before the next attack. Subaru had to decide quickly whether to fight or flee.

If I'm fighting, I need to hire Louann at the bar. That drunkard might be my best chance right now.

If I'm fleeing, I have to return to the inn, grab Rem, and leave the city immediately. Even if Flop and Medium don't want to come, they're in danger, too. I can't just leave them behind.

And if he was running inside the city, the only place he could run was…

"…So that's it."

"Buddy?"

Subaru's eyes suddenly turned bloodshot as he stared into the alley behind them.

In that moment, everything else faded away—his fear of Todd, his guilt over involving Flop, his concern for Rem, and even his desire to see Emilia and Beatrice again.

He forgot it all and latched on to the feeling inside him, squeezing his eyes shut.

"We're leaving Guaral. Right away. Before he sees through my bluff."

3

Having decided on the next course of action, Subaru immediately sprang into motion.

Even after they exited the alley and started moving, Todd didn't make a move. It seemed safe to assume that Subaru's bluff had worked, forcing Todd to act cautiously.

But the reprieve wouldn't last.

"He'll definitely see through it before long. We gotta run fast…!"

Determined, Subaru hurried back to the inn he had left five deaths ago, dragging Flop—who had only been given a vague explanation—along with him. They raced up the stairs, and Subaru banged on the door of the room where Rem and the others were staying.

"Rem! Are you… Whoa?!"

The moment Subaru opened the door, the cold blade of a sword pressed against his neck.

"Whoops! It's just you! I was about to kill ya there!" Medium said apologetically, lowering her sword.

Deeper inside the room, Rem looked on with wide eyes.

"Wh-what is it all of a sudden? Weren't you going out...?"

"Rem!"

"Gh."

Rem seemed annoyed at Subaru's sudden return, but he ignored that completely. Instead, he rushed to her and wrapped her in a hug.

Caught off guard, Rem stiffened in his grasp, her shoulders shrinking as she held her breath.

"...Please let me go."

"...Ugh, sorry, I just... The feelings got to me..."

"I...understand that. Judging from your appearance, it seems something serious has happened."

Rem calmly peeled Subaru off her. He half expected her to scold him for losing control, but instead, she sighed deeply.

"So," she said, not addressing his impulsive action. "What happened?"

"...We were found by a dangerous guy. For now, I've managed to buy us some time, but we can't stay here."

"Leaving town, then? Very well. Louis, please carry the bag."

Sensing Subaru's urgency, Rem smoothly accepted the situation without asking for details. Even Louis reacted to her instructions, shouldering the bag.

—*Wait, that doesn't make sense.*

"Why didn't you unpack? We just got into the inn..."

"..."

"Rem, did you..."

Rem said nothing, but her silence was confirmation enough for Subaru.

"So that's how it is... Makes sense why you'd accept this so easily."

"Buddy, seems like you've got something on your mind, but this isn't the time for it, right?"

"Flop."

Shaking off his thoughts, Subaru covered his forehead with his hand. He couldn't let the time he'd bought with his performance go to waste.

"Little Sister, we're leaving the city with these three," Flop announced to Medium. "There's apparently some jilted paramour after this guy here! We've gotta make sure he, the missus, and their niece can get away!"

"Uuooh, really, Brother?! But I just took off my boots!"

"Then put them back on, Little Sister! Boots are a wonderful thing—you can use them as many times as you want just by putting them on! That's their strength!"

"Ooooh! Wow, Bro! Are you a shoe genius?!"

Accepting Flop's reasoning, Medium quickly began putting her boots back on. Subaru couldn't help feeling dubious about whether they had truly communicated what needed to be said. Still, he lifted Rem into his arms.

"Wait! At least carry me on your back…," Rem protested.

"This is an emergency evacuation! Flop! Where's your cart?!"

"In the inn's stable! And for the record, it's no exaggeration to call our farrow, Botecliffe, a third sibling—a cute little brother we'd never leave behind!"

"Brother! Botey is a girl!"

"A cute little sister!"

"Uuu! Uuu!"

Even in this urgent situation, the O'Connell siblings remained boisterous as ever. With the group in tow, Subaru carried Rem down the stairs, rushing past the reception counter.

"Sorry for all the fuss! Keep the change!" Subaru shouted, leaving without bothering to ask for a refund for the unused nights.

They reached the stable, where Flop and Medium's cart stood among the others.

"How fast can a farrow run at full speed?!"

"Ha-ha-ha, we've never pushed her that hard! What do you think, Sister?" Flop replied.

"I dunno, but probably faster than you!"

Subaru sighed at the unconvincing answer but quickly helped Rem and Louis into the back of the cart. Then, he threw open the stable doors. With Flop and Medium in the driver's seat, they were now ready to escape.

All that was left was…

"Umm, what is this about a paramour? What explanation did you give Flop?" Rem asked coldly, tugging Subaru's sleeve as he climbed into the cart.

"This isn't the time for that!" Subaru deflected, turning forward. "Flop! Run Botecliffe full speed, please!"

"Understood! Run, Botecliffe!"

Flop cracked the whip, and the farrow began moving…slowly.

"This is really slow! She's just walking!" Subaru exclaimed in disbelief.

"Botecliffe! Please run! Do what your brother says, Botecliffe!" Flop pleaded.

"Perhaps she does not think of you as a brother…"

Rem's comment was probably the truth. Botecliffe's running speed, or rather her walking speed, remained unchanged. At that pace, it would be faster if Subaru carried Rem and they all just ran.

Just as that thought crossed Subaru's mind…

Before Subaru could lose all hope, Medium suddenly raised her swords, scraping them together with a threatening sound.

"Botey! Run! If you don't, I'll make you dinner!"

"—RRRGH!"

The farrow let out a deep cry and bolted forward, nearly launching the group out of the cart.

"Whoooooa!" Subaru shouted as the cart surged forward, making a sharp turn out of the stable and onto the main street.

The abrupt acceleration nearly threw Subaru from the cart, but Rem grabbed his hand just in time.

"Th-that was close! You saved me! Your hand is so smooth—"

"Huh?"

"Don't let go all of a sudden!" Subaru yelped as Rem released him, sending his head slamming into the side of the cart. Despite the chaos, everyone managed to stay aboard.

The farrow cart raced through the streets, dodging dragon carriages and other carts as crowds scattered to clear the path.

"If we make it through the main street, we'll reach the gate where the inspection happened—," Subaru started, but Rem cut him off.

"No, it looks like it won't be so simple."

"What? Wait, whoa, whoa, whoa!" Subaru's eyes widened as he saw what Rem was pointing at.

Men in armor bearing the swordwolf emblem blocked the road ahead—imperial soldiers deployed to stop them.

"Todd…! He changed plans and called in reinforcements!" Subaru muttered.

While Todd wasn't visible, it was clear the soldiers were his doing. After Subaru's challenge in the alley, Todd must have decided the odds were against him alone and gathered support. A logical and frustratingly precise move.

"Don't think you're getting away from me, you bastards!"

At the head of the group stood another familiar face. A man with a patch over his right eye who looked like the dictionary definition of a rough and violent ruffian: Jamal. He had been with Todd in the jungle, another of the men that Subaru had caught in his trap.

Given that Todd had survived, it was not surprising to see him alive, too, but…

"Thought you could get away with siccing a demon beast on me, did you? I'll destroy you!" Jamal shouted.

"…In his case, I guess it really is a plain grudge. That's a relief at least."

Jamal's bloodshot eyes and furious shout made him seem a lot more human than Todd and were almost comforting to see.

But that did not mean Jamal was not a threat. Jamal and his force of soldiers were menacing.

"How are we supposed to get through them?" Subaru wondered aloud, struggling to devise a plan in the limited time they had.

Before he could come up with a solution, the O'Connell siblings made their move.

"Bro, hold on tight to the reins. I'm counting on you," Medium said.

"Yeah, go do it, Little Sister!" Flop replied confidently.

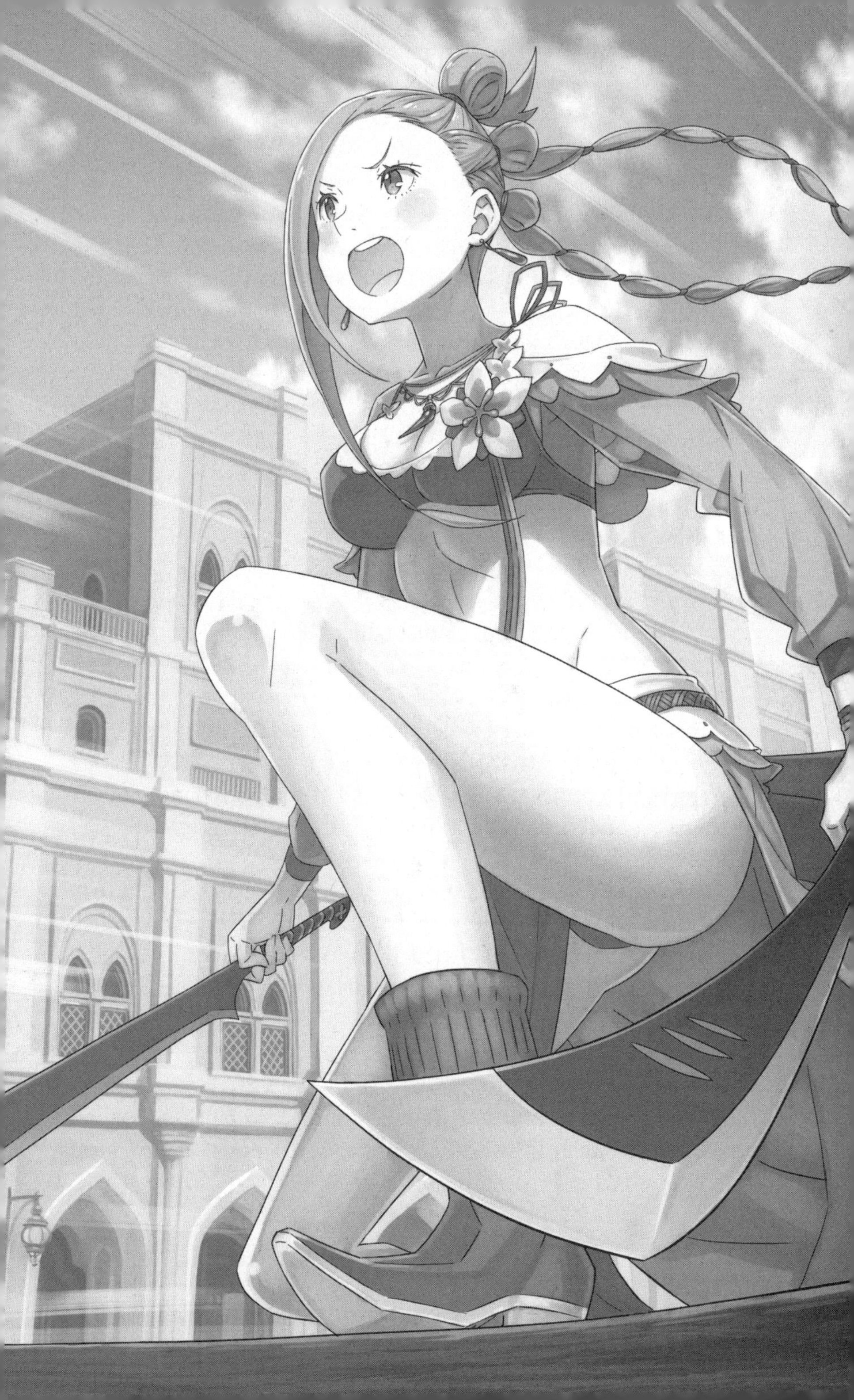

Medium placed one foot on the edge of the driver's seat, leaned forward, and then—

"Boom!"

She launched herself into the air, her swords gleaming as she charged straight into the squad's formation like an arrow.

"Orashooo!" Medium bellowed as she broke into the soldiers' lines.

Medium's feet left heavy indentations in the ground as she charged forward, each step radiating power. Her swords moved with brutal efficiency, slicing through the air and sending shock waves that scattered the fully armored soldiers. Blood sprayed as her attacks tore through the enemy ranks.

"Sh-she's crazy strong!"

"Is that supposed to be a compliment for a woman?" Rem replied coolly.

"What else should I say?! Of course it's a compliment! Medium is crazy strong!" Subaru's voice grew more animated as he watched Medium carve a path through the soldiers.

Hearing Subaru's excitement, Flop, sitting in the driver's seat, rubbed his nose proudly.

"That's my little sister's strength! I'm useless in a fight! But together, we cover each other's weak points!"

"You complement each other perfectly! I see what you mean now!"

"So you understand!" Flop's eyes sparkled, his grin wide and toothy.

Medium continued her rampage, clearing a path for the cart to pass through. The number of soldiers blocking the road dwindled, raising hope that they might actually escape.

"With this..." Subaru began to think they might make it, but a voice cut through his thoughts.

"Don't get ahead of yourself, bitch."

"Ukyaaa?!"

A blade flashed toward Medium, forcing her to block it with her sword. The force of the attack sent her reeling as if she weighed nothing. She staggered, stunned.

The attacker was a man also wielding a pair of swords—Jamal.

"Hurry up! Bow before me, you shitheads!" Jamal roared.

"Ugh! Whoa! Bro, this guy's strong!"

"Really?!"

Jamal swung his blades with unrelenting rage, and while Medium blocked his attacks, it was clear she was being pushed back.

Jamal always seemed like a yapping dog or a redshirt, but I guess he's a surprisingly good fighter.

"This is bad! There's no room left!"

Thanks to Medium's efforts, most of the soldiers had been dealt with. However, Jamal stood firm in the middle of the road, his presence alone enough to block their escape.

"Sister!"

Medium glanced toward him, perhaps hoping for some tactical advice.

"Do your best!" Flop shouted.

The simplistic encouragement left Subaru momentarily speechless, and even Jamal seemed taken aback. But Medium was different.

"I will!!!" she howled, her voice filled with determination.

Her swords swung with renewed vigor, unleashing a storm of steel against Jamal.

"You think a desperate charge'll work on an imperial soldier…!"

Despite her ferocity, Jamal parried her strikes with ease and landed counterattacks, slashing her arms and legs. She grimaced in pain as blood started flowing, but she ignored it and put everything into the attack, boldly trying to stop Jamal in his tracks. Blood seeped from her wounds, but Medium pressed on, refusing to retreat.

Subaru was worried she intended to stay behind and hold off Jamal alone. He was about to shout for her to retreat when Rem moved first.

"The one-eyed man!"

Rem stood up in the cart and hurled a wooden box at Jamal. He spun around, irritated, and sliced the box in half with his blade— only for the contents to explode in his face.

"Guoh?! What the—?!" Jamal coughed as spice powder filled the air around him.

Seizing the opportunity, Medium prepared to strike, but Subaru saw the risk. He flung his whip toward her.

"Medium!"

She grabbed the whip midair, shifting her focus from attack to retreat.

"Got it!"

"Roger!" Subaru planted his feet firmly in the cart, using the whip to pull Medium back. She leaped, using the momentum to return to the cart.

"I told you you're not gettin' away from me— Bgh?!" Jamal's pursuit was interrupted as Rem smashed him in the face with a frame—the frame that was supposed to be their payment to Flop and Medium.

"That's for down at the riverbank!" Rem shouted, her blow breaking Jamal's nose and sending him tumbling backward.

Medium landed safely in the cart, tossing her swords aside and splaying out on her back.

"Whoa, whoa, whoa, whoa, whoa! That was dangerous! Bro, that was really dangerous!" Medium exclaimed.

"Yeah, it really was, Little Sister! Buddy, I can't thank you and the missus enough!"

"Really, really, really thank you! You saved me there!"

"I-it's nothing. You're the ones saving us," Subaru replied, humbled by their bravery.

Despite everything, the siblings had been protecting them since the beginning. Subaru felt a deep pang of guilt for dragging them into his mess.

"Stop! Stop! St— Whoa?!"

The guard attempted to stop the speeding farrow cart, waving his arms frantically, but when it became clear that the cart wasn't going to stop, he dove aside to avoid being trampled.

With that, Subaru and his group barreled toward the main gate of Guaral, disrupting the orderly inspection line they left in their wake. Their goal was clear: Break out of the city in one swift move.

It was absurd. They had spent barely three hours inside the city before causing absolute chaos. But there was no time to dwell on it. They had to clear the gate and put as much distance as possible between themselves and any pursuit.

And then we can talk with everyone about what to do...

"..."

As the cart swayed wildly, Botecliffe's head pushed past the gate and a vast plain stretched out before them, the horizon wide and open. For a brief moment, it felt like they had escaped.

—But then, from above the gate, a shadow wielding an ax leaped straight toward Subaru.

"Ohhhhh!"

The ax came down, aimed perfectly to split Subaru's head in two. It was a deadly strike, too quick for Rem, Medium, Flop, or Louis to react to. It was the kind of attack that could not be blocked unless it had been predicted.

But Subaru had been expecting it.

"I thought you'd show your face," Subaru muttered as he caught the ax with one of Medium's swords, which he had hastily picked up.

He had predicted this. Todd would attack the moment their escape seemed assured, striking when their guard was down. The latent fear from Subaru's last five deaths had given him the clarity to know Todd's mindset.

"You really shouldn't be left alive!" Todd growled with murder in his eyes.

"Ghhhh...!" Subaru gritted his teeth as Todd pressed down hard on the ax.

Though Subaru had managed to block the attack, the force numbed his hands, and his grip began to falter. It was only a matter of time before Todd's strength overwhelmed him. Neither Rem nor Medium could reach him in time.

Just as Subaru braced for the inevitable—

"Aauuu!"

"Whoa!"

The pressure behind Todd's ax suddenly weakened.

Subaru saw Louis clinging to Todd's body, her blond hair swinging as she clutched him tightly, doing everything she could to stop him.

"Don't get in my way, kid!" Todd shouted angrily, elbowing her in the face with brutal force.

"Auugh!" Louis cried out as she fell backward.

"...Piece of shit!" Subaru snarled through gritted teeth. Summoning every ounce of strength, he pushed back against Todd's ax. The sudden move caused Todd to stumble, creating some distance between them.

But Todd quickly recovered, readying the ax for another swing.

"You're watching, aren't you?! Get him, Kuna! Holly!!!" Subaru shouted with all his might, his voice echoing across the plains.

See you, Subaru. Don't forget, I'm watching you.

That's right!

Before Todd could bring his ax down again, there was a sudden sound—*something splitting the air.*

The noise came from the distance, and a fraction of a second later, something struck Todd's side with incredible force.

"Kh...!"

The impact sent Todd flying off the cart. His body spun wildly through the air, crashing to the hard ground and rolling uncontrollably. He tumbled two, three times, coming to a stop far away.

"Wh-what was that...?"

With Todd gone, Subaru dropped the sword and fell to one knee in the back of the cart. Rem, cradling a shaken Louis, looked equally flustered, completely unaware of what had just happened. But Subaru had been confident all along that help would come if they made it outside the gate.

"That piece-of-shit emperor...," Subaru muttered. "I'm gonna clock him if we make it back..."

As exhaustion overtook him, Subaru imagined the smug face of the man who had likely anticipated this exact scenario.

4

—The man sprawled across the hard ground remained still.

He wasn't dead, nor was he sleeping. He was merely lying there, eyes closed, carefully regulating his breathing, sorting his thoughts.

Building and composing, building and composing...

"Hey, you alive?"

"...Yeah, I'm alive."

Opening his eyes at the voice above, Todd saw a familiar face. Upside down, it looked just as rough as it did right side up. The man had a terrible nosebleed, but the vibrant crimson seemed more a badge of manliness than anything else.

"What's with the nosebleed? Did you take one to the face?"

"Piss off. It's just a little blood in my nose, so leave it alone," the man replied, blowing a clot of blood out with an irritated snort.

"So touchy." Todd chuckled lightly. "...What about them?"

"They got past us and ran off after they dropped you. You...should do something about that thing in your side. Just looking at it hurts."

"'That thing'? ...Oh, this?"

Todd scratched his head as he sat up, glancing at the thick arrow embedded deep in his side. It had struck just below his heart—any higher, and it would have killed him outright.

It was a wound that could have cost him his life, but Todd barely reacted to it. Neither the sight of the arrow nor the fact that it had hit him seemed to bother him much.

"It doesn't hurt as bad as it looks. It'll just make moving around harder for a while."

"Dumbass, who cares how you feel about it? *I'm* saying it hurts *me* to look at it. Pull it out already." Jamal grimaced.

"So rough on an injured man... Ahh."

With a sigh, Todd grabbed the arrow. The trick with these sorts of wounds was to remove the arrow before the flesh compressed around it. Fortunately, it hadn't been in long. With a sharp tug, he pulled it free.

He stuffed a torn piece of cloth into the injury to stop the bleeding.

"There, arrow's out like you wanted. What now?"

"If it's bad, fall back and rest. I'll take a group, chase them down, and smash 'em. Show 'em who the prey is."

"...I'm telling you, that's a bad play, Jamal."

"What?"

Todd raised a hand to stop Jamal's explanation of his plan. He understood the desire for revenge and the urge to chase down a fleeing enemy, but such rashness only invited disaster.

"Think about it. They just waltzed into Guaral. Given what they did, they had to know we'd be in the city."

"...Unless they're just dumbasses not thinking ahead," Jamal muttered skeptically.

"They planned it. Even set up an ambush outside the city."

Jamal glanced at the arrow Todd had pulled from his side, his expression darkening. A skilled fighter like Jamal could gauge the force and precision behind the shot, and he realized the same thing Todd had.

"In that case, they were trying to...!"

"Lure soldiers out of the city to hunt them. If we attacked with all our forces, it'd be one thing, but sending a small squad after them? That's playing right into their hands. So who's the prey here?"

"..."

Jamal gritted his teeth, glaring in the direction their opponents had fled. Rage boiled within him, threatening to take over.

Todd didn't share that anger. What he felt was closer to wonder. Using himself as bait to draw out an enemy was a daring tactic—one that required nerve and resourcefulness.

He's a tough one, all right. A real child of war, Todd thought to himself, staring in the same direction as Jamal. "I really messed up by not finishing him off."

"Well," Todd continued, taking a deep breath, "there'll be another chance to get them back. They'll definitely come again."

"I won't have any mercy when they do," Jamal growled quietly, his rage tempered but not extinguished.

Todd nodded silently in agreement. The next step was to assess their losses and prepare for what came next.

"Jamal."

"Yeah? ...What's with the arms?"

Todd was still sitting on the ground, legs splayed, holding his arms up toward Jamal.

"Isn't it obvious?" Todd cocked his head. "Carry me."

"Just die out here alone!" Jamal snapped.

Todd shrugged, unfazed by the heartless retort.

CHAPTER 4
EMPEROR, MERCHANT, SUBARU NATSUKI

1

Subaru stepped forcefully upon the hard ground, his shoulders cutting through the wind as he advanced with long strides.

As they approached their destination, Subaru had leaned farther and farther out of the farrow cart, unable to contain his growing impatience. Finally, when the moment came, he'd leaped out energetically.

Voices seemed to call out around him, trying to stop him, but he paid them no heed. Pushing through, he made a beeline for the building he had set his sights on.

Bursting into the slightly larger wooden structure at the center of the village, he found the gazes of the people inside turning toward him.

And then—

"…So you're back? That was unexpectedly fast."

That arrogant tone came, of course, from the man wearing the pompous oni mask.

Without even acknowledging the comment, Subaru marched straight toward him. The heat of the moment propelled him, and he reached up to yank the mask off the man's face without mercy.

The mask came away with no resistance, revealing a beautiful face beneath. Subaru grabbed the smug man by the front of his shirt, yanked him to his feet, and drew back his clenched fist—

"Wait, Subaru."

Before he could throw the punch, his cocked right fist was seized from behind.

It was Mizelda, the tall, red-haired chief of the village, who had stopped him. Subaru started to object, trying to say something about why she shouldn't intervene.

But before he could—

"Listen," Mizelda said. "Not the face. I'll allow the rest."

"Oraaaah!!!"

Accepting Mizelda's condition, Subaru hesitated only for a split second before slamming his fist into the man's torso.

Perhaps expecting a punch to the face, the man staggered back with a groan when the blow landed lower.

It wasn't enough to vent all of Subaru's pent-up frustration, but—

"Don't you dare think we're even now, you piece of shit…!"

"Hmph. You are a covetous man."

Always with a comeback.

The man bent down and picked up the mask that had fallen to the side, then put it back in place.

Subaru, breathing heavily after throwing the punch he had raced so desperately to deliver, glared at the man.

He had retraced a path that had taken three days the first time— just for the sake of that single punch.

2

"Look, Sister! This is apparently the famed Shudrak village! The rumors weren't wrong! It's deep in unexplored lands! This is an enormous discovery!"

"Oooh! Incredible, Bro! Look, look! Everyone's abs are totally ripped like mine! Super ripped, Bro! The most ripped!"

"Indeed!"

The carefree voices of the O'Connell siblings echoed through the village, carefree and unbothered as ever, rising into the sky.

Their ability to chatter so freely was a sign of how much the Shudrak had gradually allowed them into their village.

Together with their farrow cart, the two were surrounded by curious Shudrak in the middle of the clearing. Yet, unbothered by the stares or any potential danger, they continued their boisterous exchange.

"You've brought a terribly discordant pair back with you. Are they necessary for your travels? If so, you and I value things quite differently."

"I'm not gonna deny that our values are different, but I can't say I like that attitude, either."

"Oh?"

Subaru and Abel were seated on the floor of the gathering place, facing off as they had a few days prior. Even after Subaru's punch, Abel showed no sign of remorse or reflection. Subaru hadn't expected an apology, but he certainly wouldn't have minded one.

However, what Subaru couldn't let slide was Abel's dismissive attitude toward Flop and Medium.

"Abel, those two got dragged into our mess. They were considerate and helpful when we were stuck in front of the city…that's all," Subaru began, though before he could fully articulate his frustration, Rem chimed in with a calm explanation instead.

Unlike the last time Subaru and Abel had faced off, the gathering place was not clear of others. Rem sat politely beside Subaru, while Kuna and Holly, who had accompanied them back, sat nearby. On Abel's side were Mizelda and Talitta.

Louis was being watched over by Utakata, who was close to her age. They were probably still in the clearing near the farrow cart where Flop and Medium were surrounded by other curious Shudrak.

Either way…

"Thanks to the help of those two, we managed to get back here safely. Because of that, Flop and Medium are now also targeted by the city's soldiers—"

"No, let me correct you," Abel interjected coldly. "It is not merely the city's soldiers. It is imperial soldiers. People who serve this country have now become your enemies."

Abel's dry words pierced Subaru and Rem. Rem averted her light-blue eyes weakly while Subaru gritted his teeth. It was a truth difficult to deny, even if it was hard to emotionally accept.

"Getting spotted by a soldier from the imperial camp was my mistake," Subaru admitted. "And the fact they've turned on us is a result of my actions."

"That is correct. This was set in motion before you even contacted the Shudrak."

"I'm not making excuses for that. I'm the one who made those enemies. But it should've been me alone paying the price for it."

Subaru's frustration wasn't just with himself—it was also with Abel's attitude. Abel had clearly anticipated the risks of their trip to Guaral. He'd known the odds of encountering surviving imperial soldiers were high and had still let them go.

"That's why you told Kuna and Holly to wait outside the city, wasn't it? To cover for us if we got chased out of Guaral," Subaru accused.

"Yeah, it was really dangerous. If it hadn't been for me and Kuna, Subaru's head would've been split in two by an ax," Holly chimed in, chewing on a round dango.

Holly's nonchalant attitude contrasted with Kuna's demeanor. She looked uneasy and awkward, clearly feeling guilty.

Subaru was grateful for their help. Without their intervention, the odds were high he'd have fallen victim to an ax.

"Kuna's sharp eyes for lookout, and Holly's strength to save us… A combo optimized for long-distance sniping," Subaru muttered.

"…I didn't realize it would be that dangerous," Kuna added softly, guilt heavy in her voice.

Her parting words to Subaru outside Guaral had been critical. Without her warning, they might not have made it to the support waiting beyond the city walls.

However…

"That only applies to Kuna and Holly. You knew exactly how things would turn out. Don't think I have any forgiveness left for you."

That was why, the moment Subaru had returned, he'd thrown a punch at Abel.

But as he'd predicted, Abel showed no sign of remorse or guilt. Instead, he sniffed dismissively, as if to say, *What of it?*

"You came rushing back just to throw a punch, and now you're complaining? I warned you from the beginning: *That is no easy path*," Abel said, his tone dripping with disdain.

"Gh…!"

"You clung to the false stability before your eyes without thinking, and now you've paid the price. A captured camp's closest town? Naturally it would be the first place surviving troops would regroup. That is simple logic."

"Then why didn't you just say so from the start?!" Subaru shot back, his frustration boiling over.

Abel, sitting with a knee propped up, continued to roast Subaru's naivete with pinpoint accuracy. If Abel had anticipated these dangers, then he had essentially let them walk into a trap.

"You knew everything from the start. The likelihood of running into survivors in Guaral, the possibility we'd have to flee for our lives, too, and you caught Rem…"

"…"

"Anyway! You knew it all, and you still kept quiet."

At first letting his mouth run free, Subaru then stopped himself, almost saying something he shouldn't.

Shaking his head, Subaru made a point of not looking at Rem. Instead, he funneled all his anger toward Abel.

Even as Subaru's anger flared, Abel remained calm and cold.

With that sharp gaze of his, how much had he foreseen? And if he saw so clearly, why had he still let them walk into danger?

"Answer me, you bastard. Why did you—"

"To avoid unnecessary extra effort."

"Unnecessary…?"

Abel responded to Subaru's heated demand with a bored sigh. Subaru blinked at the unexpected answer, watching as Abel calmly scooped some dry dirt from the ground into his hand.

"The likes of you pay more attention to your own foolish eyes than to the warnings of the wise. The harsh drops of rain are far more eloquent to you than any words from my mouth."

"..."

"Thanks to this, you've learned a painful lesson, I imagine... Now you know you have nowhere to run."

As he spoke, Abel let the dry dirt trickle from his palm. That simple gesture alone made Subaru painfully aware of how trapped they truly were.

The emperor of the Holy Volakian Empire wielded words as deftly as a weapon, manipulating those around him with ease. Before his cunning, Subaru's complaints felt like the helpless cries of a caged animal.

"...So what do you want to do, then?"

"My goal remains unchanged. To take back what was stolen from me. To that end, the empire as it currently exists is my enemy—and, by extension, yours as well."

"...So what, you're telling me to work with you?"

"For now, I have explained that I have no reason to cause you harm."

Abel's words seeped into Subaru's mind like poison, leaving him struggling to formulate a clear response. His phrasing and deliberate vagueness kept Subaru perpetually off balance, as if testing him.

Abel never stated anything plainly but kept talking as if urging Subaru to think for himself and choose his own course of action.

"...So everything's playing out in the palm of your hand, huh? I don't like it."

"Unfortunately, only some people move within my palm. My failure to fully control those outside it is why I'm sitting here on the ground."

For a brief moment, Abel's response sounded almost self-deprecating. Subaru couldn't see his expression behind the oni mask, and his tone betrayed no clear emotion, but his words felt like self-criticism. It was rare—perhaps this was the first time Subaru had sensed something like this from Abel.

"..."

Looking at Abel directly, Subaru fell silent, lost in thought.

I don't know. Not what we're going to do, not what path to take, and not what he's really thinking. I don't want to get caught up in his plans and face more misfortune.

What is he really after?

Subaru doubted Abel saw any real value in him personally. If Abel wanted him around, it had to be for some secondary benefit, not for Subaru himself.

"Buddy! The people here really are pleasant and broad-minded! I'm astonished!"

"Whoa?!"

Flop's cheerful voice burst into the gathering place, interrupting Subaru's serious thoughts. Looking around, Flop greeted the assembled group with his trademark energetic charm.

"Oh dear, my apologies for failing to introduce myself! It seems I've stumbled upon a gathering of this village's representatives! And you all bear a striking resemblance to Ms. Kuna and Ms. Holly!"

"Because we are."

"That's right."

"Oh, really! That was rude of me!"

Tugging at his long forelocks, Flop briskly walked to the center of the room and offered a bow, his amiable smile beaming.

"Allow me to introduce myself! I am Flop O'Connell, a traveling merchant accompanied by my sister, Medium, and our trusty Botecliffe! Through a series of events, we've joined the buddy, his wife, and their niece on a challenging journey. I am in your care!"

"He sort of understands his position and sort of doesn't… Sister, what should we do?"

Talitta, listening to Flop's enthusiastic introduction with a pained expression, turned to her older sister, Mizelda, for guidance.

"Hmm… No, he's a looker, so we should put him in a room."

"Sister…"

Crossing her arms, Mizelda made her judgment based purely on Flop's appearance, her reasoning extraordinarily simple and easy to understand. Talitta's slight unease hinted at the challenges of supporting Mizelda, the chief.

Of course, if Mizelda's standards were purely superficial, Subaru would never have been allowed to stay in the village. So there was likely more to her decision-making than met the eye.

"Right, Mizelda, there's something I wanted to check," Subaru interjected. "Flop here is my guest—or more like I brought him here on my own judgment. But are you going to make him take the ritual of blood, or…?"

"Ritual of blood? Is that some sort of legendary welcoming ceremony passed down in this village? If so, I'd love to experience it!"

"It's legendary, all right, but I wouldn't call it welcoming."

Flop's eagerness contrasted sharply with the true nature of the ritual. If it involved battling a demon beast, Subaru suspected Flop's enthusiasm might wane—or, equally frightening, it might not.

"I knew he was noisy from a single wall away," Abel muttered coldly, clearly unimpressed by Flop's presence.

Flop's radiant, sunlit warmth clashed completely with Abel's cold, calculating demeanor. Unsurprisingly, Abel showed no interest in the cheerful merchant.

"Oh! You have quite a unique look… Are you the chief of this village, perhaps? I've read that people with distinctive appearances often hold special statuses!"

At Flop's enthusiastic comment, Subaru's blood ran cold.

Flop's observation wasn't unreasonable, given Abel's striking oni mask, but there was no way anyone would mistake him for a Shudrak. The mask aside, everything about Abel clashed with Shudrak culture.

"The logic isn't bad, but you lack attention to detail and consideration. You said you're a traveling merchant…?" Abel began, his sharp critique cutting through Flop's introduction.

"Ah, yes, that's right!"

Almost singing, Flop placed a hand on his chest as he answered.

"I travel around the empire with an oxcart pulled by my little sister Botecliffe, loaded with items for sale… We siblings wander with the wind!"

From outside came an enthusiastic response:

"That's my bro!"

Even through the walls, the siblings' bond shone brightly. However, that heartwarming display of familial love did nothing to thaw Abel's frozen heart.

"Hmph," he sniffed. "Subaru Natsuki, you mentioned picking these up in town."

"Don't talk about people like they're inanimate objects. And technically, Flop picked us up."

"The crucial point is one of nature. I have no time to dawdle on trivialities. However, for the first time, I will praise your returning here. You've done excellent work."

"That doesn't really feel like a compliment… You're planning something."

Subaru had expected Flop and Abel to clash like oil and water. That was why he'd had Flop wait outside, looking for the best moment to introduce him. However, Abel's reaction was entirely unexpected.

Abel didn't care about Flop as a person, nor Medium, whom he only knew by her loud voice. Which meant the answer was clear.

"Merchant, how familiar are you with Guaral?"

"That is a good question, chief! I can say with some confidence that I'm fairly well connected in the Guaral area. I've learned not to stray too far afield—I stick to what I know. A traveling merchant must know the roads, after all!"

"There's a thin line between caution and cowardice," Kuna muttered at Flop's unabashed response.

Abel, however, fell silent behind his oni mask. Or rather—Subaru's ears caught something else.

It was a soft noise from Abel's throat.

"What fortune," Abel said. "You've stumbled upon a windfall, Subaru Natsuki… A traveling merchant who knows the city must surely know a hidden path or two."

"Whoa, wait a second, Abel. Hidden path? What are you talking about?"

"Again seeking answers from others? It appears you've failed to grasp the meaning of my repeated questions. I have no words to offer such ignorance."

As infuriating as Abel's attitude was, Subaru knew he couldn't sever their connection or walk away. Alone, he would be helpless.

Still, the question Abel asked Flop had made things clear.

"Abel, are you…" Subaru's cheeks tensed, his lips trembling.

"Even with that poor head of yours, you've arrived at a useful conclusion. Yes, precisely what you're thinking," Abel said, his gaze piercing through Subaru from behind the oni mask.

As if to make his intent clear to everyone present, Abel continued.

"The capture of the fortress city of Guaral. I require that city as my next base."

3

The capture of Guaral. That was Abel's next move.

Digesting that bold declaration, Subaru came to an immediate conclusion:

This is absurd.

"…Do you mean to use a hidden path to attack the city?"

Rem's quiet voice cut through Subaru's swirling thoughts. Sitting neatly with her legs tucked under her, she fixed her gaze on Abel, not glaring but studying him.

"It goes without saying," Abel replied with a shrug. "You saw it yourselves—the town is surrounded by walls, with the lone main entrance heavily guarded. A stratagem is needed to bypass those defenses and infiltrate the city."

"Even if you get in, there are still a significant number of imperial soldiers inside. Ignoring the inspection point, the disparity in numbers is simply too great," Rem countered, her argument calm and logical.

Abel sniffed at her reasoning, while Subaru's confusion deepened.

Why was Rem engaging Abel so directly? She seemed aligned with Subaru in opposing the attack, yet her arguments were startlingly precise—as if she had been mulling over the city's defenses ever since their brief stay in Guaral.

"Subaru Natsuki. What is your understanding of the balance of forces between attack and defense?" Abel suddenly asked.

"Huh? Balance of forces…? Oh, you mean the three-to-one rule?"

"Three-to-one rule… I see. A fitting expression." Abel nodded thoughtfully at Subaru's reflexive answer.

The three-to-one rule was a general military principle. An attacking force usually needed at least three times the numbers of the defending force to have a reasonable chance of success. Defenders had the advantage because they could win simply by enduring the attack, while attackers had to decisively defeat their opponents to claim victory.

In this situation, Abel and the Shudrak would need to occupy the city to capture Guaral, while the defending imperial soldiers only needed to hold out.

"There's no way you can muster three times the city's forces. Mizelda, how many people are there in the village?"

"Eighty-two all told. Including Abel and Flop…an even hundred."

"I don't know how heavily you're weighing appearances in your math, but okay, a hundred it is. Even at a rough estimate, there must be over three hundred soldiers in that city, right?"

Mizelda's calculation aside, Subaru judged Guaral's military strength based on its size. The city likely housed thousands of civilians, with a full complement of guards to maintain order and surviving soldiers from the burned-out camp bolstering their ranks.

Including Todd…

"It seems you at least grasp the fundamentals," Abel said. "However, I sense there's a different fear stopping your tongue—aside from the disparity in forces."

"…It's true I'm scared. But the difference in forces is very real, too."

Subaru's fear wasn't just about the odds. It was about the terrifying implications of what Abel was planning.

Subaru scoffed awkwardly, feeling exposed.

Abel had read him like a book. It was true—when he thought about capturing Guaral, the first obstacle that came to mind wasn't the city walls or the soldiers. It was Todd. Just the thought of facing him again made Subaru's insides churn.

But beyond that fear, the three-to-one rule still held.

"The only way I can see us bridging that gap in fighting power is if we either find some world-class warrior to fight for us or hope the enemy commander is the most incompetent idiot imaginable."

"Unfortunately, neither of those scenarios is likely. The Shudrak are certainly formidable against disorganized masses, but they will falter when surrounded and overwhelmed by superior numbers. As for the enemy commander, it is Zikr Osman, from what I have gathered. A steady and unremarkable tactician, but one who does not leave openings."

"Zikr… I've heard that name before."

Todd had mentioned him—before their relationship collapsed. Back at the imperial camp, Todd had told Subaru that someone named Zikr was in charge of the operation. Subaru had assumed he had been caught up in the camp's destruction.

"There were only expendable troops in that camp. They were given minimal information to obscure the army's true intentions. A general second-class would not deploy to the front lines for a mere jungle tribe."

"Then the command post has been inside the city the entire time."

"In truth, had events unfolded as planned, it would have been a flawless campaign. The only disruptions in his strategy were my intervention and your existence, Subaru Natsuki."

Abel forced Subaru to confront his own responsibility for the chaos. The very thing Subaru wanted to forget was now laid bare before him.

Grinding his teeth, Subaru covered his mouth with his hand.

So this General Osman was in Guaral. If imperial military ranks followed a structured hierarchy with first-class generals at the top, then Zikr was far from a nobody.

"So what does that mean? Not only are we outnumbered, but the enemy commander is high-ranking enough that it's easier to count down from the top. And on top of that, they're on high alert because we already kicked the hornet's nest?"

"Precisely. Do you understand the weight of your actions?"

"I'm saying your plan is impossible!"

Abel continued poking at Subaru's mistakes, but the real issue was elsewhere—Abel was still planning to fight despite the overwhelming odds.

More than anything—

"I'm not fighting. I made that clear when I left here. I...I just want to take Rem and go home."

"But you've already seen how difficult that is. Do you think the soldiers in Guaral are your only enemies? Can you truly say any other city or town would be safer?"

"..."

"No matter where you go, you will no longer find a safe haven. I have given you ample time to let that reality seep into your bones. Or do you need more suffering before you understand?"

Abel's sharp words pecked away at Subaru's fragile defenses.

Taking a deep breath, Subaru felt as if his very being were being whittled down. And yet—he couldn't deny the truth in Abel's words.

His experience in Guaral had shattered his confidence. Even if he tried to flee with Rem and escape across the border, the same fear and paranoia would follow them.

The five deaths he had suffered had stripped him of any illusions.

"...In that case, what if I just sell you out to your enemies?"

Feeling cornered and overwhelmed, Subaru spoke with venom in his voice.

The moment he said it, the air in the room turned razor sharp.

From the corner of his eye, Subaru saw Rem's expression freeze, her eyes widening in shock. But the one being threatened—Abel—merely smirked.

"Hmph. So your mind is finally beginning to function properly. However..."

"That is out of the question, Subaru."

Before he could react, a blade was at his throat.

He gulped and looked up to find Mizelda, the tall, imposing chief, who had moved in an instant. Her cold, piercing gaze was that of a hunter.

"We have already chosen to fight alongside Abel. If this is the wish of a brother who has been accepted through the ritual of blood, then there is no other path."

"…I know it's rich coming from me, considering I borrowed your strength to get Rem back. But is this really okay with all of you?"

Mizelda was the chief—an embodiment of the Shudrak way of life. Convincing her would be impossible. But what about the others?

Talitta, Kuna, Holly—did they all feel the same?

"He already admitted it. The difference in numbers is obvious, and the enemy is a seasoned commander. If you know you can't win, then—"

"You're misunderstanding, Subaru."

"…Misunderstanding?"

The unexpected response came from Holly.

She had been listening quietly from the side while chewing on dried meat, her big, round eyes focused on him.

"If we're just talking about winning or losing, we already lose just by staying out of the fight. Our souls would be tarnished if we didn't fight for our brother."

"Tarnished… You mean like pride? Or honoring your ancestors?"

"Right, right! You get it."

Holly nodded with a grin.

But that wasn't proof that they understood each other. It was proof that they couldn't understand each other.

Subaru knew that kind of thinking existed. Concepts like pride, honor, and family legacy—intangible things that some people valued more than life itself.

But to Subaru, nothing was more important than staying alive.

"Kuna! Talitta! Do you both feel the same?!"

"I'm not as extreme about it as Holly or the chief," Kuna admitted.

"…I obey my sister's decisions. That is my will."

"I…see…"

Subaru didn't get the response he had been hoping for.

He had thought maybe Kuna, being somewhat removed from the strict Shudrak way of thinking, might hesitate. But that had been a misjudgment. And Talitta's unwavering obedience to Mizelda went without saying.

It seemed the deadlock would continue—until…

"Mizelda, please withdraw your weapon. He does not intend to sell Abel out to the other side."

Of all people, it was Rem who spoke up.

Mizelda's sharp eyes narrowed at the unexpected request.

"You're giving me orders, Rem? You have not undergone the ritual of blood. You are only allowed in this village because Subaru requested it. You have no right to speak."

"Then all the more reason you should withdraw your weapon. This person has undergone your ritual—the ritual of blood—and has been acknowledged as a brother. It wouldn't be good to injure him."

"Mrgh…"

Mizelda had tried to silence Rem with her gaze, but Rem remained unfazed. In the end, Mizelda withdrew her knife and returned it to its sheath.

Letting Subaru go, she fixed her gaze on Rem.

"You were correct. However, if Abel and Subaru remain at odds, I will take Abel's side. Do not forget that."

"Is that because his eyes or body stench make him villainous?" Rem muttered.

"A little bit of a nasty gaze is a charm point. But I prefer a handsome man."

Though it helped ease the tension, the final exchange left a deflated feeling in the air.

Regardless, Subaru was finally free from the immediate threat of having his throat slit. He instinctively rubbed his neck where the blade had been and then turned toward Rem.

"...What?"

"I just wasn't sure how to react. You covered for me, but then you roasted me right after."

"I said nothing about your face. It was your eyes. And your stench. It's unbearable. Please sit farther away from me."

"Now you say that...?!"

Rem's attitude had shifted into its glacial phase again, and Subaru found himself exiled to a greater distance. However, a more complicated feeling gnawed at him.

Why did she speak up for me?

She had been indifferent back in Guaral, unwilling to rely on him.

"Our conversation has gone astray," Abel interrupted, dragging them back to the topic at hand. "However, even if you were to slip past the Shudrak unnoticed, selling me out would be meaningless."

"...You're good at steering the conversation back. Fine, then tell me why."

"Though you were in Guaral for only a short time, surely you heard how the empire is currently being governed."

"How it's... Ah! Right! Right! You—"

A sudden realization struck Subaru, and he smacked his knee. All eyes turned toward him.

"Flop!"

"Huh?" Flop, still catching up with the rapid shifts in conversation, blinked in confusion. "What is it, buddy? Honestly, I feel like I've been thrown into a whirlwind! The topic's been spinning out of my grasp!"

"Sorry for leaving you in the dust. I just need to confirm something. That official notice from the capital you mentioned in Guaral... The emperor's declaration."

"The declaration... Oh! You mean the trouble in the capital?" Flop snapped his fingers.

Subaru nodded. The chaos he had endured at Todd's hands had burned itself into his mind, but he had also spoken to Flop about this back in Guaral.

"The disturbances in the capital spreading beyond the city…and the emperor riding out to resolve them personally. That was the official announcement, right?"

"That's right. Actually, it's the first proclamation to be issued since the current emperor took the throne! But he's handled everything up until now. I'm not worried at all! Hail Volakia!"

Raising both hands, Flop shouted cheerfully, unintentionally reopening an old wound for Subaru.

The issue wasn't Flop's enthusiasm. It was the emperor's supposed presence in the capital.

"If the emperor is showing himself to the masses…then who the hell are you?! Can you prove you're not just some crazy pretender?"

"Proof? What need is there for such a thing?"

"What?"

Still seated, Abel snorted and dismissed Subaru's doubts. He then placed a hand to his chest, as if to emphasize his presence.

"I cannot speak for the fools who have turned against me, but if you believe me a mere madman after all this, then how would you explain our current situation?"

"I—"

"Cease clinging to delusions that you yourself cannot even believe. If you eliminate all impossibilities, what remains must be the truth."

Abel's words were harsh, but Subaru had to admit—his logic was sound.

If Abel was a fraud, that meant he had fooled not only Subaru but also the Shudrak, manipulated them, and successfully outmaneuvered the imperial army. That was a level of deception that would be nearly impossible to maintain.

In reality, Abel had already used the Shudrak's strength, combined with information from Subaru, to defeat an imperial force. That alone was not something a simple con artist could pull off.

"But in that case…what's happening in the capital? If the emperor is taking direct command, that means someone is standing in front of people as you."

"I am sure someone will appear. Someone with a sufficiently similar appearance. They will use the most complete imitation possible…Chisha Gold."

"Chisha…?"

It was an unfamiliar name. But Subaru understood immediately. That was Abel's body double.

A country ruled by the strong would naturally have an emperor wary of assassination attempts. Having a body double in place was a logical precaution.

But if that double was being used by the enemy, then—

"Wait. That completely defeats the purpose of a body double."

"Silence. I am well aware of that."

"Really? Well, it's a huge pain in the ass for us. If you'd at least kept things stable here…"

Subaru's problem was simple: Rem's cold attitude, caused by her memory loss.

In order to reunite with Emilia and the others, he just needed to travel across Volakia. That was all it should have been.

Yet somehow, everything had spiraled into this mess.

"Uh, umm, buddy."

Flop, his handsome brow furrowed, wore a troubled expression. His head tilted at an extreme angle as he tried to process the conversation.

"I've been listening, and you and the chief here are having a pretty wild discussion. Honestly, I was already shocked by the joke about capturing Guaral, but…"

"Joke… No, yeah, right. Umm, Flop, I was going to explain, but—"

"Oh, then please do! Because otherwise, I'm just gonna have to accept what I'm hearing and assume—"

Flop pointed at Abel.

"—that masked village chief over there is actually His Highness the Emperor. And that would be impossible!"

"…"

"What's this? If you clam up now, I'm gonna be in real trouble. Fortunately, I'm known for jumping to conclusions. The good thing about that is I'm flexible enough to take back my thoughts just as quick..."

"You have clearly come in bad faith."

Abel was clearly displeased that Subaru had spoken about sensitive matters far too freely. It was only natural that Flop correctly deduced the truth.

However, hearing Abel accuse someone else of dishonesty made Subaru snap.

"Bad faith?! That's rich coming from you! I know this isn't something to go running my mouth about!"

"Then you should have completed any necessary assessments before returning. It seems you still do not comprehend your situation. Even after ample time to think while fleeing for your life from Guaral."

"..."

"How can you compromise on rational thought when you have something more precious than your own life at your side?"

The moment Abel said "something more precious than your own life," Subaru's thoughts immediately went to Rem.

And every word that followed cut into him like a blade.

Abel's stance was cruelly clear. If Subaru's priority was protecting Rem, then why had he acted so thoughtlessly?

Subaru didn't believe he had been careless. He hadn't compromised. But Abel thought far more strategically and from his perspective, Subaru's judgment had been lacking, shortsighted, and naive.

He was blaming Subaru for bringing someone untrustworthy into the fold.

In Abel's eyes, Subaru's attempt to keep Flop and Medium uninvolved wasn't a kindness—it was an absurd foolishness.

"I..."

"Chief, mind if I interrupt the conversation for just a bit?"

Subaru was at a loss for words, but Flop, ever energetic, raised his hand. He stepped forward, then sat cross-legged facing Abel.

"Or maybe not 'chief.' What should I call you?"

"I have no title at present. I go by Abel, but you may address me as you wish."

"That so! Then, just based on the mood, I'll stick with 'chief.'" Flop grinned and slapped his knees with both hands. "Now, I am scared of rejection, but I'd like to circle back on this chat a bit. Chief, you asked me about hidden paths into the city, right?"

"Yes. I did. Do you know of any, merchant?"

"I do! And I'm very tempted to say what they are, but I'm sorry—if you're planning to use them to attack Guaral, then I refuse!"

Flop held his palms out, rejecting Abel outright.

Even Subaru widened his eyes at the flat refusal. And behind the oni mask, Abel's gaze seemed to narrow ever so slightly.

Flop's words were serious, despite his usual lighthearted tone.

"..."

Flop was loud, expressive, and theatrical, but he was no fool.

He had already deduced that Abel was someone of noble—or even imperial—status. He couldn't confirm or deny it outright, but the possibility was clear.

And yet, despite that, Flop was looking directly at the man who might be the emperor of Volakia—and saying no.

"...Are you aware of the meaning behind that decision?" Abel asked.

"Of course, Chief Nobody." Flop shrugged. "If it means dragging others into a battle, then I refuse. I won't let my knowledge be used to hurt people."

"Ignorant fantasy. In the real world, malice strikes without concern for your wishes. Would you hold your hands out and plead for it all to stop?"

"If that's what I have to do!"

"Even if you do, it will accomplish nothing. This is a country of wolves."

A suffocating pressure filled the room. It wasn't just power—it was presence. Abel's aura of sheer, overwhelming menace settled over them like an oppressive weight.

Even Rem and the Shudrak, who could physically overpower Abel, gulped and froze.

Subaru, of course, was no exception. He forgot to breathe.

And Flop, caught in that same dread, was no different.

Yet—despite the tension pulling at his cheeks, despite the terror looming over him—

"Even in a land of wolves, the sheep still live," Flop said. "If a wolf bites me in the butt, I'll get in my farrow cart and run away with my sister. Just like I've always done, chief."

Flop never lost his smile. Even as the weight of Abel's authority bore down on him, his response didn't waver.

At those words—Abel's menace suddenly dissipated. The pressure vanished. The air became breathable again.

Subaru, still reeling, gasped for breath. But even with oxygen returning to his lungs, his composure didn't return.

"F-Flop…"

The smile Flop gave him in response was dazzling. A bit wry, maybe, but it held no regret.

Even if Flop himself had no regrets, Subaru did. Because Flop had just refused the Emperor of Volakia to his face.

If Abel was displeased, he could order the Shudrak to turn on Flop. He could have him imprisoned. He could do anything to him.

And yet—

"…Despite your absurd words, you appear to be steadfast in your beliefs."

Abel's voice was calm.

"You are a troublesome one, merchant."

"Really? But I have a friendly sort of face, if I do say so myself!"

"I agree," Mizelda said, suddenly cutting in.

Abel did not turn his ire on Flop, and Flop responded in a way that made it unclear whether he truly grasped the nature of the tightrope he had just crossed.

As for Mizelda—well, no comment.

It was a surprising exchange, though. Flop's sheer audacity and Abel's unexpected willingness to let it slide.

Subaru had thought—

"I thought you'd be more obstinate, Abel."

"Whoa, *Rem*?!"

Subaru's eyes widened at Rem's comment, which perfectly echoed his own thoughts.

He had thought the same thing but had chosen not to say it—because he didn't see any benefit to voicing it. But Rem had had no such hesitation, drawing Abel's masked gaze.

"You have misjudged me. First of all, what would you have me do?"

"…I assumed you would have him beaten to get the information, at least."

Rem was far too honest.

But Subaru couldn't deny that he had also considered that possibility.

If Abel truly wanted to force Flop to talk, he could order the Shudrak to torture him. It wouldn't be shocking.

"It would be pointless." Abel merely shrugged. "There are times when pain is the most effective method of negotiation. However, information obtained through torture is notoriously unreliable. People will say anything to escape pain."

"…"

"And your eyes make it clear—you would risk your life to shield him if I tried."

Abel's words were aimed at Rem, and Subaru, following his gaze, realized something.

The usual softness in Rem's features was gone.

Instead, her expression was tense—grim determination overtaking her usual cold indifference.

She was willing to fight to protect Flop.

Abel saw it. Subaru saw it.

"I shall not engage in foolish self-harm for the sake of unreliable information," Abel stated. "So instead—we negotiate."

"Negotiate?"

"Merchant, I shall buy the knowledge you possess. Let us discuss terms."

Lowering his knee, Abel crossed his legs, adopting a more formal pose.

Flop blinked in surprise but kept his smile as he faced Abel.

"Well, that certainly gets my merchant blood pumping! But let me be clear—I'm very stubborn! If I don't like the deal, I won't agree to it, even if my head gets split open!"

4

"That's not really funny… That one isn't funny, Flop."

Subaru grimaced at Flop's casual remark. Flop didn't realize it himself, but the words hit hard—because Subaru had already seen Flop's head get split open. Twice.

"…"

Subaru narrowed his eyes as he looked down at the gathering place from a small hill. Inside, Abel and Flop were deep in negotiation. Abel wanted information—routes into Guaral, weak points in its defenses. Flop, however, remained resolute in his refusal.

The reason Subaru wasn't inside? Abel had benched him. It irritated him, but he had no solid reason to argue his way back in.

"…Looks like negotiations are taking a while."

"…"

A voice spoke from behind him. A voice he could never mistake. A voice he would love to hear—anytime, all the time.

But only when his heart was at peace.

"Rem…"

Turning, he saw her standing on the slope, leaning on her staff. Her steady gaze locked on to him, pinning him down. He couldn't look away. For days, he had focused all his frustration on Abel. But now that anger faded—leaving behind something much heavier.

Rem's puzzling decision in Guaral.

He had ignored it, pushed it aside—but the inconvenient truth always caught up. Just like now. No matter how much he wanted to avoid it, he had to face Rem's earnest gaze.

"…No matter what Abel says, Flop does not yield. He is a surprisingly stubborn man."

"…Yeah. He's a great guy. The guts it took to say he wouldn't let his knowledge be used to hurt others, even when surrounded by the Shudrak… He's incredible."

Having watched some of the negotiations, Subaru admired Flop's stance. Even when Abel offered to limit casualties, Flop had still refused to give in. That stubbornness reassured Subaru. Someone else was standing against Abel—someone besides him.

However—

"I do not think this is a situation where you can simply call him a great person," Rem said softly.

"…What?"

Subaru blinked.

But Rem's expression remained calm as she looked up at him.

"Not wanting to let your knowledge be used for harm—I understand that feeling. But what of the harm caused by refusing to share knowledge? Can you not say that is harm inflicted by his knowledge?"

"That's…just cheap sophistry. Blaming everything on him is unfair."

"Perhaps. But I do not believe running away forever is a viable solution."

When Abel had declared this a country of wolves, Flop had insisted that sheep could survive by running away.

But Rem pessimistically—no, realistically—questioned whether that was true.

She had been in Guaral.

She had seen how relentless the imperial soldiers were.

She doubted they could escape pursuit indefinitely.

"But wait. Wait, Rem. You're not making any sense," Subaru stammered. "You also opposed fighting, didn't you? So why are you…?"

"…"

"It's almost like…you've accepted it."

Subaru's voice trembled. The words didn't come out clearly. But some things didn't need words.

Subaru and Rem's fragile conversation was not just in their voices, but also in their eyes.

To Subaru, the grim heroism in Rem's eyes looked the same as when she had defended Flop against Abel.

"...It hurts...not being able to understand you."

Seeing her like that, Subaru simply voiced what he felt.

From the bottom of his heart, he had been overjoyed when she woke up. He had grieved her lost memories, but he had believed—truly believed—that he could find a way to fix it.

But here, in the empire, where he couldn't rely on anyone from the depths of his soul, Rem's unwillingness to cooperate in returning to the people waiting for them was like a knife in his leg.

That constant source of anguish made him want to curl up into a ball.

"...You didn't unpack at the inn in Guaral. Thanks to that, we managed to save time running away. But it's been eating at me ever since."

"That was..."

"Most people either relax when they get to a room or start unpacking. Maybe you're just not one of those people. But..."

He didn't want to say it.

He wanted to keep ignoring it.

But because he had to acknowledge Rem's inexplicable behavior, he couldn't keep looking away.

"You were trying to run away from me again."

"..."

Rem's silence was like a dagger to Subaru's heart.

And once a wound was reopened, there was no use pretending it wasn't there. There was no choice but to finish peeling it back, let the blood flow, and endure the pain.

"...It's fine if you don't believe me. It hurts, but I can understand. You don't remember anything, and to you, I smell like someone unforgivable. There's no reason for you to believe me, no matter what I say. I get why you'd want to get away from me."

"..."

"But there really are...really are so many people who care about you...who are waiting for you to come back."

His voice trembled.

"If you hate me, you don't have to talk to me. I'll deal with it if you push my hand away. But please...please stop trying to disappear from my life."

"..."

"I'm begging you..." His eyes clouded with tears. "Please don't shut me out of your life."

—I just keep looking pathetic and helpless in front of Rem.

It was a side of himself he would never show to Emilia, Beatrice, or any of his other friends.

At the very least, he tried not to let them see it. Whether he succeeded or not, he had made that choice—because he had decided that the only person who could witness his weakness was Rem. But not because he wanted to burden her. Not when she was already lost and helpless, with no memories or anything to rely on in this foreign land.

"..."

Rem said nothing.

But even as the tears blurred his vision, Subaru didn't look away.

And neither did she.

After a long, painful silence—

"I..."

"..."

"I...was not trying...to abandon you."

Carefully, slowly, she chose her words. That was something she had not done since waking up. There was a concern in her tone—a careful effort not to wound him. It wasn't just a desperate answer blurted out on impulse. Or maybe...maybe that was just Subaru's wishful thinking.

"You..."

A fragile thread of hope. A single, slender, unreliable thread to cling to. Subaru wanted to choose his words carefully. What did she think? What did she want? What did she mean by that? He didn't know. He didn't even know if he should know. But he didn't want this conversation to end.

He wanted to keep talking.

However—

"Aaaauuu!!!"

"Guh?!"

Before he could continue, something slammed into his hip, sending his body tumbling down the hill.

The serious atmosphere shattered.

Dazed after coming to a stop, Subaru lifted his head to see what had happened.

"Lou! It's not good to ride on Suu! I stopped her, but Lou just did it anyway!"

"U-Utakata…? Then this is…"

Standing at the top of the hill was Utakata, looking down innocently.

And perched right on Subaru's chest—

"We're having an important conversation here. Get off me already."

"Aaa?"

Louis, sitting on top of him, lightly slapped his cheeks.

Knocking her hands away in annoyance, Subaru glared at her from up close.

"Don't give me that 'aaa.' Utakata, gimme a hand."

"Since you ask, I'll do it. I'm a good wife and a wise mother."

It was unclear whether she really understood what she was saying, but Utakata pulled Louis up by the arm, lifting her off Subaru.

Louis, however, was not happy about it.

Subaru let out a heavy sigh as he sat up.

"I still have no idea what to make of you…"

An Archbishop. A monstrous being. Gluttony. Louis Arneb.

So many curses could be thrown at her.

And yet—the girl in front of him felt nothing like that. That monstrous Louis—the one responsible for Rem's fate—would never have tried to help him. Would never have worried about him. Would never have smiled at him so innocently.

But…

"Louis."

"Uuu!"

Louis beamed and ran straight to Rem.

She had learned how to jump on Rem carefully while she used her staff. She slowed herself just enough that Rem could catch her without struggling.

Gently, Rem stroked her head.

It was…complicated.

The very being responsible for Rem's suffering was now the one clinging to her most.

Subaru stared, unable to make sense of it.

And then—

"Your eyes…"

"Huh?"

"Your eyes, when you look at her, are bewildering to me," Rem said. "Even though she is so affectionate to you…"

Rem's voice was quiet.

Rem murmured softly as she held Louis against her waist.

Was this the continuation of what she had been about to say? Was she finally revealing her real thoughts? But no matter how long he waited, she didn't continue.

Subaru closed his eyes.

"…What do you want me to do?"

Those words were a disgrace. It was a cowardly retreat—forcing Rem to answer. But every word, every action he chose seemed to drive her further away. He had nothing else left.

All he could do was ask—what did she want? What did she want him to do?

And deep inside, he was terrified.

What if she asked for something he couldn't give?

Would that be the final break between them?

Her voice caught for a moment. Then—

"...I do not want it to become a battle."

Subaru could accept that much.

She had already given him hell when she thought he was behind the burning of the imperial camp.

Rem hated fighting. She did not want war. That was an absolute. That much—he could accept.

"But," she continued, "I don't think it's possible to just keep running away. I don't think Flop's words are realistic. And..."

"You can't accept Abel's opinion, either?"

"...That's right."

She nodded slightly, a small movement, but enough to show she understood she was asking for two contradictory things.

Of course she understood.

She wanted to reject war, but she also knew escape wasn't realistic. It was the answer of someone who couldn't commit to either side. If only Subaru could be like that, too. If only he could just wait and see which way the wind blew.

But the two truths in front of them were about to collide.

He did not want to fight. But there was a battle about to happen right in front of him, and there was no way to avoid it.

"If it were you..."

"Mhm?"

Subaru grimaced while agreeing with the contradictory thoughts she was holding.

Rem was looking at him—light-blue eyes steady, still holding Louis at her side. And then, making up her mind one last time—

"If it were you...could you do something?"

It sounded desperate.

The moment she asked, it was like lightning struck Subaru's soul.

It was too much. Too selfish.

Even for Subaru, who had always cursed his own cowardice, this was an unreasonable request.

She was asking for a third option. A choice between not wanting

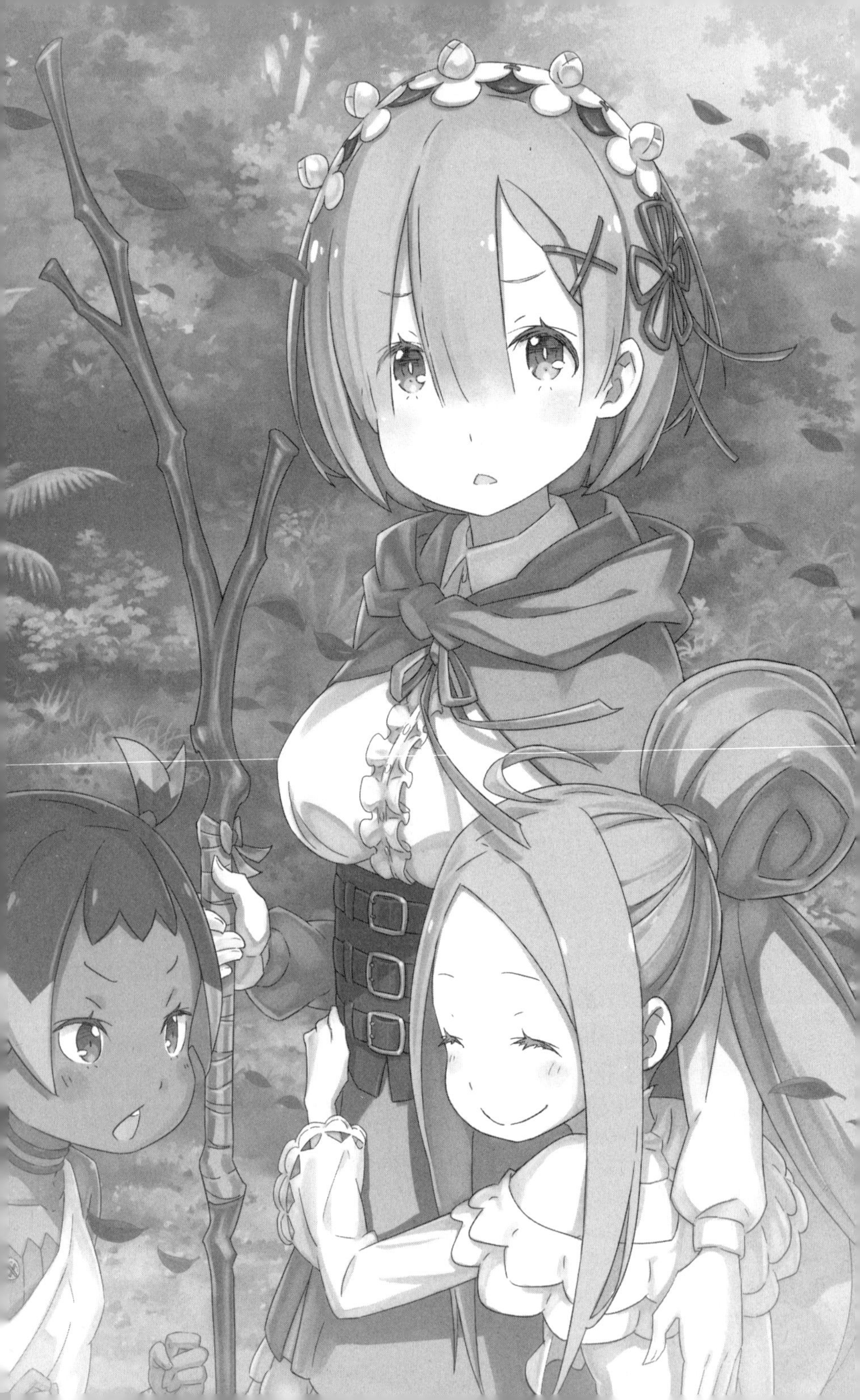

to fight and accepting that they had to fight. That was what Rem was asking of Subaru.

But why?

Why was she asking him? She had forgotten everything.

She had lost all trust in him, all kindness toward Subaru Natsuki. She was suspicious of him, wary of him—so why?

Why was she looking to him for an answer?

"..."

He might have been forgiven for getting angry, for raising his voice, for giving her hell for her selfishness. That was how self-centered her choice was. But what sprouted in him in that moment, what welled up from the depths of his soul, was a sense of purpose.

"I..."

We must fight. And we must not fight.

Both of these things were true. Subaru had to find a way through. Flop O'Connell refusing battle, withholding his knowledge. Vincent Abelks preparing for war, doing everything to survive.

Each of them had chosen the natural path for himself.

But Subaru Natsuki—Subaru Natsuki had to find another answer.

Because...

"...I'm the hero you always believed in."

Because he was a man who fought against the absurdity of this world with nothing but stubbornness. Because his principles were not so weak that they would be shaken simply because he had crossed a border or two. Because he had met Emilia. Because he had been saved by her. Because he had promised her. Because he had taken Beatrice's hand. Because he had led her out of the Archive of Forbidden Books. Because he had sworn to always stay by her side. Because he had saved Rem. Because she had saved him. Because she had loved him. Because she had believed in him.

—*I'll turn this situation around!*

His blood boiled.

There has to be something. Anything.

Everything he had experienced—the people he had met, the

enemies he had faced, the allies who had stood by him, the ones waiting for him far away—

—it was all fuel for the fire.

Think. Consider. Imagine. Grasp some possibility.

That was the only way Subaru Natsuki could fight in this world, where he was weaker than everyone else.

His only weapons were his tenacity and craftiness.

In which case...in which case...in which case...

"...Ah."

Subaru, who had felt powerless and defeated after being thrown out of the negotiation—

—that very same Subaru felt something crackle through his mind like electricity.

An idea so ridiculous—but maybe, just maybe—

He reeled it in.

He thought hard about whether he could actually turn this madness into a plan.

"..."

Rem's eyes watched as Subaru fell silent.

Louis, about to make a sound, had her mouth covered gently by Rem's hand.

Utakata, tilting her head in confusion, was quiet.

As if they believed Subaru Natsuki could find an answer that no one else could.

"...Rem."

Hearing his voice, Rem straightened.

She said nothing. She knew he wasn't asking her for an answer.

Instead, without even noticing her reaction, Subaru took a deep breath.

"I found the answer to what I'd do if it was me."

5

Walking firmly across the hard ground, Subaru pushed open the door to the meeting place.

Inside, the masked man glanced at him, then sniffed in annoyance—as if to say that no one had called for him.

"What, Subaru Natsuki? There is no role onstage for those who cannot offer a constructive opinion."

Abel made it very clear—Subaru was not welcome.

But Subaru didn't stop.

Even if Abel had tolerated Flop's irreverence, he had no patience for Subaru, who stood for nothing.

Subaru walked right up to him and stared straight down at the fearsome oni mask.

"You make any progress, you pompous asshole?"

Reaching out without hesitation, he ripped the mask from Abel's face.

Mizelda and the other Shudrak gasped at the brazen act.

Flop, too—seeing Abel's face for the first time—widened his eyes in shock.

But Subaru paid them no mind.

Abel's cold, calculating expression twisted ever so slightly—a barely perceptible reaction—before he shook his head.

"No, the negotiations are moving with difficulty. This merchant is unexpectedly steadfast."

"I see." Subaru smirked. "In that case, if you're so bad at convincing people, then let me do it for you."

"What?"

Seeing Abel's brow actually arch was deeply satisfying.

Then, turning to Flop, Subaru met the merchant's startled gaze.

Though he couldn't know for sure, Flop had likely suspected the truth about Abel for a while now. And yet even he looked shocked at Subaru's sudden shift.

"Buddy?"

Both Abel and Flop looked at him with their own unspoken questions.

"I have a plan to take Guaral without spilling a single drop of blood. If no blood is spilled, then both of you can work together on it, right?"

INTERLUDE
ZIKR OSMAN

1

—Volakian General Second-Class Zikr Osman was infamous as a skirt chaser.

A sex maniac, lascivious, a disciple of love—he had been called all sorts of things. For an imperial officer who needed the respect of his subordinates, such labels were nothing short of derogatory. However, Zikr Osman embraced his reputation as a skirt chaser.

—In fact, he was proud of it.

The reason was simple: He despised the nickname he had been given before. For a soldier, that name had been unbearably humiliating, and so he took on the moniker of skirt chaser as a badge of honor, wearing it proudly until his old nickname was forgotten by officers and enlisted alike.

Yet despite being called a skirt chaser, Zikr was unlike those men who held a low opinion of women. The Osman line had produced generations of fine soldiers who served the empire, but in some twist of fate, Zikr's family was made up almost entirely of women. He was born and raised in a home with four older sisters and six younger sisters, growing up as the lone male among them. In that environment, it was almost miraculous that he came to see all women as nearly sacred.

When he left home, parting from his sisters—who adored their only brother—Zikr embarked on the path of an imperial soldier. It was then, upon first meeting a woman outside his family, that he "burst."

From that moment on, Zikr Osman saw women as a forbidden fruit—a blend of love and hatred, existing like an ephemeral dream between reality and ideals. Unlike the domineering men of the empire, he believed it was right and good to devote himself to women, just as women should devote themselves to him.

His skill in battle, marked by solid tactics and safe, unremarkable victories, led to both envy and scorn. Many twisted his beliefs into the roots of a whisper campaign against him. Yet Zikr took pride in the name they gave him.

—Was it not splendid?

After all, more men liked women than hated them. His reputation even gave him a common topic of conversation among fellow officers and soldiers.

Zikr held no doubts about his pragmatic stance, and those who served under him respected the man known as a skirt chaser.

—And so Zikr Osman climbed to the rank of general second-class with a certain reputation.

When the emperor was driven from his throne and his enemies sought to snuff him out for good, the best weapon his political adversaries could wield—within their limited authority—was none other than Zikr Osman.

The menacing, workmanlike General Zikr Osman, a known skirt chaser.

2

From the very start, Zikr had found this deployment suspicious.

The army held annual exercises in the Badheim Jungle, located in the eastern part of the empire, but this year, they were being conducted earlier than usual. Moreover, the objective—shared only with Zikr and a select few other high-ranking officers—was negotiations with the Shudrak nation. These factors only deepened his doubts.

"The Shudrak, deep in the Badheim Jungle…"

The Shudrak were an indigenous tribe with a long history, known for rarely leaving the jungle. Though Zikr had never encountered one himself, he had long been intrigued by them, especially knowing that they were a matriarchal society.

And yet…

"Negotiate their complete submission or destroy them… What is the capital thinking?"

That was the secret order given to Zikr just before his departure.

Lupghana's true objective was to either pacify or eliminate the Shudrak. Seeking confirmation, Zikr had questioned the order, but the capital had not changed it, leaving him no choice but to comply.

Still, he had heard rumors of unrest in Lupghana, and he suspected that this deployment was somehow connected to it. The secrecy surrounding his orders—to be kept hidden from his subordinates—only reinforced his suspicions.

Zikr could not even begin to guess what His Imperial Highness was thinking.

"Not that anyone can tell what he is thinking."

Vincent Volakia, the seventy-seventh emperor of the Holy Volakian Empire.

The man who sat atop the empire, known as the most cunning mind of his generation, was said to oversee the entire nation from the crystal palace in Lupghana.

The empire thrived under a brutal principle: The strong devoured the weak, climbing ever higher in their greed. Across the land, uprisings and tribal conflicts were commonplace, and the sparks of revolution were ignited daily. Yet Vincent quashed every problem before it could flare into an uncontrollable inferno.

In the eight years of his reign, Volakia had experienced an unprecedented level of stability. Blood still flowed, flames still flickered, and lives were still lost—but compared to the past, this was an era of relative peace.

That was why this drastic approach toward the Shudrak puzzled Zikr.

Despite being a child of war, the emperor had avoided conflict whenever possible. Though Zikr had no proof, he believed it wasn't because Vincent feared war, but because he saw it as meaningless.

Perhaps the reason Zikr felt uneasy was that this mission seemed to betray that belief.

"—No, that's not it at all, sir. I can understand where you're coming from. Even a simple grunt like me has his own thoughts on the matter."

A low-ranking soldier had been listening to him with a friendly smile.

It was a random evening in Guaral, the walled city serving as headquarters for this deployment.

On nights when he couldn't spend time with women, Zikr enjoyed drinking with his subordinates. He particularly preferred the company of enlisted men like this one over the general staff and officers in his retinue.

Of course, most soldiers would rather not drink with their superiors, but Zikr had his reasons. This informal ritual—repeated every deployment—helped him understand his men's thoughts and personalities.

—However, tonight he had likely spoken too much.

This particular soldier was an exceptional conversationalist, naturally talkative. Even as he drank, he kept scanning his surroundings with a curious gaze. When Zikr had asked him what he was thinking, the man had joked about what would happen if the bar were suddenly attacked.

His constant readiness for battle, his lack of hesitation in speaking with a superior—Zikr admired these traits as the embodiment of the Imperial Way. Combined with his natural charisma, they had loosened Zikr's tongue more than usual.

While he hadn't explicitly disclosed the secret order regarding the Shudrak, it felt as though the soldier had skillfully led the conversation to uncover much of it indirectly.

Had this man been a spy for another country, Zikr's blunder would have warranted the death penalty. But...

"You don't have to worry about me, sir. I'm heading to the front lines tomorrow on your orders... I'm sure the higher-ups have their reasons, but that's none of my business."

As the buzz faded and Zikr regained his senses, the soldier reassured him.

And just as he had said, the next day, the man was sent to the forward camp—right on the edge of the jungle.

After confirming this, Zikr once again faced the bitter taste in his mouth.

The empire's unyielding stance against the Shudrak, Lupghana's ultimatum of submission or death—if possible, he hoped to persuade both sides.

That was Zikr's hope—and a sign of his near-religious faith in the emperor.

However...

"The camp was burned down in a Shudrak attack?"

Zikr was stunned by the unexpected report he received at the city hall.

Until the night before, he had been formulating an accommodationist policy toward the Shudrak, hoping to win them over without bloodshed. But now the camp at the western edge of the Badheim Jungle had been attacked by multiple Shudrak warriors. The soldiers stationed there had been routed, suffering heavy casualties without managing to mount any counterattack.

"Absurd..."

He couldn't tell whether he was referring to his own misjudgment, the Shudrak's actions, or simply the harsh reality before him. Either way, his plans for negotiation had collapsed. The Shudrak nation had made itself an enemy of the imperial army—no, enemies of His Royal Highness himself.

"It is a shame, but we will await reinforcements from the capital and then crush the Badheim rebels."

That was the decision Zikr made after taking in the surviving soldiers and reorganizing his expedition. He could have chosen to immediately march into the jungle and retaliate, but that would have been suicide. The jungle was the Shudrak's domain, and any minor numerical advantage the imperial army had would be meaningless there.

A decisive victory would require not just a slight edge in numbers, but overwhelming superiority.

"Foolish though they may be, they have rejected the hand of peace. In response, we must deliver the iron fist of His Imperial Highness."

With this self-admonition, the last traces of kindness vanished from Zikr Osman, the skirt chaser. Even if the Shudrak were a matriarchal society, he would wipe out every last one of them to ensure that the empire never again had to concern itself with such rebels.

For that purpose…

"Secure the gates. The Shudrak are skilled with bows, but they cannot overcome the city walls. Do not leave them any openings to break through."

After questioning the returning soldiers and analyzing the attack on the camp—apparently carried out by a small, elite force—Zikr decided on a purely defensive strategy.

From what was known about the Shudrak, they likely lacked large numbers. To stand against the imperial army, they would have to rely on tactics such as night raids, exploiting any opportunity to inflict disproportionate losses.

But such tactics only worked against an opponent that let its guard down.

"Seal every opening! The city walls are not solid cliff faces. Given the Shudrak's long history in this region, it is entirely possible they have ways to breach the city without using the main gate. Do not overlook any hidden passages!"

"A report on that, sir. A unit of surviving soldiers from the burned camp is already searching for and securing any back passages in preparation for an attack."

"I see. It is reassuring to have soldiers in the rank and file who can anticipate what lies ahead. Depending on how this unfolds, I may consider them for a promotion. However, for now…"

"Yes, sir. We will focus entirely on defense until reinforcements arrive."

Acknowledging Zikr's orders, the general third-class bowed deeply.

Most generals would have scoffed at such a passive strategy. In fact, Zikr had endured such ridicule in the past. But he had already suffered a stinging blow from the Shudrak, and he knew he would face some form of punishment upon his return to the capital.

With his back against the wall, there was no reason not to play the most optimal hand.

His subordinates understood this as well. That was why none of them criticized his decision.

3

"…What did you say?"

Zikr arched an eyebrow at his subordinate's report.

Tension had been mounting in the fortified city of Guaral as they waited for reinforcements from the capital. But now, this report brought an unexpected surge of emotion.

"Yes, sir. It seems a troupe of traveling performers has become the talk of the town."

The report was almost idyllic, entirely devoid of the tension that had defined their days. It seemed ill-fitted to the wartime atmosphere, but Zikr had no reason to rebuke his subordinate. After all, it had been his own policy to avoid imposing an oppressive military occupation on the city.

Just having an army quartered in the city was enough to create resentment. If they failed to maintain some level of morale among the residents, it could, in the worst-case scenario, lead to a complete collapse in support.

With that in mind, Zikr had chosen not to impose too much on daily life. While maintaining vigilance along the city's perimeter and rigorously searching for potential entry points the Shudrak might exploit, he had largely left the civilians undisturbed.

It was a compromise—one between his instincts as a soldier and his sense of good judgment.

As a result, city inspections and the treatment of traveling merchants had remained relatively unchanged, which explained how a troupe of entertainers had been able to enter.

"...What exactly is your point in telling me this? If you're suggesting we arrest them, I see no reason to. Given the circumstances, I can understand why the people would welcome such a distraction."

Several soldiers had been assigned to patrol the city alongside the local guards. Many of them, having barely survived the Shudrak assault, were both hostile and wary of their jungle-dwelling enemies. Despite orders to keep their emotions in check, skirmishes between soldiers and civilians had become a daily occurrence.

It wasn't difficult to imagine why the townspeople might find comfort in a troupe of performers. To arrest them now...

"That would be a disaster. The civilians' resentment would boil over. Surely you understand that much."

"Of course, sir. You're absolutely right. I wouldn't dream of suggesting their arrest. It's just..."

"Just what? Speak plainly."

Zikr narrowed his eyes as his subordinate hesitated. After a brief silence, the man exhaled, seemingly resigning himself to whatever consequences might follow.

"The truth is...the musicians and the dancing girl are quite remarkable. So what do you say? Would you like to see their performance for yourself, sir?"

"Me? I will not deny that this talk of dancing girls is intriguing, but…"

Zikr blinked at the unexpected suggestion.

His subordinate was a man he had known for a long time—one who had fought beside him on numerous battlefields. He wouldn't have made this proposal without a reason.

Still, Zikr found it difficult to believe he was being invited purely for entertainment's sake.

The subordinate straightened his posture and spoke in a softer tone.

"Sir, there is growing discontent among the troops—though for now, it is only in whispers."

"Mgh…"

Zikr's eyes sharpened. He gestured for the man to continue.

"The capital's reluctance to send reinforcements, combined with our prolonged defensive stance, has led to some murmurs among the men. Many are questioning your decision to hold our position, especially after the camp was burned."

"…Really? No, I suppose that is only natural."

A heavy weight settled in Zikr's chest.

His failure to anticipate the Shudrak's preemptive strike had cost dozens of lives. The survivors who had regrouped in the city had been denied any opportunity for retribution, which had left them simmering with frustration. It was only logical that their anger would turn toward him.

"Among the more gossipy men, some have started—"

"Don't say it."

"…My apologies, sir."

Zikr raised a hand to his forehead, cutting his subordinate off before he could finish.

He could already guess the kinds of insults being thrown his way. It was the same mockery he had endured in the past—including an obvious, humiliating title that he loathed beyond all else. Even as a general second-class, he couldn't bear to hear it.

Now, however, he understood his subordinate's true reason for making this suggestion.

"I see. You're proposing a way for the men to vent their frustrations."

"Yes, sir. If we allow them to enjoy the performers' songs and dances, I believe it will boost morale among both officers and enlisted men."

"Ho-ho, I see. Your description makes it sound as if you've already seen them perform," Zikr mused, narrowing his eyes.

The subordinate coughed, avoiding a direct answer. But his silence spoke volumes.

Regardless, Zikr was caught between the resentment of his soldiers and the need for discipline. And given that his subordinate—who had actually seen these dancers—was personally recommending them, it was clear they were of considerable talent.

"It seems these dancing girls are quite beautiful."

"Yes, sir! Er, I mean, I believe they will be to your liking, sir. And their music and performance are also…quite impressive."

"Hmm, that certainly raises my expectations."

Though the description seemed a little over the top, Zikr recognized the sincerity behind the proposal. His subordinate wasn't simply trying to entertain him—he was attempting to defuse a brewing crisis. That was a good thing.

Besides, in the midst of all this tension, Zikr himself hadn't had the company of a woman in some time. It was unreasonable to expect the soldiers to practice restraint when even he was feeling the strain.

"Very well. I'll go along with your little proposition. Send an invitation to this troupe and arrange a venue where the men can enjoy the performance. However," he added sharply, "make sure to search them thoroughly before they enter. No weapons, no surprises."

4

With Zikr's approval, his subordinates moved swiftly.

A grand banquet was arranged in the great hall of the city administration building, complete with an abundance of drinks, food, and women to attend to the guests. Naturally, an invitation was extended to the troupe of performers as well.

"...You will soon be treated to the beautiful queen of dance, a vision from beyond the Great Waterfalls. Lustrous black hair that has absorbed the light of the sun, radiant pale skin blessed by spirits—a supreme beauty, as if heaven itself had descended to earth. Tonight, she shall dance for you."

With this grand introduction, the musician gestured, and the dancer slowly, captivatingly, lifted her veil.

The troupe, composed entirely of female performers, had already gained admiration in town for its enchanting dances. But the true spectacle was the veiled dancer, whose face had remained hidden—until now.

Zikr's eyes widened the moment he saw her unveiled face.

"..."

Porcelain skin, long black hair cascading down her back, and a visage so breathtaking that it surpassed all expectations. The musician's florid introduction had not done her justice—no words could.

Her striking black hair and fair skin, her body draped in thin, flowing garments, possessed a magnetic allure, enchanting all who beheld her. Yet those were merely surface elements of her beauty.

What struck Zikr most was her eyes. Almond-shaped, framed by long, delicate lashes, they were the focal point of her exquisitely proportioned face—the golden ratio in human form.

If she could captivate a crowd without even moving, then the moment she began to dance would surely be nothing short of mesmerizing.

Zikr longed to witness that magic unfold.

"—If we may now present our queen of dance's performance..."

The musician with long black hair bowed deeply on behalf of the dancer.

Standing beside her was another performer, a blond woman, equally beautiful. Yet to Zikr—who had been utterly bewitched by the queen of dance—they were little more than accompaniments.

It was a discourteous thought, one he ordinarily would never have indulged.

But Zikr was, after all, a skirt chaser. Faced with such extraordinary beauty, he could not remain composed. His heart burned with anticipation as the banquet began.

As the supreme commander, Zikr was seated at the head of the hall, surrounded by his subordinates. Every officer in attendance indulged in drink and food, but the true centerpiece of the evening was the performance.

Originally, the banquet had been planned as a way to lift morale and ease the frustrations of the men. But Zikr had long since forgotten that purpose. All that mattered now was witnessing the dance of the queen of the evening.

So captivated was he that he found his throat dry, which prompted him to lift his glass and sip, wetting his lips before exhaling in anticipation.

"...Tonight we present a dance from our lady's distant homeland, far beyond the Great Waterfalls. From the very edges of the world, she brings you a vision of elegance. Please enjoy to your heart's content."

As the two musicians strummed their instruments, a delicate melody filled the hall—a tune foreign to all who heard it.

The once-boisterous officers, who had been chatting loudly moments before, fell silent, their flushed faces turning toward the stage. Not a single eye dared to stray, lest it miss a single moment of the dance about to unfold.

With an elegant step forward, the queen of dance began to move.

"..."

Everyone was speechless as she moved—her long arms and legs flowing with effortless grace, her black hair dancing through the air like silk caught in the wind.

Zikr forgot to breathe. He was captivated—no, enthralled.

How could anyone remain in full possession of their senses while witnessing a dance like this? Only a beast, incapable of comprehending the true majesty of the art, would remain unmoved.

And within the imperial army—the den of wolves—there were no such beasts. Every officer in the hall sat frozen, breathless, their words stolen by the sheer magnificence of the queen of dance.

All were enraptured.

Her pitch-black hair, her flawless porcelain skin, her face—so exquisite that an artist would surrender an arm just to capture it on canvas.

Yet none of those were what truly held Zikr's gaze.

What consumed him—what stole his very soul—was her eyes.

He could not look away.

Those eyes, sharp and commanding, swept across the stage as she danced. They pierced through the crowd, locking on to Zikr as he sat at the far end of the hall. She never once broke her gaze, her eyes gripping his mind in an unshakable hold.

Then, as if guided by fate, the queen of dance slowly cut across the vast hall, her movements carrying her directly before him.

She knelt gracefully, extending both hands toward him.

She was asking for his sword.

Zikr knew this without needing to be told. It was an instinctive understanding, a truth as natural as breathing.

She continued dancing all the while, her movements intensifying. The energy of the room shifted. The very air itself seemed to vibrate with expectation. She held the world in the palm of her hand as she prepared to move to the next stage.

And she needed his sword.

A blade for the final act. A weapon to transform her performance into something even greater.

There was no refusing her.

No one in the hall—not Zikr, not his direct subordinates, and not the assembled officers—moved to stop what was happening.

It felt natural and inevitable.

And so…

"…It is your loss, Zikr Osman."

The words were quiet, absolute.

The cold steel of a drawn blade pressed against his throat.

Even then, Zikr could not comprehend his own defeat.

He had lost—not as a soldier, not as a strategist—but simply because he was a skirt chaser.

"..."

Even in that final moment, at death's doorstep, he could not look away from her eyes.

That cold, intoxicating charisma.

That gaze—vaguely familiar, yet impossible to place—etched itself into the mind of the defeated general, Zikr Osman.

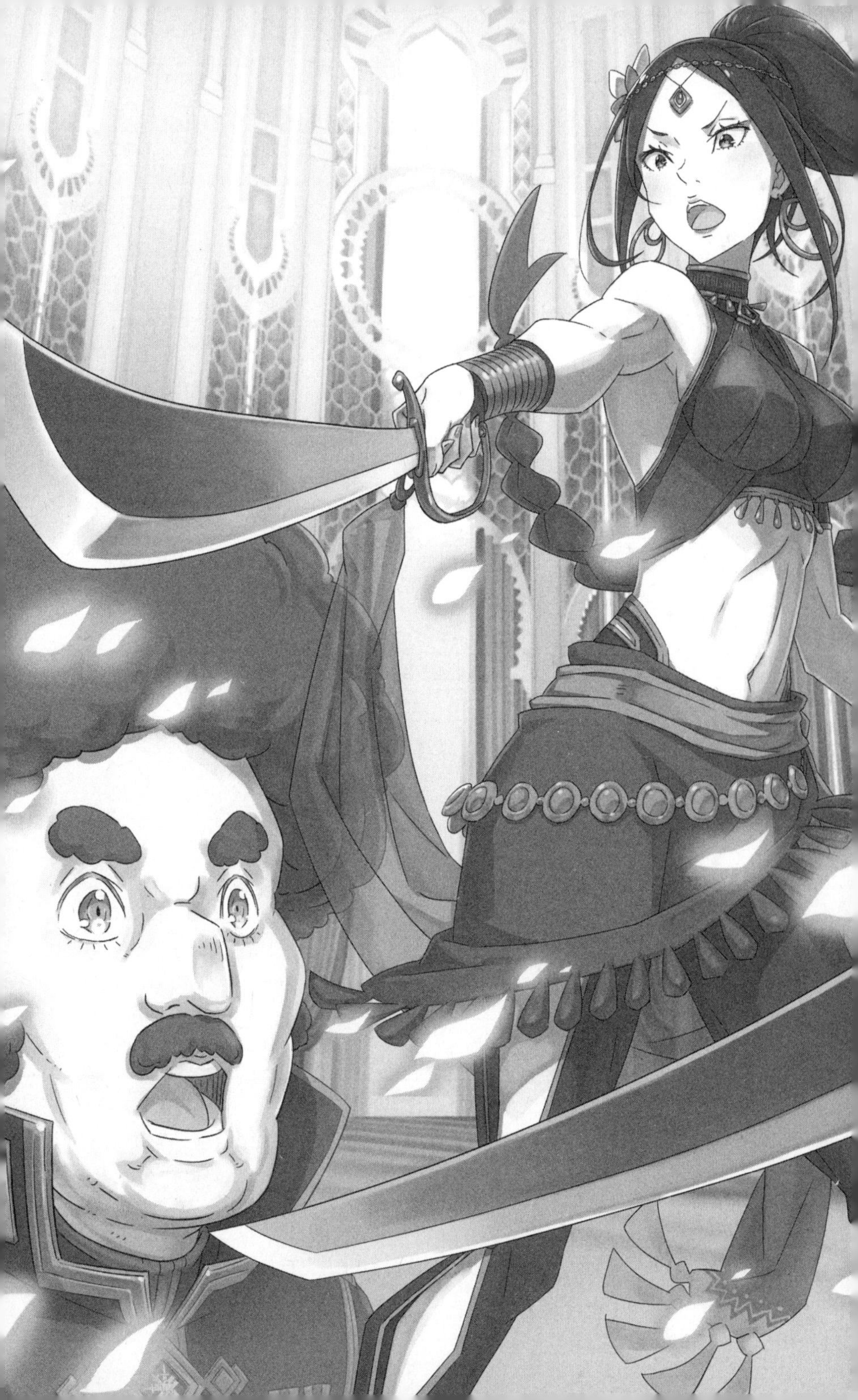

CHAPTER 5
THE MUSICIAN NATSUMI SCHWARTZ

1

—Rewinding time to before the queen of dance performed in the banquet hall of Guaral's city hall building.

Subaru Natsuki boldly strode into the meeting place and made a confident declaration.
"A bloodless victory?"
After Subaru removed his mask, Abel looked up at him and, in a cold voice, dismissed this as fantasy once again. Subaru understood how laughable it sounded.
"While you're thinking about reducing sacrifices, you have no intention of eliminating them entirely."
"Of course. Whether you accept it or not, we are at war. Death is inevitable, no matter what you or I do. Even with efforts to avoid wasting personnel resources."
"I don't really like that way of thinking," Subaru scoffed, looking down at Abel, who sat beneath him.
It was a detestable combination of words—*personnel* and *resources*—as if people were just numbers. Maybe Abel needed to think that way as someone leading a country, but…

"I won't accept it. You feel the same, right, Flop?"

"...So instead, you suggest a bloodless victory? That's quite the bold proposal, considering how exhausted you were earlier," Abel said derisively.

"I'm not gonna deny I showed my pathetic side before," Subaru admitted, looking down at his palm. "It's been one catastrophe after another since I washed up in this country."

His right arm, newly replaced, had been involved in those endless catastrophes. Or maybe—just barely—losing the arm could be considered one of the few fortunate events.

The replacement arm, Rem waking up, and meeting Flop and Medium—those were the only unambiguously good things. Everything else had just been silver linings in a storm.

Abel, the Shudrak, Todd, the imperial soldiers...

"My spirit was being ground down by all these troubles"—Subaru clenched his fist—"but the friction lit a fire in me."

At that moment, Rem appeared at the entrance behind Subaru, leaning on her staff, with Utakata and Louis in tow. She had come to witness the decision Subaru Natsuki had reached—the one ignited by her selfish request.

"Using a back door Flop knows about to launch a surprise attack... that won't go how you want. The people in that city won't overlook something so obvious."

Subaru bluntly shot down the plan they had likely been working on while he was outside. The reason? Todd—the terrifying enemy waiting inside the fortified city. He would have already sealed off any obvious back doors and weak spots. Or he might even be leaving them open as traps.

"If you try to use one of those back doors, he'll be there waiting with an ax to split your head."

"Wh-wh-why are you looking at me when you say that, buddy?! That's terrifying!"

Subaru had intended the warning for everyone, but he had ended up staring intensely at Flop.

He vividly remembered the two times he had seen Flop felled by a murderous ax before his eyes. He would rather die than witness that again. And he would not let it happen.

"If it's just a surprise attack, then yes, they'll be on guard." Abel was the first to agree with Subaru's assessment.

"...Weird. Are you really the kind of person to admit your own mistakes so easily?"

But despite Subaru's surprise—

"Fool," Abel fired back coldly. "Who said anything about a mistake? I simply said that planning a surprise attack in that way is foolish."

"...? Then what were you planning to use the back door for?"

"There is no rule that an entrance must be used by people. To paralyze the soldiers inside the city, we only need to bring something in. Such as poison."

"All the more reason I can't let you do this!"

Abel's indifferent tone made it sound inevitable, but Subaru outright rejected it.

Poison was out. Way out.

Subaru knew firsthand just how powerful the Shudrak's poison was, and he absolutely refused to let it be used.

That kind of hellish pain—it was more miserable than dying in battle.

"Aren't you trying to limit casualties to convince Flop?"

"Of course. That's why I prepared a strategy that wouldn't impact our combat strength. Even if a surprise attack succeeds, we could still suffer losses. But with poison, there's no such risk. What's so strange about that?"

"How can you talk about limiting casualties without considering the townspeople?!"

"Now, now, calm down, you two! Don't glare at each other like that!"

The discussion was about to break down completely due to the vast difference in their perspectives, but Flop stepped between them, forcing them to move apart.

Looking between their faces, he placed a hand on his chest.

"Let's calm down and talk! The chief and I weren't getting anywhere close to agreeing! But I'd love to hear about this bloodless plan of yours! If it's really possible, it'd be like a dream come true!"

"Flop…"

Seeing Flop's beaming smile and hopeful expression, Subaru suppressed the anger welling up inside him. It seemed even Abel was taken aback by Flop's optimism.

"Hmph. Very well, let's hear it. If your plan can convince this merchant and get him to reveal the hidden routes, it'll save time."

"Eh?! Buddy?! Are you—"

"No! Not at all! We didn't plan this! And you—quit trying to make me look like the bad guy here!"

Abel, as usual, showed no sign of shame over his comment, which was bound to make Flop misunderstand the situation. Seeing that unperturbed, immovable expression, Subaru grumbled, "Do you even really need that damn mask…?"

Just then—

"So then…"

A faint voice broke the tension.

Rem, standing at the entrance, watched Subaru's back. Unbothered by the shifting mood, she focused solely on him.

"So then, what will you do? Can you find a path other than a fleeting dream or a bloody reality?"

"…You really know how to set my heart on fire, don't you?"

As Rem's expression softened, Subaru grimaced but then steeled himself. He swept his gaze across the faces in the room—Abel, Flop, Mizelda, and the other Shudrak warriors.

"My plan doesn't need a back door or any bloodshed. But Flop, I need your help."

"Buddy, I'm just a powerless traveling merchant with a knack for words. You know that."

"Yeah, of course. But you're not just a traveling merchant. You've got a special talent… Your good looks."

"…Huh? My looks?" Flop's eyes widened as he instinctively touched his face.

The others in the room tilted their heads, puzzled by Subaru's remark.

"I see. That's certainly true."

"...! Sister, did you realize something?"

"No, I was just agreeing with Subaru's comment."

"Sister..."

Talitta slumped in disappointment as Mizelda crossed her arms and nodded sagely.

To varying degrees, everyone had the same reaction—they didn't quite grasp Subaru's intent. Even Flop and Abel were at a loss.

However, Mizelda, who held strong opinions about beauty—or the lack thereof—wasn't entirely off the mark. Her occasionally disheartening eye for attractiveness had given Subaru a crucial clue.

Her taste in men had sparked the idea for his bloodless plan.

"Seeing is believing. Just go along with me and give it a try, Flop."

"Go along with you? I don't mind, but what exactly—"

"Just roll with me," Subaru cut in forcefully. He turned to Mizelda. "You use cosmetics to dye your hair and create the patterns on your bodies, right? Any chance you could lend me those and the tools you use?"

2

"..."

Returning to the gathering place after a short while, the group fell into stunned silence at the sight before them. Not out of confusion or exasperation—Subaru could tell it was pure, simple surprise and wonder.

He could take pride in the fact that he had done well enough to earn such a reaction.

"...This is the key to winning without spilling any blood. My trump card."

There was still no response as Subaru rubbed his nose. Everyone remained speechless, struggling to process what they were seeing.

"B-buddy." The very source of their shock—and the only one aside from Subaru who wasn't dumbfounded—spoke up hesitantly. "I can't really see the results for myself, so…what's the outcome, generally speaking?"

"C'mon now, you don't need to worry about a thing, Flop…no, Flora."

"Flora?!"

Flop—or rather Flora—gasped, eyes widening in disbelief. Her surprised expression, however, was unexpectedly adorable. Brimming with confidence, Subaru nodded and touched her cheek.

Her long, soft blond hair was brushed out, and her eyes were now accentuated with eyeshadow, which made them stand out more than usual. Neatly arranged eyelashes framed her gaze, while a slight blush highlighted the paleness of her skin. Red lipstick added a finishing touch, complementing the new outfit.

By emphasizing her natural features and refining them for full impact, Subaru had proven a simple truth—

"Beauty can be created."

"…Is this some kind of bad joke?"

"Eh?!"

Rem's icy stare pierced through Subaru as he proudly presented his masterpiece. Just moments ago, her eyes had been filled with warm expectation—but now they carried the coldest scorn she had shown since waking up.

"Wait! It's not a joke! I'm completely serious, so don't look at me like that!"

"I was a fool for trusting you even a little."

"You're jumping to conclusions! That immediate disillusionment is just like Ram's!"

"Huh?"

She might not remember, but the way she'd so quickly lost faith in him made her seem just like Ram. It was almost endearing, a reminder of how close the sisters were.

But more importantly, Subaru needed to win back Rem's trust—because this wasn't just some dumb joke.

The purpose of the makeup was—

"…So your target is Zikr Osman."

Abel was the first to figure it out.

Unlike the others, who were still struggling to process Flop's transformation into Flora, Abel had already begun analyzing Subaru's intent.

—The goal was Zikr Osman.

A second-class general and the commander of the forces stationed in Guaral. A seasoned leader who favored reliable, safe tactics. And also...

"I've heard he's a notorious womanizer. Apparently it's well known among the soldiers."

Subaru recalled his time imprisoned in the imperial camp. Jamal had threatened to "gift" Rem and Louis to the general—a warning that had stuck with him. If Osman's reputation as a womanizer was so well known, even among lower-ranked soldiers, then...

"A beautiful, nonthreatening woman can get close to him. In other words, Flora can definitely do it."

"B-buddy, you keep calling me Flora with this awkwardly intense expression, but...what exactly are you planning? I'm getting scared here!"

"Don't worry, Flora. I won't make you go alone. I'll be with you, of course."

"That's way too much, Subaru!"

Mizelda shot to her feet, her intense expression clouded as she grabbed Subaru by the shoulders, shaking her head.

"Your eyes are charming, but the raw materials you were born with are..."

"Mizelda, I get your concern, but I told you—beauty can be created."

Placing his hand over hers, Subaru answered firmly. Mizelda's eyes widened, and she swallowed hard. Then, looking at Flora's made-up face, she narrowed her gaze as if staring into something dazzling.

"...It's my loss. Let me see your potential."

"Just you wait."

"I have no idea what you two are talking about," Kuna sighed in exasperation.

Either way, the main concern was—

"What do you intend to achieve by appealing to Zikr Osman's proclivities?" Abel asked. "He's still a wolf, not some puppy who will obediently come begging for whatever bait you dangle before him."

"Yeah, if we just present ourselves without a strategy, it won't mean much. That's why we need a plan to get him to bite. Maybe by inviting him to a party or something."

"A banquet? But he won't be easily swayed. He has no reason to leave the safety of the city walls until reinforcements arrive from the capital. He won't accept a suspicious invitation."

"Yeah... I'm still working on narrowing down the options..."

"W-wait a moment!"

Rem suddenly interrupted. She still looked visibly shaken as she glanced between Subaru and Abel.

"Are you serious? Discussing this ridiculous scheme as if it isn't a terrible prank on Flop?"

"Huh? A prank on me? What's going on? If the missus thinks it's a joke, then...little niece, what's happening?"

"Auu? Uu! Uuu!"

Flora—who still hadn't seen himself in a mirror—turned to Louis for comfort, but she panicked at the unfamiliar face and hid behind Rem.

From her perspective, Flora and Flop were two entirely different people.

"Setting aside whether her reaction is a valid test, I don't believe this is a joke. This is finally a plan worth discussing."

"So you acknowledge Flora's beauty, too?"

"...What I acknowledge is the idea you arrived at—one I had not considered. What an unexpected angle."

Subaru frowned at Abel's stubborn response, but the emperor ignored him, placing a hand on his chin in thought.

Then Abel turned his sharp gaze on Subaru.

"Subaru Natsuki, I will ask this once—is your makeup limited to just the merchant?"

For a moment, Subaru was stunned. But after digesting the meaning behind the question, he shook his head.

"Like I said, if we go with this plan, I'll be doing it, too."

"Fool. Who would expect anything from you? Spare me your prattle until you've seen your own face in a mirror."

"Phrasing!" Subaru shot back, appalled by the sheer brutality of Abel's words.

But then Abel placed a hand on his own chest.

"...It would be too much for the merchant alone. I shall go as well."

"Y-you will?!"

His bold declaration caused a stir among Mizelda and the others. Subaru was, of course, just as shocked. He never would have dreamed that Abel would volunteer himself.

"...Honestly, I thought convincing you would be the biggest hurdle."

"Under normal circumstances, this would be a foolish ploy, unworthy of consideration. However, given our limited options, we must take advantage of any effective strategy available."

"Tch. What a nasty way to put it. This is the problem with charismatic guys..."

Even after being driven from his throne, Abel remained an emperor through and through. This was his creed, his unwavering philosophy.

From their first encounter in the jungle through the ritual of blood and beyond, he had repeatedly made massive bets with his own body on the line. And from the looks of it, he had no intention of stopping now.

"An outlandish scheme only works when it shatters the enemy's expectations," Abel continued. "We will exploit the general's proclivities and use the negligence it invites to our advantage. It is worthy of consideration."

"Yeah, I read something similar in an ancient book called the *Kojiki*. Dressing as a woman is one of the best ways to target an enemy's top commander."

"…Blindly accepting the contents of such a dubious book…" Rem sounded unconvinced.

It is from an actual historical text, but there's no way I'll be able to convince her with that. Winning back her trust won't be so easy.

Still, Subaru had braced himself for outright rejection—so Abel's response was both unexpected and welcome.

Either way—

"If you're willing to cooperate, that makes things easier. As for your name…Abel Volakia…how about Bianca?"

"I have no attachment to an alias. Call me whatever you like. More importantly—you, I, and the merchant alone will not be enough."

Abel's gaze shifted to Kuna and Talitta.

"Huh?"

"A necessary precaution. Even if Zikr Osman takes the bait, we need enough force to deter any immediate response. However, we must also avoid using anyone who can be easily identified as Shudrak."

Subaru quickly understood what Abel meant.

Talitta and Kuna blinked in surprise at being singled out, but they were the least obviously menacing among the Shudrak.

Mizelda radiated an aura of strength, making her a poor candidate. Holly, with her distinct look and demeanor, was even more conspicuous. Neither of them would be suitable for this mission, in which subtlety was key.

What they needed was a femininity that wouldn't put the enemy on guard…

"That much will come down to what I can do with makeup and costuming, I guess."

And then—

"…Me too."

"Rem?"

Rem raised her hand.

Rem had made no secret of her distrust of Subaru sparked by the Flora incident, but, perhaps because she saw how earnestly they were discussing the plan, her expression was serious. Determination and resolve flashed in her light-blue eyes.

"Allow me to accompany you. I will be of use."

"Rem…sorry, but that's not going to work."

"…Gh! You're still trying to keep me away from unnecessary danger…"

Rem glowered at Subaru, her resolve wavering.

He really did feel a protective instinct toward her—the kind that would undoubtedly irritate her. It wouldn't be a lie to say he wished he could keep her far from harm, sleeping peacefully in a safe, soft bed.

But that wasn't why he was saying no.

"It's true I worry about you. But the reason I'm saying no is because it would lower our odds of success. The soldiers in the city have seen your face."

"—Ah."

"Back when we were caught in the camp, and again when we escaped the city. That's the same reason we can't involve Medium, either. We made way too big a scene getting out."

Given how much of an uproar they had caused, the guards at the inspection points would never forget Rem, Medium, or even Louis. That was why Rem couldn't be part of this—she would jeopardize the entire plan.

"But…but in that case, they know your face, too, don't they?!"

"Yeah, but it's not going to be me walking through the gates of Guaral."

Subaru grinned.

"It'll be Natsumi Schwartz."

"Huh?"

Rem's eyes flashed with anger. She assumed he was brushing her off again.

She wouldn't believe it, no matter how many times he said it.

The plan was simple—just as he had transformed Flop into Flora, he would transform Subaru Natsuki into Natsumi Schwartz.

—She'd have to see it to believe it.

"Anyway, that's why we can't bring you. But, Talitta, Kuna…if you're willing to take on this dangerous role—"

"No need to ask them," Mizelda interrupted. "I'll allow it. Take them both."

Before Subaru could get their confirmation, Mizelda had already given her approval.

Subaru turned to her in surprise, but Talitta only smiled, as if intrigued by this unconventional strategy.

"Subaru, you and Abel have already proven your valor. The Shudrak take pride in strength, but that doesn't mean ingenuity is unworthy. The ultimate warrior surpasses all in both combat and wisdom… Prove yourself again."

Subaru had assumed Mizelda and the Shudrak would reject this kind of deceptive plan outright. That's why he had wanted to ask Talitta and Kuna separately.

But, in line with Mizelda's decision, Talitta and Kuna nodded as if it were completely natural.

"If the chief says so, I've got no reason to argue," Kuna said lazily, resting her hands behind her head.

"I will follow my sister's decision," Talitta added. "Also…I'm interested in this makeup as well."

Kuna was resting her hands behind her head, seemingly disinterested, and Talitta had the same answer, but she was glancing over at Flora. Apparently she was curious to see the extent of Subaru's skill with makeup.

They're a bit lackadaisical, but not getting too fired up is probably for the best.

"If there are no objections, then let's start preparing at once," Abel stated. "We need to move before those in the capital push those cowards behind the walls into action."

"…Yeah, got it. If everyone's in agreement."

Subaru then turned to Rem.

"Rem, can you accept this?"

"…It's not like you'd listen to me anyway."

Rem glared at him, frustration clear in her expression.

He felt bad for shutting her out despite her determination, but her safety and the success of the mission were on the same side of the scale—he had no choice but to keep her away from this.

He braced himself for her anger—

"...However," she said quietly, "I was the one who asked you to do something."

"Rem?"

"I have no right to complain about it now...so please make it work."

She was still frustrated, but she was respecting his judgment.

It wasn't an outright approval, but it was enough to clear the heavy cloud in Subaru's heart.

"...It might only be with Rem, but man I'm easy. Oh, then again... Hmm..."

The tiniest show of goodwill from her made him so happy he could float.

But then again—Emilia's simple smile made him feel like he was ascending to heaven.

Beatrice's smug lectures always warmed his heart.

Maybe he was more excitable than he thought.

Just then—

"Hey, Bro! It's about time we let poor Botey rest. I wanna put her away somewhere."

Medium peeked in from the doorway.

Even among the tall and muscular Shudrak, she stood out—a full head taller than most. Her big, round eyes scanned the room curiously.

"Huh? Where's my brother?"

"Oh, Sister! That's awfully cold of you, not recognizing your own brother. I'm right here!"

"...?"

Medium tilted her head.

Flora stood up and waved, but Medium furrowed her brow, staring hard.

After a few long seconds, realization dawned.

"Bro, you were really my older sister?!"

"Buddy?! What did you do to me?!"

If Medium—Flop's own sister—was completely fooled, that was a good sign the plan had a real chance of success.

3

Staring into a crude mirror, Subaru Natsuki—or, rather, the person who had once been called that—squinted, double- and triple-checking his reflection.

Heavy eyeshadow and carefully curled eyelashes. A neat application of powder to soften the texture of his skin, masking the differences between a man's and a woman's complexion. Scarlet lips, painted just enough to add a luscious sheen.

Getting the clothing right had been a real challenge—arranging layers of fabric to conceal his body shape while painstakingly adjusting them to match the styles of the southern regions.

—Always keep in mind the most beautiful version of myself.

Using every trick at his disposal, picturing everyone he had ever met.

Starting with Emilia, through Felt and the loathsome Elsa. Ram and Rem. Beatrice, Petra, and even Meili (but setting those three aside for now). Priscilla, Crusch, Anastasia… Ferris—whom, honestly, he should be looking to as his guide here.

Drawing on every instance of beauty he had seen in this world—distilling all of it into a single image in his mind…

"…This is me."

Stepping back from the mirror, he took a slow, deep breath. Then, with a resolute turn, he faced the door.

After a long and lonely battle, he had finally finished his transformation.

And now it was time for the verdict.

He pushed open the door to where everyone waited, holding their breath.

As the door swung open, revealing the results, the gathered onlookers gasped.

"...Splendid."

The first to recover was Mizelda.

Her voice carried admiration, even a hint of respect, as she began clapping.

Taking her word as a blessing, Subaru softly cleared his throat and smiled.

"It is an honor to be complimented by you, Mizelda."

"...Even your voice? How...how far did you go...?!"

"Once I've committed, it is my duty to give my all. Lives may be saved if I see this through completely—so there is but one thing I must do."

"Ohhh...!"

The smile faded as he raised a single elegant finger toward the sky.

The dense jungle canopy blocked the sun, but this gesture wasn't meant for anyone above—it was for everyone gathered here.

—Always keep in mind the most beautiful version of myself.

Follow that image. Manifest the ideal.

There was nothing to fear.

Thus I will become...

"...The second coming of Natsumi Schwartz."

"Is this some joke?"

"Eh?!"

Subaru had been completely convinced he had perfectly embodied his alias, but Rem instantly shattered his pride.

Looking closer, he realized that while Mizelda and the other Shudrak were deeply moved by his transformation...

Rem alone was looking at him with a subzero glare.

However, she quickly covered her mouth and shook her head.

"I-is there something wrong? I was quite...confident in the results, but..."

"I'm sorry. I said I wouldn't comment, since I was the one who asked you to do this."

"…It's okay, Rem. Don't feel down," Subaru reassured her. "It may be surprising, but I don't dislike it."

"Huh?"

Rem's expression somehow grew even colder.

"No, no, that was a misstatement on my part! Come on now, Talitta, Kuna!"

Desperate to change the subject, Subaru hastily nudged forward the two women standing beside him.

Talitta and Kuna had already undergone their own makeovers, their hairstyles and outfits completely transformed.

Talitta's normally imposing presence had been softened, her surprisingly childish facial features giving her a more innocent look.

Meanwhile, Kuna's long hair had been styled into twin-tails, which added a touch of sweetness to her usually cool and sharp demeanor.

"Heh-heh, you are both adorable. Plenty of excellent material for me to work with."

"Th-thank you… It feels like I'm almost someone else," Talitta murmured, blushing as she touched her hair.

Next to her, Kuna—now with a sweet Lolita style—was suddenly scooped up in a hug by Holly.

"You're even cuter than usual, Kuna! I'm so surprised at how good you are at this, Subaru!"

"I was surprised, too. He knows women better than women do."

Subaru grinned triumphantly at their praise.

Meanwhile, Rem narrowed her eyes at him, suspicious.

"…Why are you this good at makeup? And at applying it to yourself?"

"Umm, regarding that, there are reasons—reasons that run deeper than the sea and higher than the mountains—um, anyway, what about you?" Subaru stammered, quickly deflecting as fast as he could. "Why, you're the type of heroine who'd rather make people wait than wait yourself, Bianca…"

It was a little difficult to explain, so Subaru looked away while dodging the question.

Rem was about to press him further when—

"It seems everyone is finished."

A voice rich with arrogance—completely unaltered—rang through the room.

A new figure had arrived.

Everyone turned without much thought—

—and in an instant, time stopped.

"..."

Or rather, time stopped for everyone...except Subaru, who had applied the makeup.

"I left the adjustments to you...but it's almost offensive how skilled you are."

"Who would be glad to be complimented on their skill with powder and adornment?" Subaru muttered. "Still...I'll admit, even I'm astonished by the final result. You're far more striking than I expected."

"Kh, that smug winner's confidence...!"

Subaru bit his little finger in frustration. He had no doubts that beauty could be created. He had proven it with his own appearance, despite the limited tools.

However, the difference in base quality was undeniable.

"...Um, Abel, right?" Rem's voice quivered.

"Who else would it be? Do not ask such a foolish question. Then again, I suppose if I have changed that much, it might be pertinent to include your surprise in the evaluation."

Abel—or, rather, after the makeup, wig, and wardrobe change...

...Bianca had arrived.

He clenched his pale, slender fingers. His jet-black hair gleamed, perfectly complementing his sharp, almond-shaped eyes. The flowing outfit he wore—a dancing girl's attire—wasn't excessive, revealing just enough. His bare stomach and long legs were framed by fabric, accentuating his smooth, flawless skin.

A gorgeous dancing queen.

The ultimate trump card.

"...Personally, I was a little surprised you had no resistance to being made up...," Subaru muttered.

"What, did you expect me to be ashamed?" Abel scoffed. "You

should know—this isn't my first time. I've done this many times since childhood."

"...As a child?"

"Considering my position, it's only natural that I should have as many tools at my disposal for protection as possible."

Bianca—or rather Abel—crossed his arms in a decidedly unladylike pose.

Subaru could accept that reasoning. He could easily imagine that the succession process in Volakia was far more brutal than in Lugunica. A battle for survival among those with a claim to the throne, where concealing one's identity—even one's gender—might be a necessary survival tactic.

Abel's willingness to sacrifice anything for his goals, even himself, must have been instilled in him from a young age—even before he took the throne.

"Still, though...it's a little irritating that you acknowledge yourself as beautiful...!"

"That's absurd. How could one survey an entire country from its summit without the ability to objectively assess oneself?" Abel scoffed. "You, on the other hand, have managed to overcome that lack of objectivity through mere skill—but I have no need for such cheap tricks."

"Gh...!"

"Do you know why the tiger is strong? It is strong because tigers are strong."

It was a logic Subaru had heard from Garfiel before—and it utterly crushed him.

The tiger is strong because it's a tiger.

Applying that logic here, Abel was beautiful because he was Abel.

...It was a tautology.

"I...I'm sure Flora thinks the same way as you! Hmph!"

"Don't rope me into this, buddy!"

Flora—formerly Flop—was standing behind Abel, having entered with him.

Unlike Subaru's and Abel's transformation, Flop had required very few changes to become Flora. In fact, because he'd had long hair to begin with, his transformation had been the most natural of them all. With just a little styling and work, he was effortlessly stunning.

If the three of them stood in a lineup, Subaru felt he wouldn't lose in direct comparison.

But—

"The time…the time taken is so much longer… The heavens are so unfair…!"

"Sorry, buddy, but you're really incredible! I didn't recognize you at all!" Flora exclaimed. "At this point, I guess 'Ms.' would be more appropriate!"

"…I suppose I will have to content myself with that level of compliment."

"Wait, was that a compliment? I couldn't tell."

Even in Flora's body, Flop's candidness remained unchanged.

Subaru shrugged—that was fine. Though Flora would still need some guidance on how to conduct himself for the plan.

However, the biggest challenge would be Abel.

"Flora and I can play instruments. However, your role is…"

"Dance." Abel's voice was flat, as if the answer were obvious. "I already memorized the plan without your commentary. I understand the importance of my role."

"…And?"

Abel smirked.

"While I am not as gifted as my late sister, dancing happens to be a forte of mine."

His pompous, triumphant smile was annoyingly beautiful.

His overflowing confidence should have been frustrating—

—instead, it only heightened Subaru's expectations.

If Abel wielded the potential of his natural beauty to its fullest extent, he could flawlessly transform into Bianca.

And if Subaru was right about that…

…then he could get his hopes up about the dance as well.

"...Very well. If you're going to speak that highly of yourself, then I'd love to see your skills," Subaru challenged. "Just make sure you don't choke on your own spit."

"Choke...? Hmph. You mean my words are as pointless as spitting at the clouds? What a roundabout expression, but so be it," Abel said, crossing his arms. "I shall teach you. Consider it a reward for the plan you've contributed."

Even while he was cross-dressing, Abel's arrogance remained utterly intact.

It was as if he had no doubt about himself whatsoever.

Subaru was both reassured and intimidated by his presence.

He glanced toward Rem. Unfortunately, he couldn't bring her along for this mission.

However—

"Please pray for our safety. I will devote myself to this task...for your sake."

"...................Done."

"It took you a long time to pray!"

Rem had replied so slowly, with such an unfathomably deep sense of sincerity, that Subaru nearly fell over.

Peeking out from beside her, Louis blinked up at Subaru.

Apparently, she hadn't made the connection between Natsumi Schwartz and Subaru.

For now, that was enough proof that the plan had picked up serious momentum.

4

—Operation Kumaso Takeru.

That was the name of the plan to entrap Zikr Osman, the skirt-chasing general second-class of the imperial army.

There were no objections to the operation name—borrowed straight from the *Kojiki*—so the group, disguised as a traveling performance troupe, walked boldly through the front gates of the walled city.

Meanwhile, Mizelda and the others moved separately.

There was no need for a back door. If they couldn't pass through the front gate's inspection, then they had no hope of getting close to Zikr.

—The inspection was their first test.

And...

"Come one, come all, and lend us your time! We shall perform a song and dance from the far East—beyond the Great Waterfalls, beyond the vast seas, traversing through time itself! We are a traveling troupe, and we have arrived to delight you with our performance!"

A black-haired maiden raised her voice in a poetic introduction, drawing curious glances from the line of people awaiting inspection.

At her side stood:

A young woman with soft black hair.

A musician with flowing blond hair.

Two dark-skinned women of striking beauty.

Their presence was dazzling enough to earn whistles from the gathered crowd.

As a lyulyre was strummed, a clear, bright voice rang out beneath the blue sky.

"Oh? What's going on?"

"They said they're traveling performers—music!"

"Heh... They're all lookers..."

Excitement spread as attention and anticipation grew.

The guards handling inspections were completely overwhelmed.

—And that was exactly what the troupe had planned.

The moment the guards asked about their performance, their fate was sealed.

Before they even realized it, the troupe had begun a show—using the gate entrance as their stage.

"Well...the singing and playing aren't bad at all."

The guards, already fed up with their work, didn't bother stopping them.

Lately, they had grown frustrated with the imperial army's behavior. Soldiers and guards had different positions. Soldiers were subordinate to the empire, and guards were subordinate to a city. Neither of them was inherently superior, but the soldiers did not seem to understand that.

Occupying the city hall, looting people's houses under the guise of searches, carrying out night patrols only to spend all night in bars.

The entire mood of the city had soured under the military's tyrannical presence.

On top of that, the guards had recently been blamed for letting rebels escape through the main gate—leaving them bitter.

If a troupe of performers could clear the air some and lighten the mood, that was not such a bad thing.

And so they had overlooked the troupe putting on a performance, but…

"…Ah."

The guards froze as someone stepped forward.

—No.

Not just the guards. Everyone. The entire line of people awaiting inspection—every last person—fell silent.

"…"

A dancing girl lifted her veil. In that moment, the spell was complete.

"…And now, Bianca's performance!"

At the black-haired maiden's call, the dancer slowly raised her arms.

Even that single movement was irresistibly elegant—bewitching those who watched.

Then a flowing, mesmerizing, and majestic dance began.

"…"

The audience was entranced.

Breathless. Something primal in them refused to look away. It was so enchanting that they wouldn't have hesitated to say their souls were crying out—declaring that their eyes existed solely for this moment, no matter how dramatic it sounded.

—They were under an instinctual command:

Watch.

Had there been a pickpocket in the crowd, they could have stolen freely and walked away undetected.

But even a thief would be too captivated to act.

"..."

The song lasted less than five minutes. As the music faded, the dancer's feet touched the ground—the spell was broken.

And only then did the guards and the audience realize the performance had ended.

A wave of applause and cheers erupted.

"...Hopefully, we were able to relieve some of the tedium you've been feeling."

"Y-yeah..."

One of the guards snapped back to reality at the voice of the black-haired musician.

The troupe had demonstrated their skill—in both music and dance.

And, judging by the crowd's reaction, there was no way they could be turned away.

Now only one question remained—

"What do you ladies intend to do in town?"

"We shall renew the spirits dampened by the soldiers' presence."

A confident smile. A gesture toward the rest of the troupe.

The guard swallowed hard. Then, touching the hilt of his sword...

"I know a shop in town... Would you mind performing there tonight?"

"Oh my..." The black-haired musician covered her mouth in delight.

With that, their entry was secured.

The troupe stepped into the walled city.

As they walked away, the guard watched their silhouettes disappear, vowing to finish work early tonight.

5

From the very first performance, the troupe became the talk of Guaral.

The dance at the gate had merely been a preview, and the full performances had exceeded all expectations. Dozens of repeat attendees made their efforts much easier.

However...

"Do not forget—this limelight is only because we are new and different."

"Our performance is just a veneer. The appeal will fade. Right now, we are just another passing fascination."

"I see! So you're saying we need to work hard on our fundamental skills, buddy."

"Exactly. Diligence and discipline, every single day."

Visibly excited, Flop nodded with a cheerful smile while Subaru clenched his fist.

Flop really was a great listener—always engaged, responding promptly. Subaru often got carried away in their conversations, but it was fun.

That said, Flop wasn't the one Subaru really needed to be talking to.

"Are you two even listening?! Don't let your minds wander!"

"Whoa, leave me out of this."

"U-us...?!"

Talitta and Kuna looked startled at being suddenly called out.

Inside the inn, they had already discarded their performance outfits and reverted to their Shudrak clothing—which was essentially just underwear.

They managed to dress properly for their shows, but the moment they were in private, they immediately switched back.

"Listen closely. There's a saying—'God is in the details.' Every little action, every habit—mastering them is the key to realism. The secret to maintaining beauty!"

"B-beauty... That's more my sister's thing...," Talitta murmured, shifting uncomfortably.

"What are you saying, Ms. Talitta?!" Flop gasped. "Your charm and your sister's charm are completely different! Would complimenting you ever be enough to compliment Ms. Mizelda?! No! Because you are two different people! And your beauties are different, too!"

"Gh...!"

Talitta sat stiffly on the bed as Flop suddenly took her hand. His sparkling smile was almost too much. Talitta's eyes widened at his enthusiasm, her mouth opening and closing as her cheeks turned bright red.

"Oh my..." Subaru covered his mouth in mock surprise.

"Spare me." Kuna sighed. "Talitta clings to the chief and barely goes out—she's got no resistance to this at all."

"Well, it's kind of adorable in a way. But you're pretty confident yourself, Kuna."

"I get out of the jungle pretty often. Plus, I don't have a terrifying older sister." Kuna smirked. "...I do have something like a troublesome little sister, though."

There was no doubt she was thinking of Holly.

The two of them were practically family, like best friends or even mother and daughter.

Meanwhile, Holly, Mizelda, and Rem were still outside the city, waiting for news.

I can't go back empty-handed.

Currently the troupe was staying in an inn in Guaral.

Three days had passed since they entered the city, and in that time, they had performed ten times with overwhelming success.

Originally Subaru had planned to rely on the money from selling the elgina horn, but the tips they received after each performance had provided more than enough.

At least for now.

"Still...it'd be nice if things started moving soon," Subaru muttered, running a finger along his chin.

Things were almost going too well. The performances were a massive hit and the residents were adoring fans. It was all thanks to Bianca's exquisite dancing plus Natsumi and Flora's conversational charm.

Bianca's mystique was part of her appeal, so she rarely appeared outside of the shows.

Since Abel couldn't fake a feminine voice, the job of gathering intel naturally fell to Natsumi (Subaru) and Flora (Flop).

"Weirdly, no one ever questions you, even though you don't change your voice."

"I don't have your skill!" Flop laughed. "But maybe I picked up some of my sister's habits over the years. Could be that's what makes it work."

Subaru frowned.

He imagined Medium... Sure, she was beautiful. Her expressions changed constantly, and her energy was charming. ...But did that really explain how flawless Flora's identity seemed to be?

"You must be quite composed to waste time with such a pointless discussion."

A cool voice interrupted.

The star of the troupe—Bianca—sat by the window.

However, without the wig, the rest of the head was unmistakably Abel's.

After days of dancing as the lead performer, there was finally a trace of exhaustion on his stoic face.

They were living among enemies. Tension was inevitable. Subaru himself had to stay sharp as Natsumi.

Rem and Mizelda had seen this plan as just a joke at first, but Subaru had proposed it in all seriousness, and they had gone through significant debate to raise the odds of success. If he messed it up, they were not going to be sympathetic to the idea of just giving up.

All the more reason...

"Bianca, why don't you rest a little? I just realized—I've never actually seen you sleeping before."

"Eh, what are you saying, Ms. Natsumi? That's a little too..." Flop started to laugh, but then he froze as realization dawned.

"...Huh? Wait, huh? Now that you say it...I don't remember seeing Ms. Bianca sleep, either."

Abel snorted, not even sparing Flop a glance. He showed no sign of engaging in the conversation. His wariness remained unwavering— he refused to let his guard down, even around them.

He's still blinking one eye at a time...like always.

Even though no one here would do anything to him if he closed both eyes for a second.

"...Is it not exhausting? Living like that?" Subaru asked.

"...You of all people are asking me that?"

Abel furrowed his brow at Subaru's blunt question. Subaru wasn't sure what that reaction meant. Abel's way of living was undoubtedly suffocating. Subaru's, on the other hand, wasn't.

"That you don't even realize what I am talking about is especially pitiful. But I'll allow it. Continue."

"I was going to keep living whether you said so or not. Your—"

"To close both eyes is to yield the power over life and death to another."

Abel's voice was calm, final.

"I do not take my life so lightly as to allow that. Not even for an instant."

"..."

"'Do not spoil the tension'—is that not what you said?"

That shut down whatever Subaru had planned to say next.

He scowled at Abel, but Abel didn't even look at him. The wig and jewelry were gone, yet he still wore Bianca's clothes. At a glance, he should have looked unbalanced, missing that key piece of his disguise——but somehow, even like this, he was beautiful.

That battlefield discipline, that constant vigilance—it was precisely what gave him that strange, strained beauty.

As Subaru was thinking that...

"There's movement."

Abel suddenly stood up, quickly reaching for the wig hanging from the bedpost.

"Eh?"

Subaru was caught off guard, but then he heard it—loud, heavy footsteps echoing down the hallway.

Then there was a sharp, forceful knock on the door.

"Is this where the traveling troupe is? Open up. Message from city hall."

Subaru's heart skipped a beat.

"Ah, j-just one moment, please!"

"Ha! Don't make me laugh. I'm a soldier, you think I'm gonna wait?"

The voice sneered from the other side—just before the door was shoved open violently. A one-eyed man in a distinctive red-and-black uniform strode in without hesitation. Two swords on his back. A twisted smirk of ecstasy on his face. A familiar face.

Jamal.

"…Gh!"

Subaru's body froze. His breath caught.

"Don't be scared. I ain't gonna bite."

Jamal laughed as he scanned the room with a contemptuous gaze. His eyes fell on Talitta and Kuna—still in what was barely more than underwear.

His lips curled.

"Heh. The looks weren't a lie. And here I thought the chief of staff was overselling it…"

Subaru's stomach twisted.

"Ah…"

Before he could react, Jamal's hand shot out and grabbed Subaru's chin, tilting his face upward.

"You've got some good, defiant eyes."

His grin widened.

"Good glare, too. Just how I like it."

Despite his sleazy demeanor, Jamal was strong. But strong and terrifying were two very different things.

"Supposedly, you girls are pretty hot at singing and dancing." His fingers dug slightly into Subaru's jaw. "So what's your specialty? Maybe I should take you to bed tonight."

A nauseating chill ran down Subaru's spine. Still—he smiled.

"I-it is an honor to receive such an invitation. I happen to like strong men."

Jamal's eyes glittered.

He leaned in closer, eyes roaming over Subaru's body.

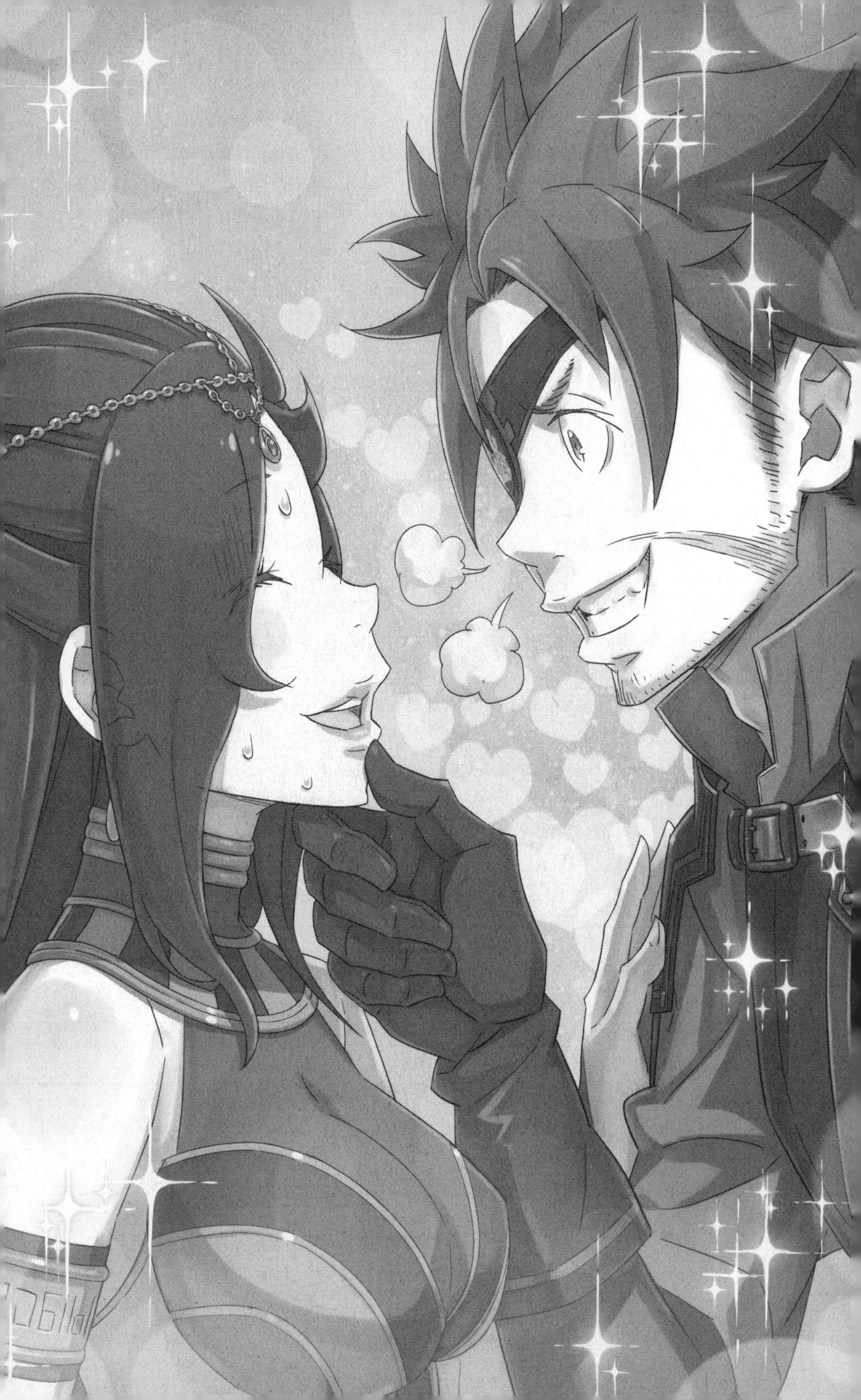

Even at this proximity—even as his gaze devoured him—he showed no sign of recognizing Subaru. That was good.

But—

—unfortunately, he had struck a chord with Jamal in an entirely different way.

Of course, during performances, situations like this had come up. Subaru had always dodged them with a smile and a few clever words. But this wasn't just any man.

And escaping this kind of situation would be far, far more difficult…

—That was when a strong breeze blew through.

"…Oh."

Subaru's hair danced in the wind, and Jamal grimaced as the strands tickled his cheek. Annoyed, he glanced toward the open window—only to freeze at the sight before him.

There, standing with arms crossed in calm composure, was the black-haired queen of dance—the very woman Guaral could not stop talking about.

Seeing her up close, Jamal curled his lips into a smirk of surprise.

Most people would be utterly captivated, rendered motionless in her presence—yet he stood unfazed. That was impressive grit.

"Ha-ha, so this is the famous queen of dance, huh?" He chuckled. "Figures they told me to bring you."

"That's…"

Subaru exhaled in silent shock as Jamal released him and thudded over to Abel.

Then—of all things—he grabbed Abel by the chin, tilting his face upward.

He had no clue that the face he was grabbing—the face he was grinning so coarsely at—belonged to the emperor of Volakia.

So this…is what "ignorance is bliss" really means.

Subaru gulped, watching silently.

"…"

"This one doesn't even make a peep, huh?" Jamal murmured. "Well, that's tempting in its own way."

Abel remained perfectly still, his expression blank.

His silence didn't betray a single ounce of emotion—he seemed completely unbothered by the crude soldier holding his chin.

Unaware of Subaru's rising anxiety, Jamal continued his blatant disrespect of the emperor.

Then, with Abel's chin still in hand, he turned to the rest of the troupe.

"Rejoice, girls! You're all invited to a banquet at the city hall."

His lips curled into a grin.

"General Second-Class Zikr Osman—the one running this town—wants you there."

"General Second-Class…!"

The name sent a shock wave through Subaru's mind.

Jamal's pompous declaration was so shocking that for a moment, Subaru even forgot about the sheer disrespect he was witnessing.

Zikr Osman.

The fish they'd been trying to hook—

—they had him.

"Ain't no way you're turning that down, right, girls?"

"Of course not!" Subaru straightened up, adopting an excited tone. "We would absolutely love to share our songs and dances with the esteemed gentlemen of the army! It is what we have dreamed of!"

Even more enthusiastic than Subaru, Flop beamed, his charm radiating as he echoed the sentiment.

Jamal nodded, pleased. "Good answer! I like you." Then, roughly releasing Abel's chin, he plodded toward the door.

He leaned against the frame, crossing his arms.

"Hurry up and get ready. I'm taking you there myself."

"Eh?! If we've been summoned, we'd gladly bring ourselves—"

"Ha-ha-ha, don't worry about it." Jamal sneered. "I was told to make sure you arrived safely. This is my job, you see. Just get changed. My men'll carry anything that needs carrying."

"…"

"The banquet tonight is only for the officers." His gaze swept the room. "Us grunts? We get the scraps tomorrow. So…"

He licked his lips.

"I'm not letting any of you slip away."

Subaru's skin prickled at the vulgar gaze Jamal cast over them.

Fortunately, he, Abel, and Flop were in the bare minimum of cross-dressing to pass.

Talitta and Kuna were the ones in real danger—but they were actually women, so at least the plan wouldn't fall apart because of a lack of preparation.

However…

"Take your time."

Jamal's smirk only deepened.

The humiliation of having to dress under his watchful eye wouldn't be forgotten anytime soon.

But—

"All right, let's get ready, everyone! We mustn't keep the soldiers waiting! Let's move along!"

"Flora…"

"That's not like you, Ms. Natsumi!" Flora smiled radiantly. "Blood and tears don't suit you."

The anger bubbling inside Subaru simmered down. That extra line, intentionally added at the end, was a reminder. A reminder of the bloodless victory Subaru had promised.

"…Yes, that's right."

He inhaled deeply.

"Come on now, everyone! And you especially, Bianca—since you're a klutz at everything except dancing!"

"…"

Abel's gaze sharpened. Subaru met it head-on—and then casually ignored it.

They quickly packed their things, changing into attire fit for the banquet.

Subaru made a show of it, ensuring that Jamal got exactly what he wanted—

A good, long look.

Go ahead. Keep whistling. Enjoy the show.

Because when the plan succeeds—this'll be the biggest regret of your life.

So…

"Oh no! You don't have to intentionally shake your bottom, Ms. Natsumi!"

6

Even to an amateur's eye, it was obvious that the city hall was not a proper military structure.

It was a government building, meant for administration, not for war. Naturally, it lacked defensive installations.

Even so, with over three hundred soldiers quartered inside and a total fighting force of nearly five hundred including the city guard, its military strength was still considerable.

"But we've already slipped inside their walls."

Subaru smirked as he mentally mapped out the building's layout.

Operation Kumaso Takeru was progressing unexpectedly smoothly.

The plan was simple:

If a troupe of beautiful women became the talk of the town, then Zikr Osman, the notorious skirt chaser, would surely take notice.

From there, they just had to wait for the invitation to a banquet and capture the commander.

However, just as the perfect opportunity was presenting itself, a major problem arose.

"We're executing the plan tonight, but…"

There was no way to send a message to Mizelda and the others outside the walls.

Jamal—the very one who had come to fetch them—had given them no chance to make contact.

Not out of caution, but out of sheer perviness.

Now that they were inside the city hall, their freedom was restricted.

They had no chance to slip away, no way to let the outside team know that the plan was happening tonight.

"We have to find a way to get the message out...somehow."

The outside group was meant to be insurance if the plan failed—

—but even if it succeeded, they would still need help disarming the remaining soldiers.

Whether Operation Kumaso Takeru worked or not...contact was crucial.

"And I still have no idea what Bianca is thinking."

Abel had barely spoken since they arrived.

He seemed focused on the banquet, but...

...ever since they were brought inside and confined to a waiting room, Abel had been completely silent.

He knows the other team is critical. He knows there's no one else to turn to.

Flop was cooperative, but he wasn't the right person to plan the taking control of the building.

Talitta and Kuna had been chosen for their brawn, not their brains.

Which meant—

"...I'll have to do something myself."

Subaru clenched his fist.

He was standing inside the restroom, where he had gone under the pretense of nerves. The guards had ordered them not to leave the waiting room—but they weren't strict enough to deny a bathroom break. Unfortunately, the window had metal bars, so escaping through it wasn't an option.

I can't panic and do anything too reckless. But at the same time—

—I can't just sit here and do nothing. Worst-case scenario, we can delay the plan...but...

"Tonight is for the officers. Tomorrow is for the rest of the soldiers..."

That was what Jamal had let slip earlier at the inn.

Tonight's banquet would be limited to high-ranking officers.

Tomorrow, the rest of the soldiers would get their turn. Which meant the person Subaru least wanted to meet would be there.

"..."

Honestly, Subaru had nearly had a heart attack when Jamal burst into the room.

If Jamal was here, then there was a good chance that other man was, too.

...But then again, maybe that arrow had actually killed him.

"Wishful thinking, huh...?"

That wasn't something he should be hoping for.

It was complicated.

Subaru knew there were people in this world who simply shouldn't be allowed to live.

The Archbishops were a prime example.

If one of them was hit, he wouldn't hesitate to wish for their death.

But this man was different. He terrified Subaru, there was no doubt about that.

But he wasn't evil.

And yet...

What about the Archbishop I'm letting go because I've got no choice?

Subaru shook his head.

"...This isn't helping. Focus on the plan."

Scolding himself, he pushed the thoughts away.

He had searched every inch of the restroom, but there was nothing that could help him get a message outside the walls. If he stayed too long, the guard outside would get suspicious.

Maybe if things got urgent enough, Abel would finally act.

For now, he had to pull back.

Subaru took a deep breath, then stepped out of the restroom with graceful poise.

"My apologies for the wait. I was just...a little nervous."

The guard at the door barely reacted, just grunted in response.

But then—

"Hm. Ah, forget it. Someone to talk to just showed up."

"Oh?"

The guard nodded at someone, and following his gesture, Subaru turned. Then his heart froze. Standing before him was the last face he wanted to see.

"...Eep."

"Huh? What is it? Why the surprised look? Hey now, I'm not going to eat you."

Seeing Subaru's throat quiver, he smiled and joked.

It was a joke Subaru had heard from Jamal back at the inn, but unlike then—when it was just Jamal's horniness on full display—this time, Subaru couldn't just let it slide.

Because this time, he wanted to ask if it was really true.

"What, did you do something to her, Todd?"

"Me? Don't be absurd. There's no way I could. The wound was deep, so I've been in bed this whole time. I only just healed up enough to start walking around."

The man, Todd, rubbed his stomach while chatting amiably with the guard.

He was the person Subaru had been wariest of—not counting the Archbishops—the one man Subaru had nearly wished death upon. Now that terrifying nightmare stood before him, chatting casually.

"...Ah."

Subaru's mind spun at high speed.

I have to say something. Silence is bad. I can't give him a reason to be wary. If he gets suspicious, he'll use it as an excuse to act. He doesn't need proof. He doesn't need evidence. If he suspects anything, he'll move.

So...

"Seriously though, what is it? Did we—?"

"M-my apologies... It's just..."

"Just?"

Todd had only repeated the question, but Subaru's heart felt like it might burst.

He had wanted to end the conversation by saying he wasn't feeling well. But right before the words left his mouth, doubt struck him—should he really say that?

Not feeling well is the usual excuse, but it's a lie. And I think he'll see through it.

Subaru had died and returned enough times to know—Todd could read his thoughts. Last time, Todd had guessed what Subaru was thinking and stabbed him without hesitation.

A lie—a lie will just get me caught.
I have to avoid lying.

It wasn't that Subaru wasn't feeling well. The real reason he was suffocating right now was…

"I'm a little, um, scared…"

"Scared? Of me?"

"You too. We…um, we were brought here a little roughly."

He averted his eyes so Todd wouldn't see them.

Every word, every gesture made Subaru question whether it was the right move, drowning him in uncertainty. If Todd saw his eyes, he'd see through the lie. If he lied, he'd be caught.

But this wasn't a lie.

Todd closed one eye as he listened to Subaru's desperate response.

"Brought here roughly? You know who brought them over?"

"Ah, I think it was Private First-Class Aurelie."

"Oh, Jamal? That makes sense. In that case, sorry for scaring you," Todd apologized.

"Eh…?"

Subaru's eyes widened at the unexpected turn of events as Todd scratched his cheek.

"He's not a bad guy… Well, not exactly. His mouth's foul, his personality's worse, and he's not the sharpest tool in the shed. But it's not malice—that's just who he is."

"Ha, haa…"

"If possible, could you try to find a little forgiveness for him? I know how he looks, but he's going to be my brother-in-law. His little sister—an absolute angel, nothing like him—is my fiancée."

Subaru was growing more and more confused. From Todd's demeanor, he didn't seem to find anything suspicious in Subaru's words or reactions. In fact, he even pretended to sympathize with Subaru over Jamal's behavior.

To think my cross-dressing skills and Jamal's shittiness would actually come in handy.

"Ah, there you are! Hey! What are you doing walking around, Todd?!"

A loud voice echoed down the hall.

Jamal came stomping over with heavy steps.

"Uh-oh." Todd put a hand to his forehead. "He found me…"

"'Uh-oh' nothing! Guys with a hole in their gut need to rest and recover! You just can't believe something unless you see it yourself, can you?"

"No, no, I believe you." Todd shrugged, raising his hands. "You're surprisingly diligent, so do your job. But even serious people can make mistakes."

"That's just another way of saying you don't trust me…!"

Jamal stomped forward angrily but suddenly stopped, noticing Subaru standing beside Todd. His scowl shifted into a grin.

"One of the party girls. You were the one most my type, too. Hey, if you don't get any invitations tonight…"

"All right, that's enough of that."

Jamal reached for Subaru's shoulder, but to Subaru's shock, Todd was the one who stopped him.

Jamal's face twisted when Todd grabbed his wrist.

"Enough," Todd said again, his voice firm. "You're scaring her with that attitude. You have to be gentle with girls."

"Ahh? Why are you getting in the way…? Wait, are you…?"

"Don't even joke about that, Jamal. I only have eyes for your sister. You know that."

"As her older brother, that's not exactly what I want to hear from some guy, either…"

Jamal scowled but shook off Todd's hand. He glanced at Subaru again, but, seeing his tense expression, he let it go—for now.

Surprisingly, Jamal seemed to have some level of understanding. Or maybe he just felt hurt that someone he'd taken a liking to was scared of him.

Either way...

"We don't get to enjoy the banquet tonight anyway, so let's just go."

"You say that, but I'm getting sick of tracking down every possible back door into the city."

"It's not boring—it's insurance. Insurance. Because that's definitely where they'll come from."

Todd smiled easily, but that one comment sent a shiver through Subaru.

The idea of using a back door had already been anticipated and shut down. Subaru silently congratulated himself for not choosing that strategy. And as that thought settled...

"By the way, what was your name?"

Did he notice I relaxed?

Subaru felt like he might pass out at that seemingly offhand question.

My name? Why? For what reason? It's just a name. But Todd wouldn't ask without a reason—he doesn't care about things like that. That was why Rem was wary of him from the start. We were never on good terms this time around, so I never told him my name, either. Should I answer or not?

"C'mon, please tell me?"

Subaru held his breath. Resolving not to delay any further, he forced a smile, feigning as much calm as he could.

"I am Natsumi Schwartz."

There was no other option. All I can do is pray and hope this was the right choice.

"Huh." Todd rubbed his chin and nodded. "See, Jamal? Aren't you glad to know that?"

"Shut up! Let's get out of here!"

Jamal's face turned red as Todd shrugged and followed him. Without looking back, they turned a corner and disappeared from sight.

They're gone. Gone.

"...R-really?" Subaru exhaled, watching carefully to make sure they weren't coming back.

"A-are you all right? You look really rough."

The remaining guard sounded genuinely concerned—proof of how desperate Subaru must have looked. But Subaru had no composure left to respond.

Somehow, he managed to gloss over the situation with the guard and return to the waiting room.

"You took quite a long time, Ms. Natsumi! ...Are you all right? Your face is..."

"I've heard that one before... For now, I weathered the storm."

Seeing Flop there to greet him, Subaru finally felt his heart slow down, his breath settling.

I made it through the sudden storm...I think. But we still haven't cleared the first wall.

"I couldn't find a way to make contact with the outside. Without that, even if the plan works..."

"If that's all, don't worry, Natsumi. Kuna and I already sent a signal that Sister and the others will understand."

"Huh?"

Subaru's eyes widened. The massive problem he had been worrying about had already been resolved so easily?

Talitta looked a bit apologetic at his reaction, while Kuna appeared completely unfazed. Subaru turned to them, silently asking for an explanation.

"About that... After you took the guard away, Bianca said she'd distract the remaining one so we could finish the job."

"Wh...wh...wh..."

Subaru's widened eyes shifted toward Abel, who was seated in the corner of the room.

Noticing his attention, Abel narrowed his eyes and shook his head slightly.

"Rather than telling you and risking an unnatural reaction, I used you as a natural distraction. Fortunately, you did your job well enough. I'll even commend you for it."

"You are so annoying! I—I was terrified out there!"

"C-calm down, Ms. Natsumi! Don't ruin that cute face!"

"Sooo annoying!"

Subaru lunged, ready to grab Abel for his infuriating attitude, but Flop held him back from behind.

He really did want to punch that smug face—but without Abel, their plan wouldn't work. He had no choice but to calm down.

Being hostage to a face... This is absurd.

But if contact had been made, all that was left was to carry out the plan and make sure it succeeded.

"If this doesn't work, it'll be a disaster."

It sounded like sour grapes, but after the past few days, Subaru was sure that it would end in nothing but bitter disappointment.

It is really aggravating, but there isn't anyone other than an Archbishop who wouldn't be captivated by that arrogant dancing queen.

CHAPTER 6
A HAUGHTY CRIMSON

1

"The banquet attendees have been seated," the guard announced. "You're up now."

Subaru and the others in the waiting room stood. The rising, suffocating tension reached its peak as the impending performance loomed closer and closer.

Everything had gone smoothly so far, but that was no guarantee it would continue that way. People aren't simple enough to think like that. Subaru had confidence in his cross-dressing, but even so…

They picked up their various instruments and underwent a brief inspection before passing into the banquet hall. Their sheer outfits left little to the imagination, and as they endured the curious and lustful gazes, they were led inside.

"…Ngh!"

"Talitta?" Subaru furrowed his brow.

Midway, Talitta's steps suddenly grew heavy.

Her face was pale, and sweat glistened on her skin. She was obviously tense. Far from her familiar village, without her reliable chief and older sister, unarmed in the middle of the enemy's camp—maybe it was all too much stress.

Subaru searched for the right words, worried she might collapse at any moment, but—

"Talitta. There is nothing to fear. Look at me."

The voice was haughty, arrogant, and brimming with confidence.

It was no more grounded in reality than the words Subaru had been about to say, but that cheap consolation pulled Talitta back from the brink.

There was power in those words—the ability to move hearts with just a few syllables. Words from one who had power easily swept aside the hard work and effort of those without it.

Subaru had felt that difference painfully many times before, and here it was again, illustrated so vividly.

"I won't let it get to me, though."

He whispered the words to himself, as if convincing himself to accept it. But when he realized his own tension had eased as well, his lips curled.

I won't say it out loud, though—that bastard would just get smug.

"—Thank you for coming. I have heard you will perform a magnificent song and dance."

They were greeted by about thirty muscular imperial soldiers seated around the banquet hall.

Supposedly, no enlisted men had been invited, so everyone present must have been an officer of some kind. And the one who had spoken—the man sitting in the chair farthest back—

"...That's General Second-Class Zikr Osman?" Subaru murmured softly.

Abel, standing beside him with his face hidden behind a veil, nodded ever so slightly. That confirmation told Subaru he had identified their target correctly. He looked closer.

Zikr Osman—the commander of all the soldiers quartered in Guaral.

With a rank as high as general second-class, Subaru had expected him to be a towering, powerful man. Instead, he was short and plump, with a distinctive hairstyle.

He stood half a head shorter than Subaru, but his hair made up for the height difference—it was worn in an Afro.

I heard he was a crafty tactician, Subaru thought. *He definitely doesn't look like someone who won awards for his sword skills.*

"We are currently grappling with a serious issue," Zikr continued. "Gathering in the city and waiting day after day is difficult for morale. Thus we have arranged this banquet. You know your role, I trust."

"…Yes. It was the highest honor to receive your summons."

Subaru knelt as Zikr propped up his chin self-importantly.

Flop, Talitta, and Kuna followed his lead.

But Abel, standing at the back of their line, did not kneel.

For a moment, Zikr's eyes narrowed, and tension spread among the officers.

As expected, one of the men set down his drink and stood.

"Why do you not kneel?" he glowered. "You stand before a general second-class and—"

"Wait. Do not lose your temper."

It was Zikr himself who intervened.

"This is a banquet. What is expected of those who devote themselves to performance is not etiquette, but the ability to provide a diversion from boredom."

"Mrgh… If the general says so…"

Begrudgingly, the man sat back down.

Throughout, Abel stood unmoving, his face still hidden behind his veil.

"Unyielding even before a warrior's spirit, hmm?" Zikr mused. "You appear quite confident in your dance. However, let me tell you now, the first impression is not favorable. I shall hope you prove it wrong."

"…I am grateful for your magnanimity," Subaru replied, still kneeling. "However, you need not worry."

Zikr regarded Abel's haughty demeanor with interest.

"Oh?" He raised an eyebrow, intrigued.

I feel a bit bad for what's about to come, Subaru thought. *But this is the perfect chance. I'll make sure he experiences a complete defeat.*

For the sake of that—

"…You will soon witness the beautiful queen of dance, who comes to you from beyond the Great Waterfalls. Lustrous black hair that has absorbed the light of the sun, beautiful pale skin blessed by the spirits—a supreme beauty descended from the heavens. She shall dance for you tonight."

With that extravagant introduction as a signal, the queen of dance stepped forward and lifted the veil covering her face.

As her visage was unveiled, the gathering—already dumbfounded by her haughtiness—gasped.

"…"

The shock was especially great for Zikr, who found himself pierced by Abel's gaze.

As for how great it was—well…

"…It's your loss, Zikr Osman."

Zikr was unable to move, powerless before the sword that he had offered with his own two hands.

Even hearing what was unmistakably a man's voice from the mouth of the queen of dance, the skirt chaser Zikr Osman could not escape the ultimate intoxication that filled his eyes.

2

—*Yes!*

Internally Subaru shouted, certain of their victory.

The sword in Abel's hand was positioned to easily slit Zikr's throat.

They had captured him perfectly. The operation was a success—achieved even faster than planned.

The original plan was to build up a reputation as performers in the city, get close to Zikr Osman, and ideally be summoned to his room or another secluded place where they could catch him off guard.

Once he was captured, they would force him to order the soldiers in Guaral to surrender.

But that plan had been upended during the banquet.

"Subdue every officer in the city at the banquet."

Abel had announced this change in plan right after they were summoned.

It was a high-risk, high-reward maneuver that would pay off immensely if successful. Subaru had agreed to it on the condition that they could revert to the original plan depending on how things played out.

I agreed, but I never thought it would go this smoothly.

"I will say it again, Zikr Osman. This is your loss. Surrender now and order your subordinates to lay down their arms. If you refuse, your glass will overflow with your own blood."

Abel demanded surrender, but Zikr remained frozen—not with fear, as one might expect of someone facing death. Nor did he bear the resolute eyes of a soldier prepared to die. Instead, his expression swirled with confusion and doubt.

"Dancing girl, you… No, you are…"

The confusion surfaced in his eyes, as if he were witnessing something incredible. It was not the reaction of a man simply faced with a dancer.

At least, that was how it seemed.

"…gh! You damned traitors! Don't you—"

One of the stunned officers snapped out of his daze and reached toward Abel. But before his hand could make contact, throwing knives struck his arm and leg—blades thrown by Kuna.

"Sorry, but the chief said to protect Abel's face."

The blades were mere table knives that Kuna had picked up during the dance.

Seeing her precise preemptive strike, the other officers hesitated. However—

"Don't make me laugh! This isn't enough to stop an imperial officer!"

The large man who had been hit yanked the knife from his arm and lunged forward.

Drawing his greatsword, he charged straight at Abel's back, completely heedless of any wounds he might suffer.

"Abel!"

Subaru shouted in panic, seeing Abel standing there with his back exposed, still focused on stopping Zikr.

The greatsword swung down toward Abel's back—

"…kh."

In that moment, Talitta took aim with a bow she had seized from one of the men. She had already nocked an arrow, her green eyes glinting with lethal intent.

To stop him, she would—

"Don't kill him!"

Just before she released the arrow, Flop shouted.

Her eyes wavered for an instant, throwing off her aim. Instead of striking where she had intended, the arrow pierced the man's right shoulder. He collapsed with a cry of pain, but his sword slipped from his grasp and spun toward Abel.

It looked like it would split his head open—but it barely grazed the back of his head before embedding itself in the floor with a loud crash.

"…Ah."

Abel's braided hair came undone and spread out.

The blade had sliced through the hairband, causing the knot to unravel. No—more than that. The wig frayed and lost its shape, and the false black hair scattered to the ground, revealing Abel's natural black hair.

With that, the soft, alluring impression of the performer vanished. Standing in its place was the unvarnished, cold emperor.

"General! Get away—"

"Stop! Don't resist!"

Zikr silenced the officer who was still thinking of resisting, even as the wounded man groaned on the floor.

With Zikr's apparent cooperation, the most feared scenario—suicidal charges, soldiers ignoring all costs—was now off the table.

"Do I have your assurance that my subordinates will be spared if I do as you say?"

"That depends on your behavior, coward."

"Gh…"

Zikr clenched his teeth, his face reddening at Abel's merciless insult.

This humiliation cut even deeper than being outmaneuvered and captured.

"I've heard of you, Zikr Osman. Before they called you the skirt chaser, they called you the coward."

"…A demeaning title unworthy of an imperial soldier. Is that why you chose this plan? Did you expect that I, who am scorned as a skirt chaser and a coward, would surrender to protect myself when threatened by a woman…?"

If so, then there could be no greater humiliation.

If that were the case, Zikr might very well die from the shame alone.

But that was not the reason Abel had believed this operation would succeed.

"Though you do not get particularly remarkable results from your skilled, steady tactics, you are a strategist who limits the casualties your forces take. A skilled commander but lacking in aggression. And thus you were called a coward."

"That's right. That is it exactly. But…"

"You seem to be misunderstanding something."

Abel's eyes narrowed.

Zikr's eyes widened, confusion plain on his face as Abel continued, still holding the sword to the general's neck.

"Those who censured you as a coward were either bluffing in the face of your results or fools who could not comprehend them. Your nature is why I considered this operation likely to succeed."

"…"

"You despise pointless losses. I judged that you, a strategist labeled a coward, would not resist in this situation... Will you disappoint me?"

Abel's sharp gaze bored into Zikr as he questioned him.

To someone unaware of Abel's identity, his reasoning might have sounded like nonsense. Trusting in an opponent's supposed cowardice and using it as a basis for victory was absurd.

However, Zikr Osman was left breathless by Abel's words.

A complex emotion flickered in his eyes. If one were forced to describe it, it was something close to surprise—almost verging on inspiration.

It was akin to the feeling of a maiden receiving a treasured gift from someone she has fallen for, a pure and almost innocent reaction...

"...I will put down all weapons. My subordinates, too. No exceptions."

"A wise decision."

Zikr obediently lowered his head, and Abel gave a quiet nod.

Even when he was dressed as a dancing girl, his presence was so solemn and dignified that no one could resist.

Their commanding officer having surrendered, the soldiers in the room followed suit, placing their weapons on the ground one after another.

And then—

"What are you dawdling about? Quickly go and burn the flag atop the roof."

"Ugh? M-me?"

"You. Just you. You're the only one who has done nothing since this started."

Subaru blinked and pointed at himself as Abel glared coldly at him.

Subaru glanced around the room.

Kuna had subdued an attacker with her knives. Talitta had shot the man who drew his sword. Flop had kept the bloodless victory plan on track by preventing the man's death. And Abel had forced the surrender.

Subaru, who had just sat on his butt while the chaos unfolded, was the only one who had done nothing.

"Quickly. Without Mizelda and the others, disarming everyone will be difficult."

"U-understood! Eh, um, pardon me!"

Subaru hurried to the balcony and climbed swiftly up to the roof.

From there, he could see Guaral spread out beneath him in the night—a majestic sight.

In the cold wind, Subaru took a torch from the wall, raised it to the empire's flag—the swordwolf flag—and set it ablaze.

This signaled that the fortress city of Guaral had been captured.

3

Todd was patrolling the city with Jamal trailing behind, glancing repeatedly toward the city hall.

The town had a long history, and despite its large walls, there were countless ways in and out. Some local families had built underground passages, while smugglers had carved out narrow routes just big enough for children. Todd had uncovered them all with precision and heightened caution, anticipating the inevitable attack.

"There's no way they'll back off. In that case, they'll definitely try to take the town. Using some hidden passage, rushing the headquarters and occupying it, or setting fire to the town... Hmm, are there any other methods?"

If their goal was simply to bring down the city, they had plenty of ways to do so—indiscriminate slaughter of both soldiers and citizens alike being the most straightforward.

People'll die in fire and water and even just from being buried. If you don't care about the how, it's easy to kill a person... What sort of trick will that black-haired boy use?

The thought unsettled him. So much so that even with a hole in his gut, he couldn't just lie around the barracks.

"Since every last one of them is careless and sloppy."

Even if not all of them were as incompetent as Jamal, most lacked a keen eye for detail. Todd didn't consider himself especially talented or intelligent, but at least he was aware of his own shortcomings. That awareness alone had given him countless opportunities to improve.

I don't understand how everyone can live their lives without questioning their own stupidity. Every last person is an idiot, and we just have to do the best we can to make up for it.

"...Wow, that's some sick joke."

Todd was about to enter the next house when an unexpectedly confused voice stopped him in his tracks.

Looking over, he saw Jamal staring, mouth agape, in the direction of the city hall.

"What is it, Jamal? Did something—?"

Todd was about to ask when he moved beside Jamal and saw it for himself.

The officers were supposed to be enjoying the banquet, entertained by the dancing girls. It wouldn't be surprising if someone had gotten a little too loose and done something reckless.

It wouldn't be surprising—except climbing onto the roof and setting the imperial flag on fire was no joke.

"No way..."

That was well beyond drunken antics. It was outright barbarism. Even Todd was speechless.

The burning flag flapped in the hot wind, sending sparks flying into the night sky.

And standing right next to it was the woman he had seen inside the building earlier.

The musician with the rich black hair and sharp eyes.

Her name was...

"...Natsumi Schwartz."

He remembered her saying it when he asked.

The weak girl who had shrunk back in fear when Jamal approached her.

Yet there she was, holding a torch, burning the imperial flag without hesitation.

There's no way she just got drunk and decided to do that. That is clearly a deliberate attack against the empire.

And if the headquarters flag was burning, it meant the city had already fallen into enemy hands.

With that realization, a possibility crackled like lightning through his mind.

"...No... You?"

Eyes wide, he carefully studied the black-haired girl—Natsumi Schwartz—his breath catching at the minuscule possibility that had taken root in his thoughts.

Who could even think of that? Trying to break through the enemy's defensive lines from the front and capture the headquarters like that?

"I thought it was impossible...slipping through right from the front."

Who in their right mind would choose such a reckless method?

Of course, he had been wary of people hiding in cargo or dragon carriages and had reinforced inspections accordingly. But just strolling into the city, drawing attention to themselves—it was entirely beyond his imagination.

He had already heightened security after their first infiltration attempt. Who would be insane enough to try a direct entry right after—

"Even that was a setup for this? Letting himself be seen, making me think a frontal breakthrough was impossible?"

Then they had simply walked into the city, gained access to headquarters in the guise of dancing girls, captured the building, and burned the flag—exactly as Natsumi Schwartz had planned.

"...Not good."

What a meticulous plan. A chill ran down Todd's spine.

He had thought he'd done everything possible, holding nothing back to secure the best position. Yet his opponent had surpassed him effortlessly, mocking him from above.

The mere thought of such a divine tactician sent a shudder through him.

"Hell! What's going on?! We need to get back—"

"Stop it, idiot. Do you want to get yourself killed?"

Unlike Todd, Jamal hadn't realized who was burning the flag. At that distance, he couldn't see what was happening on the roof. Todd had only spotted it because of his sharp eyes.

And because he saw it, he stopped Jamal.

With the headquarters flag burned, it was clear the city had fallen.

Most likely all the officers at the banquet have been killed. Even if we burst in, the best we can hope for is dying in a counterattack.

"You lost your spine? And you call yourself a soldier of the empire?!"

"Pride won't win you battles or save your life. You know it, too. Headquarters is done for. The general and the officers are already dead. The Shudrak will be in the city soon."

"…"

"If we don't get away before that, we won't have any choice left but dying valiantly in the fighting."

With his personality, he'd never accept the humiliation of laying down arms. The only other choice is recklessly rushing in, weapons in hand, and dying after taking maybe a dozen down with us.

That could be called the ideal death for a swordwolf, but to Todd it was just dying in vain.

Life is a finite resource. It would be one thing to use it to win, but using it just because you don't want to admit you lost is a waste. We've known each other for a pretty long time. We've got enough of a connection to at least warn him. I think.

"We've got a hole in the wall we just finished blocking. I'm going to escape through there. What about you?"

"Gh, gh… You're telling me to live in disgrace again?"

"If you're alive, you'll have another chance to get revenge for that disgrace. But if you're dead, that's the end of it. So I'm going. I'm not taking a fight with no chance of winning."

I wouldn't take a fight with bad odds of winning, either, to be honest, but I don't have time to explain the details or argue with Jamal about it.

Todd turned around and started to run. After a moment of hesitation, Jamal shouted, "God damn it!" and followed after him.

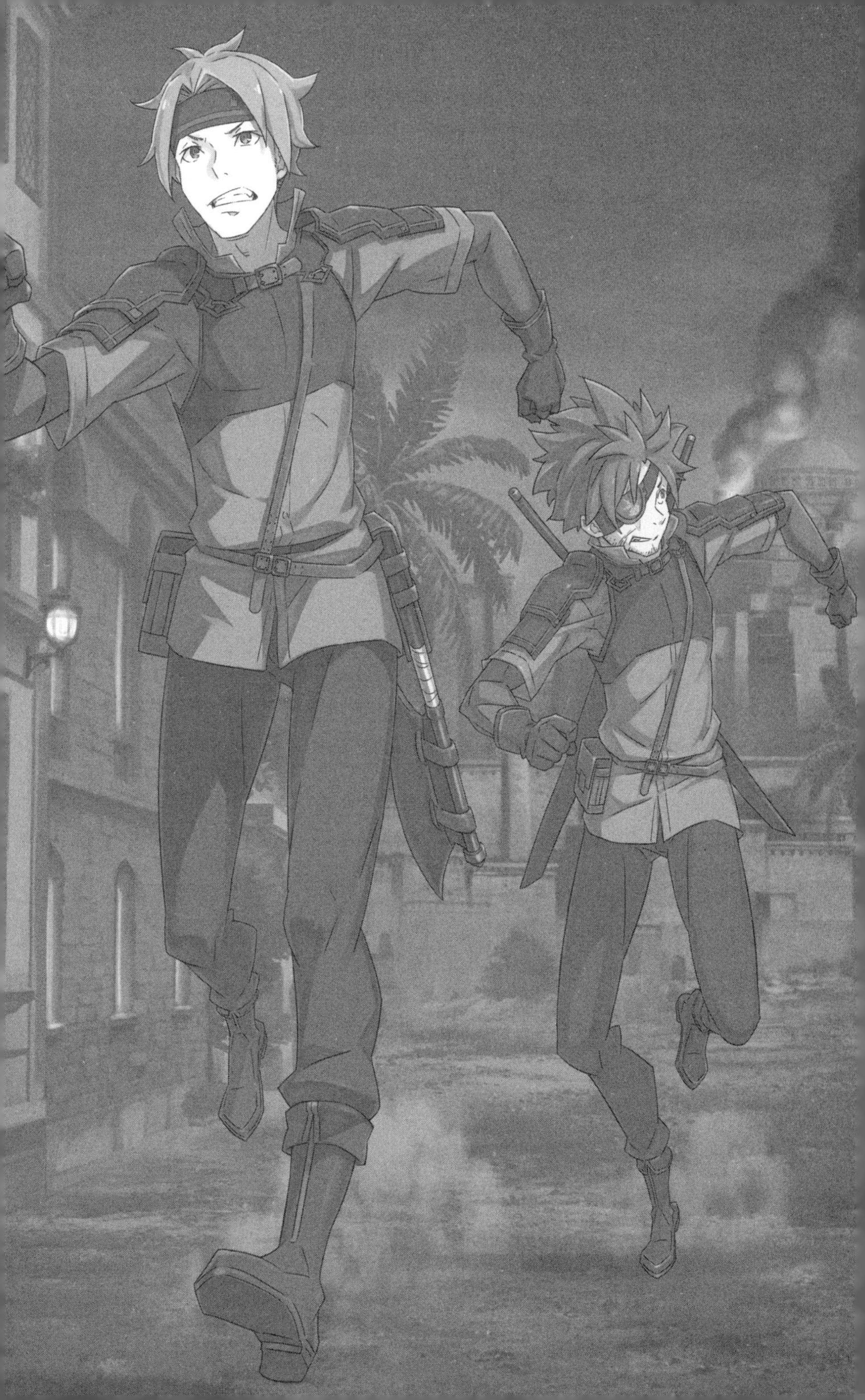

It would be nice if everyone were that simple, but the world just doesn't work that way.
Either way...
"For now, I'll have to remember the name Natsumi. Little child of war."

4

Seeing the flag burning and realizing that the city hall had been captured, the soldiers were surprisingly obedient when ordered to disarm.

The city's guards, too, complied without much resistance, which was both a great help in achieving Subaru's goal of a bloodless victory and an unexpected turn of events.

"This was quite the feat, Subaru...or, rather, Natsumi."

"Mizelda."

Still in disguise, Subaru was breathing a sigh of relief when Mizelda appeared, drinking straight from a bottle of alcohol.

She and the others had been waiting outside the city, prepared to move in once the burning flag signaled the army's headquarters had fallen. With the guards and soldiers already aware of their loss, they apparently made no attempt to stop the outside force from entering.

As a result, with the Shudrak's help, most of the soldiers had been successfully tied up.

The banquet hall had been cleaned up, with drinks and food removed, and now rows of bound soldiers filled the room.

"With this many...a head-on fight would have been difficult."

"Even when facing a numerous enemy, Shudrak pride would not waver...though it cannot overcome sheer numbers. But you and Abel did."

"..."

"Be proud, Natsumi. You have proven your courage through wisdom. That is something we could not have done."

Giving Subaru a good slap on the shoulder, Mizelda flashed him a broad, manly smile before heading over to Talitta and Kuna, who had played crucial roles in capturing the building.

Even from a distance, it was heartwarming to see Talitta's eyes shimmer as she was praised by her sister.

Kuna, on the other hand, was bear-hugged by Holly and nearly snapped in two.

"So long as the distinguished service medal winner doesn't get choked out…"

Feeling a bit relieved, Subaru allowed himself a small smile—until he turned around and almost bumped into someone standing right behind him.

"R-Rem…"

"…"

She was staring up at him from an unexpectedly short distance, causing Subaru to reflexively step back.

Leaning on her wooden staff, she slowly looked him up and down with her light-blue eyes. Feeling awkward under her silent scrutiny, Subaru coughed.

"Wh-what is it? There's nothing wrong with me, right?"

"So I have heard. However, I have the feeling you would say so even if you were injured."

"So untrusting…but I don't do well with pain, so I'd definitely say something if I was hurt. Really."

He tried to brush the concern aside with the demeanor of an innocent little princess, but then he cocked his head.

"Hmm? W-were you worried about little old me?"

"Huh?"

"Ah! I'm sorry! I got ahead of myself! That's right! It's fine, even if you weren't worried a—"

"I was."

"Eh?"

Subaru had been frantically waving his hands, trying to correct his own misunderstanding, but Rem cut him off.

Looking closer, he saw that her expression hadn't changed, but there was a slight shift in her eyes.

"I was worried. Of course I was. No matter how absurd the plan was, I was the one who asked you to carry it out. So why wouldn't I worry? How heartless do you think I am?"

"N-no, not at all, of course not! I don't think you're heartless in the slightest! You're deeply affectionate, a little extreme in your assumptions, and can be distant until you warm up to someone, but that's just part of your charm and allure..."

"..."

"Are you, by any chance, moved by—?"

"No, I was simply thinking you are disgusting."

"Ugh!"

Subaru clutched his false breast in exaggerated pain as Rem sighed, looking exhausted. Then she took a step closer.

"However, regardless of your words and conduct, you somehow managed it. You really did capture the town. And without anyone dying."

"...I would have preferred if there hadn't even been any injuries to stay faithful to the spirit of the plan. But that was too much to hope for."

"I wonder. Perhaps, with you and Abel, it might actually have been possible... Why are you making that face?"

"...It...it's...nothing."

Subaru grimaced, and Rem furrowed her brow in suspicion.

In truth, there was something to what she said. Without Abel's cooperation, the plan never would have worked. It was undeniable that he was a terrifyingly intelligent and strategic man.

But hearing her praise another guy—it really hit him in the heart.

"Even this fake breast can be deeply moved..."

"It sounds like you are saying something utterly stupid..."

Subaru quickly waved both hands and shook his head as Rem stared at him coolly.

Even if I tell her about it, it would just disgust her. That's fine and understandable, but if something hurts, it hurts. One-sided love is a painful thing.

"No, in this case, it would be reflex…? It goes straight past Emilia-tan, but at least it *feels* like she's accepting it…"

"Oh! Natsumi, there you are! I heard you were incredible! Congratulations!"

"Wah, Medium."

Medium came bounding over with loud footsteps and a booming voice. She wore a big, beaming smile and had Utakata and Louis perched on her shoulders as she cheerfully scanned the room filled with bound soldiers.

"You caught all of them, right? What a surprise! So, so, so, where's Big Sis? Did she do her best?"

"Big Sis… If you mean Flora, then…"

"I'm here, my sister!"

A loud stomp accompanied the cheerful call, and the beautiful young man made his presence known. Medium's round eyes widened as she saw Flop step into the room.

"Oooh!"

She was looking at the familiar Flop she had known for so long.

"Big Bro! It's you, Big Bro?! I thought you were my big sis, but the Big Sis I thought was Big Sis was actually you, Big Bro?!"

"Ha-ha-ha! I don't have any idea what you're saying, Little Sister! But either way, here I am. In which case, whether I'm your older brother or older sister is just a trivial matter, isn't it?"

"Right! Then maybe I'm your younger brother instead of your younger sister! I am really big, after all!"

"Brother or sister, it doesn't change the fact that we're family!"

The O'Connell siblings' conversation was as distinctive as ever, but in their own way, they made sense of the situation.

Flop smiled, wrapped his arms around Medium's waist, and spun her around. Since Utakata and Louis were still on her shoulders, they were swept up in the motion, too, and before long, Flop's feet left the ground entirely. All four of them twirled together, their laughter filling the room.

"It's surreal…"

"Medium was worried about Flop, too… So then, how long do you intend to remain like that? The rest of your life?"

"That's a little much! However cute I may be, this is just a temporary form… I am destined to return to my original self at some point."

"At some point? Meaning you're staying like that for now?"

"I just didn't have anything else to change into!"

Rem looked at him with clear skepticism—or, more accurately, like she was looking at an insect. Subaru didn't have the mental endurance to withstand that gaze for long.

The truth was, between burning the flag, greeting the Shudrak as they entered the city, and giving orders to the soldiers, he had simply been too busy to change.

It wasn't that he wanted to remain as Natsumi Schwartz.

"That isn't it at all."

"Is that so? If you're looking for Abel, he's in the back room with the commander."

"You don't sound like you believe me!"

Rem's face remained doubtful as she pointed the way, and Subaru quickly headed in that direction.

I'd love to just celebrate the operation's success with Rem and everyone, but now isn't the time for thoughtless celebration.

Guaral's capture was just a stepping stone. The real turmoil that would shake the empire's foundations was yet to come.

And I need to decide what position I'll take in all of it.

Speaking of which…

"Pardon me," Subaru said as he pushed open the door to the back room of the large hall.

This had originally been the mayor's office, but the previous occupant had been removed, and a new ruler had taken his place.

First it had been General Second-Class Zikr.

Now an even haughtier man sat in that chair.

"…You? Still dressed like that?"

Abel sniffed in mild disdain, resting his head on one hand. He had already discarded his dancer's outfit and changed back into men's clothing.

Zikr knelt before him, his hair disheveled. Aside from them, the room was empty.

"I'd appreciate it if you didn't dwell on that. More importantly, you're alone with the general? Without a guard? There should be a limit to recklessness, don't you think?"

"Of course. If he had any will to resist, I'd have him at swordpoint. However, he has no such will. Isn't that right, Zikr Osman?" Abel nodded toward the kneeling general.

"...Sir. That is correct, Your Highness."

His words carried an unmistakable reverence, proof that he no longer saw Abel as just some cross-dressing rebel.

"You've already spoken with him?"

"There was no need. It seems he realized it during the dance. Or perhaps it would be more accurate to say his head understood after the dance."

"...?"

Subaru cocked his head, not quite grasping the distinction.

Zikr, on the other hand, bowed his head deeply, as if in admiration of Abel's discerning eye.

Honestly, it had never really felt real that Abel was the emperor. Seeing someone actually acknowledge it and treat him with the proper respect was oddly reassuring.

"But this is convenient in its own way. Zikr Osman, obey me. I will see that you are not mistreated."

"Sir! If it would serve Your Highness, I, Zikr Osman, would gladly stake my life!"

"W-wait, wait, are you serious?! You haven't even heard what's happening yet!" Subaru cried.

Still seated, Abel calmly requested Zikr's loyalty—and the man accepted without hesitation.

It was convenient. Too convenient.

But Zikr shook his head emphatically.

"His Highness sits before me and asks for my service. As a general of the empire, it is my duty to answer his call. If anything, I would swear an even greater loyalty than before."

"Ho-ho... And why is that? Were you that enchanted by my dance?" Abel asked, his tone dry, not even a trace of humor in his voice.

"It was truly a wondrous sight to behold. However...that is not all."

Zikr's passion was palpable as he pressed both fists against the floor. An intense, almost burning delight shone in his eyes.

"Your Highness not only remembered my second name, one that I cursed as naught but a disgrace, but Your Highness even trusted in it..."

"Of course. As the ruler of the empire, I must understand all its extensive territory. The same applies to the subordinates who serve me. A general must always be prepared—who knows when I may need to rely on them as my arms or legs? Do you think an emperor could walk straight without understanding his own limbs?"

"Certainly not, Your Highness! That is why this is an honor—from the depths of my heart!"

Zikr shuddered with persistent ecstasy, swearing fealty to Abel with fervent passion.

To be honest, given the circumstances, his reaction was over the top. But the sheer intensity on Zikr's ghastly face left Subaru unable to doubt his sincerity.

At the same time, Subaru was overwhelmed by the sheer cohesive force of Abel's charisma—his powerful confidence and unwavering conviction.

The emperor, a being so far beyond reach, had not only *known* of him but also *grasped* his strengths and weaknesses, crafted a strategy around them, and magnificently entrapped him within it, securing his defeat.

It might be akin to how a high school pitcher would feel after giving up a home run to a major leaguer.

...Though in this case, the situation was war. A bit too intense to be compared to baseball.

Either way—

"If Zikr Osman will obey, then the officers beneath him will follow. Combined with the fortifications of the city, we finally have something resembling a proper fighting force."

"Nonetheless, if Your Highness intends to deal with other locations, then I believe it may be wise to first handle the reinforcements sent from the capital. Perhaps by luring them into the city and demanding their surrender."

Now that professional strategists with a greater understanding of Volakia's situation sat at the table, this war council was far more fully realized than any of their ad hoc planning sessions.

Unlike Abel, who accepted this with ease, Subaru still had major reservations about preparing for a real war. Before the discussion advanced too far, he wanted to talk with Abel—about what position he and Rem would hold after the city's capture.

However, before he could broach the topic—

"…Reinforcements from the capital."

The mood in the room shuddered at Abel's quiet murmur.

Subaru's and Zikr's eyes widened as he forcefully rose from his seat and strode into the hall.

"Close the front gate at once! Do not engage—even with a messenger!"

Abel's loud bellow stunned everyone in the hall.

Naturally, if Subaru and Zikr—who had been speaking with him just moments ago—had no idea what was happening, Mizelda and the others were even more in the dark.

But Abel's expression and demeanor were more than enough to convey that this was no trivial matter.

"Go, Talitta. Tell them to close the gate."

"S-Sister, what is—?"

"Go! Do not stain the Shudrak name!"

Mizelda's forceful voice cut through Talitta's hesitation.

Eyes wide at the almost murderous edge in her sister's tone, Talitta frantically dashed out of the room. Surely she would run straight to the gate and ensure it was sealed.

But would that be all he intended to do?

"What happened, chief? It's rare to see your expression change like that."

"I do not have time for your prattle, merchant. We must ready ourselves at once. Zikr Osman, rally the officers. Mizelda, you—"

"Uuuuuu!!!"

Disregarding Flop's concern, Abel quickly fired off instructions to the others. Abel instructed Zikr and Mizelda, the leaders of their respective groups, but he was interrupted by a child's loud tantrum.

"Wa, whoa, what is it? What's wrong, Louis?!"

"Uuu! Uuu! Aaauuu!"

"Lou! Calm down! I'm here!"

Medium's eyes spun as her hair was pulled. Perched on her shoulder, Louis was frantically crying out, while Utakata tried to comfort her. But she refused to calm down.

Instead, she started bawling, big tears rolling down her face, her expression tense with fear.

"Louis, please calm down! What is it? If something happened, I'll listen—so please don't cry…"

"Uuuu!"

"Hmm? There's something over there?"

Unable to bear seeing Louis cry, Rem stepped forward.

Louis, noticing her, pointed toward a corner of the room, tears still streaming.

Following the direction she indicated, Rem—and then Subaru and Abel—looked toward that spot.

But there was nothing there.

There should be nothing.

"Mizelda!"

Glowering at the empty space, Abel promptly shouted her name.

Without hesitation, Mizelda immediately drew her bow, snatching four arrows with one hand, nocking them all at once, and pulling back the string.

With the sheer strength of her stout body, she loosed a tremendous volley.

The four arrows tore through the air, bearing down on the seemingly empty space where Louis had pointed.

The sheer force behind the shot made Subaru recall the hunter's attack in the jungle—the one that had killed him.

It was that level of power.

If he had been the target, the arrows would have torn right through his torso.

The floor and wall, which should have been far harder than the arrows, shattered on impact, scattering fragments of stone in a cloud of dust.

Soldiers scrambled out of the way, gasping as they eyed the dust-filled space, waiting for whatever had triggered Louis's terror to reveal itself—

"…That can't kill me."

An easygoing voice fell gently in the room.

A…female voice. Casual, carefree, almost monotone—and quiet.

It felt incredibly out of place in such a tense moment. However, the results were powerful.

—In the blink of an eye, Mizelda's entire body was engulfed in flames.

5

"Gahhhh!!!"

Mizelda screamed as flames consumed her body in an instant.

Everyone froze, watching as she transformed into a fiery figure.

"—Holly!" Kuna shouted.

"G-got it!!!"

Holly dashed to a water jug large enough to fill her arms. With her superhuman strength, she lifted it and hurled it with all her might at Mizelda's feet.

The jug shattered, spilling water across the floor, dousing Mizelda as she collapsed.

"…Ah."

The flames had only burned for an instant, but the searing pain she had endured was unimaginable.

What had happened?

Subaru couldn't process it. Panic swirled through the hall, confusion gripping everyone—until he noticed an unfamiliar figure.

And it wasn't just him.

The others could see it, too.

—A beautiful, brown-skinned girl stood before them, wearing clothes that left little to the imagination.

She had short silver hair with a few red strands, an eye patch covering her left eye, and a bushy tail swaying behind her. In her hand she held a simple branch, which looked as if she had picked it up off the ground.

Her expression was flat, her face youthful and immature, yet her body had ample curves, creating an odd, unbalanced impression.

There was no question that she had caused what had just happened.

But exactly what she had done, what her goal was, or who she even was—all of it remained unclear.

"…So it's you, Arakiya."

While most remained frozen in shock, one person spoke her name.

The emperor, driven from the throne of Volakia, fixed his sharp gaze on the girl he called Arakiya.

Faced with the same overwhelming aura that had made Zikr immediately swear fealty, Arakiya merely swung the branch in her hand casually from side to side.

"It's been a while, Your Highness."

"You seem to be in good health. Chisha is merciless."

"Mercy? No. That's dangerous."

Her voice was lighthearted, her tone casual.

But Abel's tense expression made it clear—whatever conversation could be had with her, she was not someone who could improve the situation.

Who was she, to act so nonchalant while recognizing Abel?

"General…First-Class…Arakiya…"

"…What did you say?"

The voice belonged to Zikr, who had ended up standing beside Subaru.

Subaru twitched at those words.

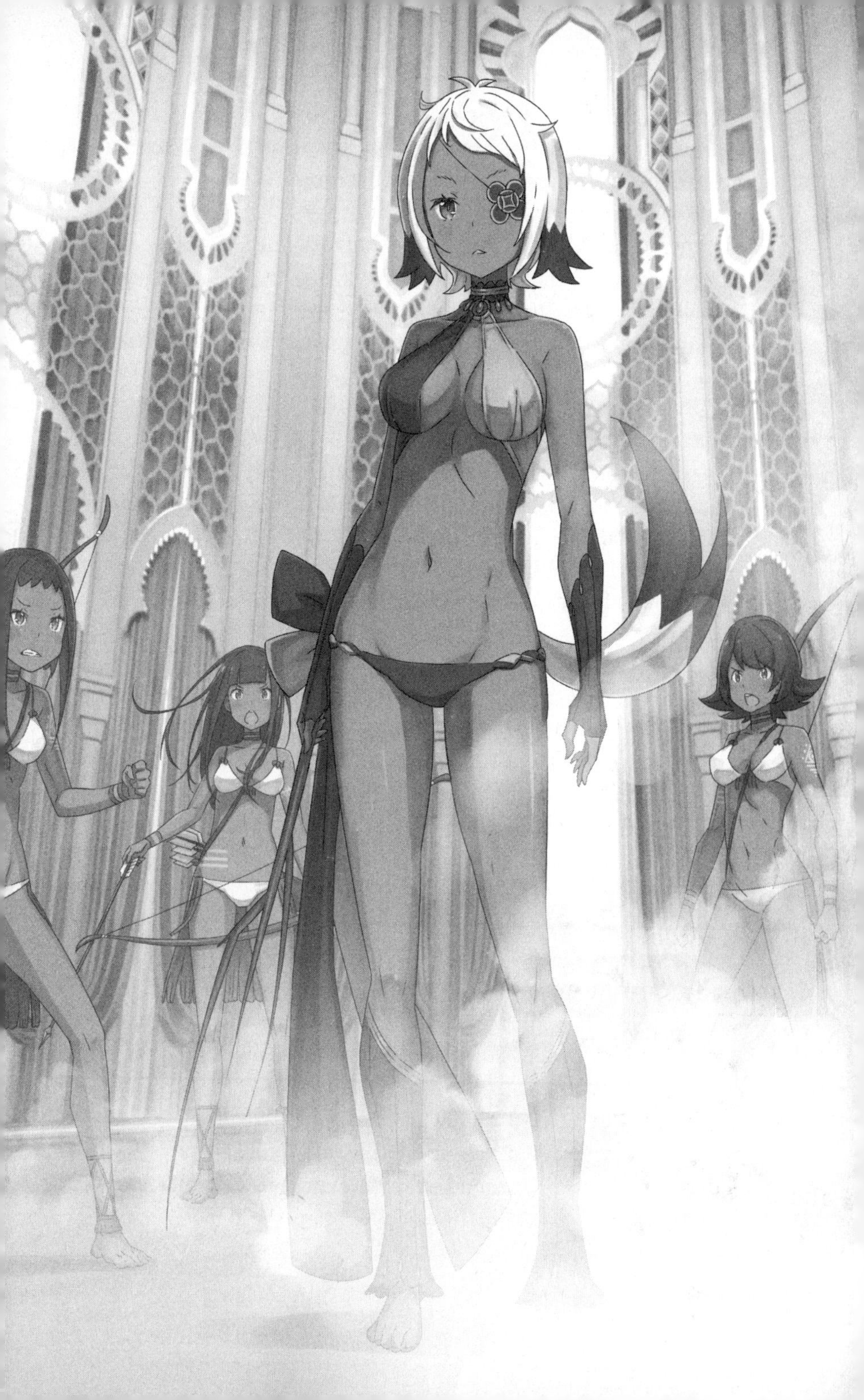

He wished he had misheard them.

But Zikr was visibly sweating, his expression deadly serious—there was no chance Subaru had heard wrong.

And to hammer it home, Zikr continued—

"General First-Class Arakiya...is one of the Nine Divine Generals!"

"Not just one of them—her position is Two," Abel supplemented. "Meaning she's the second highest in the entire empire."

"The second...?!" Subaru shouted, ignoring any concern for appearances.

With all eyes on her, Arakiya lifted what looked like a stick and puffed out her chest. "I'm important."

The Shudrak in the hall began edging around, forming a circle around her. Mizelda had fallen in the first move, but seventeen Shudrak remained—including Utakata, though it was unclear how much fighting strength she could provide. But...

"Do you think I'll let this victory be snatched away at the last minute?!"

Subaru picked up one of the swords they had taken from the soldiers. *Drive her back, beat her down, and capture her—whatever it takes, whatever we do, I won't let this win slip away...*

"Even if you try, it won't matter."

In the next instant, a powerful wind surged, twisting the entire hall. Subaru, the Shudrak, and even the bound soldiers were all thrown into disarray.

"..."

The world spun as Subaru lost all sense of direction, his body slamming into the floor, the wall, the ceiling. The intense pain nearly made him pass out.

"Kh..."

What had happened? Tossed onto the floor, staring up at the ceiling, he slowly worked to analyze the situation. —*It was probably...a whirlwind.*

A massive whirlwind had erupted inside the room, swallowing Subaru—no, all of them—and wildly flinging them about. Arakiya's storm raged without distinction between friend and foe.

The only reason Subaru had barely clung to consciousness was...

"I won't allow...a woman to...be injured any further..."

Zikr had held on to Subaru. The moment the whirlwind began, he had immediately pulled Subaru close, shielding him from the storm's destructive rampage. Meager though his body was, it had served as a cushion, keeping Subaru conscious.

However...

"No...way..."

Despair gripped Subaru as he surveyed the carnage in the room. People and objects were crumpled throughout the hall. The Shudrak, who had been ready to fight moments ago, now lay sprawled across the floor, completely incapacitated.

"...Rem..."

Enduring the pain consuming his body, Subaru searched for Rem. *She might have been knocked out, too. Depending on how she was hit, it could be really bad.*

As he scanned the room, he spotted something.

It wasn't Rem, but it caught his attention—because despite the whirlwind's rampage, someone was still standing.

Leaning against the half-destroyed balcony railing, glowering at Arakiya, was Abel.

"Abel..."

How had he protected himself?

Abel's injuries were minimal, but even so, a cut on his forehead bled, and one of his arms hung limply in a painful-looking way.

Yet his eyes remained as sharp as ever, fixed straight on Arakiya.

"The obedient puppet really overdid it. Have you forgotten why you became my subordinate?"

"...You lied, Your Highness. I was tricked. I won't forgive you."

"Did Chisha put that in your head, too?"

Lowering his gaze slightly, Abel let out a heavy, bloody sigh.

Arakiya's expression remained flat, but clear anger burned in her eyes as she slowly stepped forward, crossing the battered floor toward the balcony.

Step by step, she approached Abel...

"Uwaaaaaa!"

A loud shout rang out, and in the next moment, a massive pillar crashed down where Arakiya had been just about to step. The stone shattered with a thunderous crash as the primitive weapon, weighing several hundred kilograms, came down on her.

Rem had been waiting behind the pillar for her chance.

Even through the whirlwind, she had remained conscious, using the pillar as cover. From where Abel stood, she was almost certainly visible. She had hidden her presence, waiting for Abel's gaze on Arakiya to time her attack and push the pillar down.

It was their last, desperate move—relying on Rem's Herculean strength.

Her aim was true. The massive stone loomed over Arakiya's delicate body—

"Huh?"

"...No way."

Arakiya didn't even glance at it. The floor beneath her feet shifted, stretching upward like sugar crystals, catching the pillar and propping it steadily back into place.

The surprise attack had failed.

Rem's desperate effort hadn't just missed its mark—it hadn't even drawn Arakiya's attention.

Arakiya turned toward Rem, who was kneeling at the base of the broken pillar. Her eyes widened slightly.

"Oh, an oni. Rare."

"You are..."

"...Don't get in the way. I don't want to hurt a peer."

"A peer?" Rem's face flushed red with anger. She was unable to understand the words.

But with such an overwhelming difference in strength, anger was just an emotion—her will to resist was meaningless.

She reached for the rubble, signaling her intent to attack with a throw, but before she could, Arakiya swung her stick.

A fierce wind erupted, sweeping away all the rubble near

Rem—not just the debris, but the wall and ceiling behind her. Pieces of the building were torn away one after another.

"I'm not good at holding back. You'll fly, too."

"Then—then why not just do it?! After all this, what reason do you have to hesitate now? This—"

"...Unfortunate."

Arakiya's shoulders slumped at Rem's defiant response.

But while the gesture seemed almost cute, what came next was neither gentle nor kind.

Slowly, she raised her stick—an extradimensional force poised to shatter Rem's very being.

—There was no way Subaru Natsuki could allow that to happen.

"Aah, aaaaaaah!!!"

Shouting and suppressing all the pain, his body leaped into action.

In this one moment, the paralyzing fear and the anxiety of what might come—it was all just in the way. Abandoning all thought and moving forward on pure instinct, he stepped between Rem and Arakiya.

It's fine if I die. If I can protect Rem, it's fine if I die.

He did not want to die, and it was his cursed fate that everything would be wasted if he did, but in that moment, he wouldn't mind dying.

Dressed as a girl, with false breasts, makeup, a wig—using every trick he knew to make his skin look paler and more beautiful—even in that ridiculous form, Subaru Natsuki stood his ground to protect the girl who had to be protected at all costs.

"—Ngh!"

He spread his arms wide, shielding Rem with his body. He heard her gasp as she realized he had moved in front of her. However, he would never get the chance to know what she thought of it, what she felt.

In the face of Arakiya's destruction, it would all be swept away in an instant...

"...What an absurd self-sacrifice. But not bad."

As everything was about to be stolen away, as he steeled himself for the nothingness that awaited, a voice reached him.

Squeezing his eyes shut, he had tried to accept impending doom—but the heat, the emptiness, or whatever force was meant to take his life never reached him. He gulped.

Slowly he opened his eyes.

Subaru stood in front of Rem, arms spread as he shielded her with his back. And in front of him, there was another person's back.

Not Arakiya. Arakiya stood beyond that figure, her face frozen in astonishment.

The one who had stopped it all held a gleaming red sword in her right hand, having sliced through the destruction that would have consumed Subaru.

Arrogant, pompous crimson eyes that knew—without a doubt—that everything in this world knelt at her feet.

One arm wrapped around her chest, accentuating her abundant bosom, an embodiment of cruel beauty with a sneer on her lips—someone who should not be there.

Subaru held his breath, staring at the impossible sight before him.

With Subaru behind her, the manifestation of the word *crimson* sniffed.

"You need not speak your name, fool. Simply call my name instead."

Priscilla Bariel flashed a blood-colored smile.

<END>

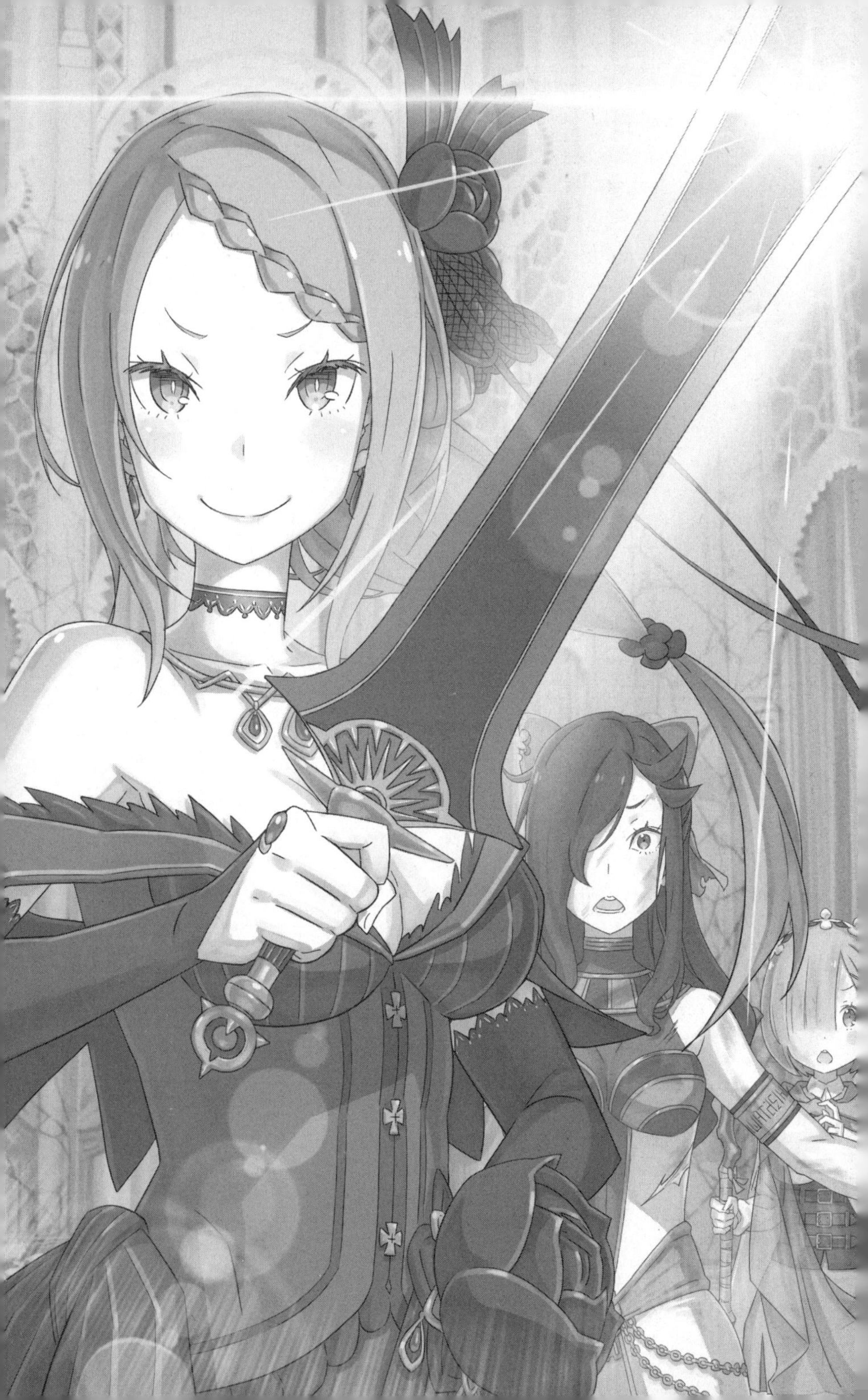

AFTERWORD

Hello! This is Tappei Nagatsuki! Also the mouse-colored cat!

In the last volume, we charged into the seventh arc, and it has been an arc of new and different developments, but hopefully you have enjoyed it.

Sent flying from the tower in the sands all the way to the empire to the south, in a new land without any familiar characters, Subaru is feverishly rushing hither and thither with a cold Rem. Those who read all the way to the end of this volume witnessed the appearance of one familiar face at the end, and I hope your heart is racing in anticipation of what will come. Because I am, too!

As I mentioned in the last volume, the gap between the web version of *Re:ZERO* and the books is practically nil! That means only the author and God know what comes next. And depending on how things go, it might only be God.

But it is also true that I feel satisfaction as an author at having finally reached the developments I've been wanting to do. If it feels like my pen was flowing particularly smoothly this time, then I will be glad!

But it is a series of difficult situations in which Subaru can't afford to be smiling, so I hope you will continue to watch over this series, this author, and Subaru Natsuki as he continues to experience terrible situations.

AFTERWORD

* * *

As ever, the page length looms, so allow me to move on to the usual thanks!

To my editor I, what happened to my resolve from last time? I am so sorry for pushing up against the deadlines again this time! My intention is to work seriously and consistently on the next one…!

To the illustrator, Otsuka, thank you for all the new characters again this time! I was just fresh off the farm, but thanks to your illustrations, I might be promoted to a regular…I think! I look forward to your work with the lively and varied empire cast in the next volume, too!

To the designer, Kusano, thank you for taking the scene from the road and working it up just beautifully! That feeling of being on the road might just continue in the seventh arc!

In manga news, Atori and Aikawa's adaptation of the fourth arc is ongoing in *Gekkan Comic Alive*. Tsubata Nozaki's *Love Ballad of the Sword Devil* and Minori Tsukahara's *The Frozen Bond* in *Manga UP!* are both reaching their climaxes. Thank you all so much!

And to everyone else at MF Bunko J's editorial department, the proofreader, and all the bookstores, thank you very much for all your work. I'll be in your care next time as well!

And finally, my greatest thanks to all the readers who continue to support this series!

I hope you will follow along with this new arc woven from new encounters and new difficulties!

May we meet again in the next volume! Thank you!

June 2021
<<*Even with the end of a busy month, the busyness never ends*>>

CHARACTER DESIGN

JAMAL

First Draft

170cm
155cm

ZIKR

Secret Boots

"So technically this is the combo from the cover. Me and…"

"Me! Apparently, if we work hard, we'll get lots of meat as a reward!"

"This doesn't come with any reward that obvious…but you tell me to get it done and I'll get it done, whether it's announcements or infiltrations."

"Kuna, you did so much! Talitta did, too, working so hard without stopping."

"I wouldn't say there was no stopping, but… Right, we have to do the announcement."

"Oh yeah! The next book after this is scheduled to be *Re:ZERO Ex*, Vol. 5 in September."

"Supposedly it digs deeper into what's going on around the empire. Probably because that woman who showed up right at the end came out of nowhere and surprised everyone."

"But, you know, if she wasn't there, Subaru and Rem would have been turned into meatballs."

"So it'll explore why those two didn't end up minced meat."

"Ohhh, I see. Ah! Also, there are other announcements, too. Shinichirou Otsuka, who provides the illustrations for *Re:ZERO*, has a second *Re:ZERO* art book going on sale!"

"There were a bunch of illustrations that couldn't fit in the first one. It's the same for this book, but isn't Otsuka having to work too hard on *Re:ZERO*?"

"The preorders start on June twenty-fifth, so be sure to reserve your copy and check out all of Otsuka's beautiful pictures. I want to make sure all that hard work gets rewarded."

"I doubt everything will fit into this book, either, so show your support and there can also be a third art book. If any pictures of us make it in, that's where they would show up."

"Oh, also, Emilia's birthday event…is already happening! We don't really know who Emilia is, though."

"From what I've heard, she's got some connection with Subaru. Even though he already has Rem and Louis. Men are just like that, I guess."

"Uh-oh, Kuna's starting to grumble. You really are the same as ever."

"Who asked you?! There will be more details to come later! Anyway, just remember that it's happening!"

"That's right! That's all the announcements."

"Sheesh, I'm tired… Why is everyone making me do everything?"

"I'm sure it's because everyone knows how reliable you are. But I'm the one who relies on you the most, so don't forget."

"You didn't need to say that! Hurry up and let's go!"

"Kuna, it's cute how you get embarrassed."

HAVE YOU BEEN TURNED ON TO LIGHT NOVELS YET?

86—EIGHTY-SIX, VOL. 1–13

In truth, there is no such thing as a bloodless war. Beyond the fortified walls protecting the eighty-five Republic Sectors lies the "nonexistent" Eighty-Sixth Sector. The young men and women of this forsaken land are branded the Eighty-Six and, stripped of their humanity, pilot "unmanned" weapons into battle...

Manga adaptation available now!

WOLF & PARCHMENT, VOL. 1–10

The young man Col dreams of one day joining the holy clergy and departs on a journey from the bathhouse, Spice and Wolf. Winfiel Kingdom's prince has invited him to help correct the sins of the Church. But as his travels begin, Col discovers in his luggage a young girl with a wolf's ears and tail named Myuri, who stowed away for the ride!

Manga adaptation available now!

SOLO LEVELING, VOL. 1–8

E-rank hunter Jinwoo Sung has no money, no talent, and no prospects to speak of—and apparently, no luck, either! When he enters a hidden double dungeon one fateful day, he's abandoned by his party and left to die at the hands of some of the most horrific monsters he's ever encountered.

Comic adaptation available now!

THE SAGA OF TANYA THE EVIL, VOL. 1-13

Reborn as a destitute orphaned girl with nothing to her name but memories of a previous life, Tanya will do whatever it takes to survive, even if it means living life behind the barrel of a gun!

Manga adaptation available now!

SO I'M A SPIDER, SO WHAT?, VOL. 1-16

I used to be a normal high school girl, but in the blink of an eye, I woke up in a place I've never seen before and—and I was reborn as a spider?!

Manga adaptation available now!

OVERLORD, VOL. 1-16

When Momonga logs in one last time just to be there when the servers go dark, something happens—and suddenly, fantasy is reality. A rogues' gallery of fanatically devoted NPCs is ready to obey his every order, but the world Momonga now inhabits is not the one he remembers.

Manga adaptation available now!

VISIT YENPRESS.COM TO CHECK OUT ALL OUR TITLES AND...

GET YOUR YEN ON!